PRAISE FOR *NORMAN MAILER'S LATER FICTIONS*

"The bewildering profusion of novels and non-fiction works that Norman Mailer published in his last twenty-five years, on subjects ranging from ancient Egypt to Adolf Hitler, has been comparatively neglected—and sometimes too easily dismissed—by Mailer's critics. Whatever the failures among them, these books demand and deserve closer attention. This well-edited collection of essays should provide both a needed corrective and a very useful road map to this protean body of work."—Morris Dickstein, author of *Gates of Eden* and *Dancing in the Dark*

"This collection of provocative and thoughtful essays by a new generation of Mailer critics addresses what is so often overlooked: the run of major works Mailer published over the last twenty-five years of his life, beginning with *Ancient Evenings*. Superbly edited."—J. Michael Lennon, coauthor, with Norman Mailer, of *On God: An Uncommon Conversation*

"This is an important study of one of the most influential and controversial writers or our era. Mailer's eclectic career—as novelist, journalist, historian, religious writer, and, of course, celebrity—comes alive in vibrant, thorough readings of his life and work. The essays in this volume are vital for anyone interested in the ever-shifting conceptions of what it means to be a public intellectual in the American cultural imaginary."—Tony Trigilio, Columbia College Chicago and author of *Allen Ginsberg's Buddhist Poetics*

"Sometimes novels are ignored for good reason, but in Mailer's case, they deserve attention, and this focused, well-organized collection is a sensible way of tackling the books, some of them huge. Mailer is ambitious, bold, original, irritating, and at times, tasteless and silly, but less often (and for better reasons) than hostile critics like to imagine. These essays make a very useful argument: when Mailer presents a behavior (male warrior-mentality or CIA mentality, for instance), he does so not necessarily to uphold it, but rather to question it, and scrutinize its origins or its dangers. This approach to the subject matter puts a lot of critics and book reviewers in the wrong. Odd though that sounds, the essay writers make a good case that Mailer has been read naively—this collection starts to right the balance."— Kathryn Hume, Edwin Erle Sparks Professor, Department of English, Penn State University

"A spirited defense of this tantalizing writer's late work. Lawrence Shainberg's portrait of Mailer on the road in his seventy-ninth year is itself worth the price of the ticket."—Carol Polsgrove, author of *It Wasn't Pretty, Folks, But Didn't We Have Fun? Surviving the '60s with* Esquire's *Harold Hayes*

AMERICAN LITERATURE READINGS IN THE 21ST CENTURY

Series Editor: Linda Wagner-Martin

American Literature Readings in the 21st Century publishes works by contemporary critics that help shape critical opinion regarding literature of the nineteenth and twentieth century in the United States.

Published by Palgrave Macmillan:

Freak Shows in Modern American Imagination: Constructing the Damaged Body from Willa Cather to Truman Capote
By Thomas Fahy

Women and Race in Contemporary U.S. Writing: From Faulkner to Morrison
By Kelly Lynch Reames

American Political Poetry in the 21st Century
By Michael Dowdy

Science and Technology in the Age of Hawthorne, Melville, Twain, and James: Thinking and Writing Electricity
By Sam Halliday

F. Scott Fitzgerald's Racial Angles and the Business of Literary Greatness
By Michael Nowlin

Sex, Race, and Family in Contemporary American Short Stories
By Melissa Bostrom

Democracy in Contemporary U.S. Women's Poetry
By Nicky Marsh

James Merrill and W.H. Auden: Homosexuality and Poetic Influence
By Piotr K. Gwiazda

Contemporary U.S. Latino/a Literary Criticism
Edited by Lyn Di Iorio Sandín and Richard Perez

The Hero in Contemporary American Fiction: The Works of Saul Bellow and Don DeLillo
By Stephanie S. Halldorson

Race and Identity in Hemingway's Fiction
By Amy L. Strong

Edith Wharton and the Conversations of Literary Modernism
By Jennifer Haytock

The Anti-Hero in the American Novel: From Joseph Heller to Kurt Vonnegut
By David Simmons

Indians, Environment, and Identity on the Borders of American Literature: From Faulkner and Morrison to Walker and Silko
By Lindsey Claire Smith

The American Landscape in the Poetry of Frost, Bishop, and Ashbery: The House Abandoned
By Marit J. MacArthur

Narrating Class in American Fiction
By William Dow

The Culture of Soft Work: Labor, Gender, and Race in Postmodern American Narrative
By Heather J. Hicks

Cormac McCarthy: American Canticles
By Kenneth Lincoln

Elizabeth Spencer's Complicated Cartographies: Reimagining Home, the South, and Southern Literary Production
By Catherine Seltzer

New Critical Essays on Kurt Vonnegut
Edited by David Simmons

The Emergence of the American Frontier Hero 1682–1826: Gender, Action, and Emotion
By Denise Mary MacNeil

Feminist Readings of Edith Wharton: From Silence to Speech
By Dianne L. Chambers

Norman Mailer's Later Fictions: Ancient Evenings *through* Castle in the Forest
Edited by John Whalen-Bridge

Norman Mailer's Later Fictions

Ancient Evenings through
Castle in the Forest

Edited by

John Whalen-Bridge

palgrave
macmillan

NORMAN MAILER'S LATER FICTIONS
Copyright © John Whalen-Bridge, 2010.

First published in 2010 by
PALGRAVE MACMILLAN®
in the United States—a division of St. Martin's Press LLC,
175 Fifth Avenue, New York, NY 10010.

Where this book is distributed in the UK, Europe and the rest of the world,
this is by Palgrave Macmillan, a division of Macmillan Publishers Limited,
registered in England, company number 785998, of Houndmills,
Basingstoke, Hampshire RG21 6XS.

Palgrave Macmillan is the global academic imprint of the above companies
and has companies and representatives throughout the world.

Palgrave® and Macmillan® are registered trademarks in the United States,
the United Kingdom, Europe and other countries.

ISBN: 978–0–230–10024–4

Library of Congress Cataloging-in-Publication Data

Norman Mailer's later fictions : ancient evenings through castle in
the forest / edited by John Whalen-Bridge.
    p. cm.—(American literature readings in the 21st century)
Includes bibliographical references and index.
ISBN 978–0–230–10024–4 (alk. paper)
    1. Mailer, Norman—Criticism and interpretation. I. Whalen-Bridge,
John, 1961–

PS3525.A4152Z825 2010
813'.54—dc22   2009039193

A catalogue record of the book is available from the British Library.

Design by Newgen Imaging Systems (P) Ltd., Chennai, India.

First edition: May 2010

10 9 8 7 6 5 4 3 2 1

Printed in the United States of America.

For Barry Leeds—Road Trip Buddy

CONTENTS

Part III   Politics

Part IV   Fame

Foreword: Our Byron

Jason Epstein

Norman was unlike any other author I've dealt with, and I've dealt with many. He was a performer and one of his arts was writing. Of course, there were many like him. For example, Lord Byron. Like Lord Bryon, he was—when I first knew him, God knows forty years ago or more—mad, bad, and dangerous to know. I was a very young man then, and only as time went by did my anarchist possibilities begin to emerge. Despite that, Norman and I became friends. We had much in common, we liked each other, we went to the same places, knew the same people. Of course, I admired him but I didn't think to work with him until much later, when I became his editor.

Norman was very easy to work with. He listened politely, he paid attention, he took notes and he ignored everything you said. In this respect he reminds me of Stendahl who, as some of you may know, was asked by his publisher to write a sequel to *The Charterhouse of Parma*. He didn't want to do that nor did he want a discussion with his publisher on the matter, so he simply killed off all his characters in the last paragraph and made a sequel impossible. So that gives us two writers Mailer can justly be compared with, Byron and Stendahl.

An editor's job is to do the most he can for his writers, try to find a narrative if the writer can't find it himself all the time. Try to create voice. Just keep him from going off the deep end. And often it can be a pleasure and rewarding. In some cases I find it useful to tell an author that he has to imagine himself standing on a pitcher's mound, all by himself at Yankee Stadium with 37,000 people out there. And hold them in their seats without any props, through the length of what he's writing. That's what's going to have to happen—he's got to do this not when they're all in the stands together, but one by one, if he wants to make a success of his book. And not 35,000, but many,

many more. But with Mailer, an editor really wasn't much more than a valet—I would have to make sure that his trousers were pressed, his shoes were polished, that there's at least some money in his pocket before he went out. That's really what it came down to. We dealt with the financial side, but actually we had very little to say about that part—Norman made his own decisions that way, too. A strange character. I don't think we ever won a contractual debate with him over anything. He'd say, "No I want it this way, so you'd better make it that way. No, I'm going to have it...." That was always his way.

I remember that we talked at length about the first chapter of *Harlot's Ghost*—which I thought put him in a terrible narrative predicament—how was he going to get out of that mess. And this novel—how was he going to solve that crime, and what did it have to do with the rest of the book? But there was nothing I could do. I warned him that he would never finish that novel. Of course, he didn't. And, he found a solution—he simply didn't finish it and never had to confront the problem.

I remember arguing with him at length about his book on Jesus. I had no interest; like my Hebrew ancestors, I believe that you don't discuss God or even use his name as something out there. It might be something, and it may be nothing. I think it's very hard to make fiction out of that. And Jesus was simply a very smart Jew at the time who got picked up by the wrong people. We were very far apart on that issue. But he was shrewd—he saw the beginning of this Jesus boom, which I didn't. He was right there at the birth of that.

The relationship an editor has with an author is confidential like the one a client shares with a lawyer, but we can be not too fussy about that. An editor lives vicariously through his writers. They do the work, they spend hours, months, days in the library. They take the risks. The editor's rewards are derivative and secondary. But so are his punishments if they come to pass. For me, being an editor has been like having a personal university all my life, where I could choose my own curriculum, the books I want to publish, and choose my own professors, the authors I want to work with, and I've learned everything I know from them. It's been a thrilling life. Whatever I may have contributed to Norman's understanding is nothing compared to what he contributed to mine.

ACKNOWLEDGMENTS

I would like to thank Morris Dickstein, Jason Epstein, Ross Forman, Robbie Goh, Kit Hume, Mike Lennon, (Cindy) Lim Lay Hoon, Loh Wai Yee, Norris Mailer, Jane Nardin, Lee Norton, Angela Faye Oon, Jeff Partridge, Linda Furgerson Selzer, Phillip Sipiora, Kelvin Tan, Edwina Quek, Heidi Virshup, Linda Wagner-Martin, Helena Whalen-Bridge, Cyril Wong, and Wong Yeang Chui (a.k.a. The Jane Person) for various kinds of encouragement and in many cases a great deal of work. Without the sort of help that they provided, books wouldn't see the light of day. Norris Mailer painted the portrait of Norman Mailer that appears on the cover of the book and helped me figure out how to get the image from her wall to this book's cover. Brigitte Shull agreed to take the picture of the painting.

Two of the essays in this book are extended versions of articles that appeared in *Journal of Modern Literature* 30:1 (Fall 2006). Scott Duguid's essay draws on "The Addiction of Masculinity: Norman Mailer's *Tough Guys Don't Dance* and the Cultural Politics of Reaganism" (23–30). James Emmett Ryan's essay fleshes out and revises ideas first treated in "Insatiable as Good Old America": *Tough Guys Don't Dance* and Popular Criminality" (17–22).

I worked on this project while at the Huntington Library with HEH grant support, while at Naropa University with Lenz Foundation grant support, and while on sabbatical from National University of Singapore with full support. I'm truly grateful for the help.

Thank you, reader, for reserving some moments for this book. May it serve you well!

CHAPTER 1

Absolutely Dauntless: A Quarter-Century of Sex, God, Politics, and Fame

John Whalen-Bridge

> *He was absolutely dauntless ... He was quite weak in the end, but he still planned to write a seven-volume novel about Hitler.*
>
> *Jason Epstein*

The essays in *Norman Mailer's Later Fictions:* "Ancient Evenings" *through* "Castle in the Forest" testify to the vitality of Mailer's fictional engagements in the last quarter-century of his writing career. After his 1979 masterpiece *The Executioner's Song*, Mailer's work did not receive adequate critical attention, largely because he relished the role of America's least politically correct author past the time when gatekeeper's found this amusing. Yet the volume of his work developed steadily. Mailer's contributions to what was once called the "New Journalism" are uncontested, but his lifelong attempt to assert himself as a novelist of the first rank never earned widespread critical consensus in spite of an astonishing variety of work. The developments of his last quarter-century have gone unnoticed.

The fictional hero of his infamous 1965 book *An American Dream*—a novel about a man who murders his wife, written by a novelist who had recently stabbed his wife almost killing her—claims with gravitas that "magic, dread, and the perception of death" are the roots of motivation. There is a provocative contradiction running through Mailer's work that many readers simply refuse to accept. As with Melville's *Moby-Dick*, Mailer's fictional universe is characterized by a stench of mortality, and an astonishing, simultaneous levity. Magic, dread, the perception of death, *and* an unapologetic fidelity to cavalier humor—these are the roots of Mailer's own motivation.

The Naked and the Dead (1948) is an obvious case in point, and we forget that *Advertisements for Myself* (1959) had such a strange, reckless playfulness to it that many readers considered it the book-length equivalent of a professional suicide note. Perhaps Leroi Jones was thinking of the serious side of Mailer's play, in part, when he wrote "Preface to a Twenty Volume Suicide Note."[1] The stench of death runs through *An American Dream*, as does its shocking vision of freedom. The cavalier freedom of *Armies of the Night* (1967) without the smell of death explains why this has been Mailer's signature work for many readers, while *Why Are We in Vietnam?* (1967) is perhaps the purist expression of the Mailerian mix of death and laughter.

Mailer has associated himself strongly with "the death penalty" in both literal and figurative ways, and many critics have very much wanted to give him the chair. Between *Executioner's Song* and his own death in 2007, Mailer's vision, so often written off as pataphysical fantasy or artistic self-indulgence, underwent a series of bewilderingly varied permutations that *must* in retrospect receive due recognition as a stable, carefully articulated, vision. It is often said that Mailer's vision of life is "Manichean," but this word is much too narrow for world Mailer presents. For Mailer the universe is a vast game of musical chairs in which we are profoundly undercertain about the meaning of the chairs. We think we know what a chair is, at least until we have to account for the ways in which people might struggle for a mere chair. Are we struggling for sexual gratification? Do moral questions of the largest possible significance animate us, or are human beings selfish agents who use words like "God" and "Devil" to manipulate perceptions for mere personal advantage? Everyone wants to have a chair when the music stops, and maybe the chair is nothing more than raw attention: perhaps the common denominator, dramatically presented as "fame" or "celebrity" in Mailer's work, is merely the hunger for attention. *Sex, God, politics,* and *fame*: in Mailer's imagination, they are interchangeable commodities, but this interchangeability is troubling indeed, because it denies us the protection of *mere* cynicism.

Writing novels was at once a joke and a demonstration of profound faith. Mailer's novels show, again and again, that our attempts to *empty* the world, to reveal it as an absurd joke, are just one more effort to escape the pain of the game in which we are all trapped, for the essence of the game is that we cannot be sure whether or not it is a "mere" game. In his last quarter-century he published five novels that recombine sex, divinity, political struggle, and human vanity, and the artistry that went into these efforts prove the seriousness of the game: *Ancient Evenings, Tough Guys Don't Dance, Harlot's Ghost, The Gospel According to the Son,* and *Castle in the Forest.* During this period, Mailer continued to work with narrative forms such as biography (*Oswald's Tale* and *Portrait of Picasso as a Young Man: an Interpretive Biography*), and he also assembled retrospective anthologies of his work and of his insights into the writing process (*The Time of Our Time* and *The Spooky Art: Some Thoughts on Writing*).[2] He also found time to write about the second war in Iraq (*Why Are We at War?*), attacking the neocons for inventing a conflict in order to build up the white male national ego! Mailer's nonfiction writing continued steadily and reliably, and at the same time his experiments with narrative forms and subject matter took some startling turns. According to Mailer, a novelist must not repeat but rather must develop: "I don't think it's an accident that I'm a novelist. Novelists have a wicked point of view—wicked as opposed to evil. They are interested in upping the ante. They are interested in more happening, not less" (Mailer *Conversations* 329).

If we think of "sex," "God," "politics," and "fame" not as arbitrary signs of a Saussurian sort but rather as hungry beings such as ourselves, perhaps these beings engage in literature's longest orgy in Mailer's 1983 novel *Ancient Evenings.* It is more prestigious to discuss the interrelations of signs with other signs; we behold "orchestration" from a disembodied distance. John Dewey was criticizing this sort of distance when he described the "museum aesthetic" in *Art as Experience*: the predominant aesthetic values train us to forget that we have bodies at all until concert's end, when we can clap. Sex, God, politics, and fame: Mailer's late work develops the relationships between these areas of interest obsessively and with a cavalier joy.

Ancient Evenings is usually approached as a book about *Sex*, which is a rather daft reduction; it was to have been Mailer's epic achievement, and the commonplace view was that the next novel *Tough Guys Don't Dance* was dashed off quickly to make money. Mailer fed this notion, but critics have found *Tough Guys* to be an interesting novel— there are two essays on the novel included in this collection. Scott Duguid's "From Egypt to Provincetown, By Trump Air: The Historical Return of the Repressed in *Ancient Evenings* and *Tough Guys Don't Dance*" challenges received notions about Mailer's ideological stance, with special attention to cultural shifts that Mailer readers have, to date, ignored. A partial critical shift occurred with the postfeminist 1990s and the parallel rise of masculinity studies, when critics such as David Savran tended to view Mailer's work as being critically engaged with exploring maleness in its historical and cultural manifestations. In the visual arts, Matthew Barney's continuing relationship with Mailer's work illustrates a certain, if hardly wholesale, rehabilitation of his ideas on sexuality and maleness in at least one corner of contemporary advanced art.

With close attention to cultural contexts, Duguid looks at *Ancient Evenings* and *Tough Guys Don't Dance* in relation to America's assimilation of literary Modernism, and, in so doing, finds a more progressive and reflective Mailer than critical histories of contemporary culture typically recall. Attention to the actual texts, Duguid demonstrates, shows very clearly that Mailer, in this portion of his writing career at least, has been anything but an uncritical defender of patriarchal privilege. Duguid uses the psychoanalytic concept of the "return of the repressed" to "move beyond a 'nostalgia' reading of *Ancient Evenings*, taking up Mailer's retention of a modernist aesthetics and historicity in its own terms." The scuttlebutt of reviewers is that Mailer worked long and hard on the former book and then dashed out the latter, but Duguid is able to connect the two works as no critic has before: "to the extent that *Tough Guys Don't Dance* represents a return of the repressed, the central metaphor the novel employs for Mailer's return to American themes is a structure of *addiction* and *withdrawal*." Duguid's shrewd attention to Freudian insights into censorship and unsayability allows us to see the connections between the exoticism of *Ancient Evenings* and the parodic topicality of *Tough Guys Don't Dance*.

It is often claimed that Mailer's achievements as an innovative journalist outstrip his accomplishments as a novelist.[3] James Emmett Ryan turns matters around, however, in "Mailer and the 'Diet of Reality': *Tough Guys Don't Dance* and American Values," which compares *Tough Guys* with Mailer's true-crime works such as *The Executioner's Song* and *Oswald's Tale* in order to explore the ways in which "popular criminality has been mainstreamed." Extending outward from *Tough Guys*, Ryan looks at "the extralegal maneuverings of the CIA in *Harlot's Ghost*" as an index to "the colonization of American culture by the criminal impulse." Ryan finds in *Tough Guys* "an extremely revealing sort of cultural barometer," one that marks the cultural moment in which tattoos, pot-smoking, and obscenity ceased to be markers of transgression and became more acceptable to mainstream tastes.

The section on *God* includes three essays, all including some discussion on *Gospel According to the Son* and one of three extending the
discussion of Mailerian theology into *Castle in the Forest*.
Mailer's religious themes are usually approached as an expression of Mailer's
religious views, but the three essays here connect Mailer's personal
theology (which was, one could say, his private business) with public
concerns such as the continuing role of anti-Semitism in cultural
evaluation, the connection between the Holocaust and contemporary
spirituality, and, relatedly, the ways in which we define "evil." In the
Fall 2006 issue of *Journal of Modern Literature* Brian McDonald has
approached *Gospel* in relation to post-Holocaust theology, and Jeffrey
Partridge from a specifically Christian point of view—Partridge
delineating the ways in which Mailer's text is and is not faithful, as it
were, to the spirit and letter of the biblical originals.

Ashton Howley's "Mailer's 'Gnostic' *Gospel*" provides a state-of-
the-art overview of Mailer's syncretic spirituality. He carefully reviews
"Manicheanism" to show that Mailer fits the category insofar as we
privilege dualism as the defining aspect but complicates our attempts
to define him when we take into account his refusal of Manicheanism's
stark polarization:

> Although the Manicheans were "obsessed with duality" (Walker
> 1983, 125), they were anxious to resolve "this dualism," by placing
> "great emphasis on self-control and asceticism, and by "oppos[ing]
> marriage, sensual indulgence, the eating of animal food and the drink-
> ing of wine." Mailer, in his writings, early and late, is everywhere dual-
> istic, but he is nothing like ascetic. No litany of Manichean's
> anti-materialist doctrines could accurately describe his exuberant
> verbal-formalizings of the phenomena of lived experience in his
> novels.

Just as Mailer refuses to despise the body and favor the disembodied
spirit, he complicates the split between darkness and light with his
own brand of Kierkegaardian uncertainty. Howley prefers to call
Mailer a Gnostic, but then he wisely distinguishes Mailer's home-
grown gnosticism from the sort popularized by Elaine Pagels—Mailer
is heterodox even among heretics! After carefully establishing this
framework, Howley reads *Gospel* in relation to Gnostic and Jungian
sources to show how Mailer's Jesus "unites good and evil within himself" in ways that make the psyche and the cosmos each an analogue
of the other.

Approaching matters from a Jewish rather than a Christian perspective, Mashey Bernstein's "A Jew for Jesus? A Jewish Reading of

Norman Mailer's *The Gospel According to the Son*" takes up the issue of Mailer's reworking of the archetypal Christian narrative (if we can take the synoptic gospels as a single narrative). "Jewish writers have not shied away from using the Gospels or the image of Jesus in their text." But Bernstein demonstrates, through discussion of the earlier writer Sholem Asch, that Jewish-American authors who take up such material face the risk that they will be dismissed as outsiders or even desecrators. Bernstein pays close attention to Mailer's stylistic decisions in relation to commentaries by the book's initial reviewers to show the ways in which subtle religious sensitivities have conditioned the book's reception: "While I am not implying that anyone who didn't like Mailer's version of the text is an anti-Semite, criticism of the novel carried an undercurrent of suspicion and cynicism that went beyond what one would might expect when dealing with a literary work." Critical misapprehensions notwithstanding, Bernstein Mailer's novel offers us an especially Jewish Jesus.

"There is more resemblance between Norman Mailer and Saint Augustine than one might suspect at first blush"—thus begins Jeffrey F.L. Partridge's "Augustinian Evil in Mailer's Final Novels: A Case for Non-Dualism," a consideration of the evolving theological imagination in *Gospel* and *Castle in the Forest*. Partridge concludes that "dualism" is a misleading word to describe Mailer's position. Like Howley, Jeffrey Partridge finds it necessary to revisit the notion that Mailer is a Manichean dualist. While Mailer did not verbally repudiate Manicheanism when the word was used to describe him, for example, in interviews, Partridge argues that Mailer's aesthetic practice was, in fact, a repudiation of Manichean dualism: "Mailer embraced a Manichaean-type Dualism to the end—unless one considers, as this paper does, the non-dualist, Augustinian representation of evil in Mailer's final novels, *The Gospel According to the Son* and *The Castle in the Forest*." Partridge argues that Mailer followed "the whisperings of the unconscious rather than the logic of his theological pronouncements" and thus "came to understand evil in his final novel in a way that unwittingly cancels out Manichaean Dualism and embraces Augustinian privation and perversion." Partridge pays careful attention to Mailer's slow and careful presentation of character development in *Castle* in ways that bring theology, aesthetics, and historiography together: "The novel suggests that even an Adolf Hitler is not born evil. Even an Adolf Hitler is not catapulted into evil by some trauma or cataclysmic event. Rather, evil is the slow erosion of everything that is good." Partridge readily admits differences between Augustine and Mailer—one believes God is all-powerful and the other that God is embattled, vulnerable. Nonetheless, he offers a fresh approach to this important aspect of Mailer's career by showing that Mailer's theological imagination shares ground with some of the most influential thinkers of the West.

Politics begins with Ashton Howley's second contribution. "Imperial Mailer: *Ancient Evenings*" considers Mailer's most ambitious book, the little-discussed novel that was to be Mailer's own *Moby-Dick*. Critics of Mailer's work often play Mailer's egotism against his political acumen to argue that his narcissism spoiled his chances of becoming the novelist of his dreams, one who ranks with Tolstoy or Joyce. Howley takes up the notion of the "imperial ego— meaning both the acquisitive ego of the ego-maniac and the national ego of a state threatened with dissolution—to examine Mailer's own reflections on the relationship between his individualistic and macho imperatives of personal growth and the fate of empires (whether Egyptian or American). Howley is not arguing that Mailer himself is an imperialist—"Yet the author of *Ancient Evenings* was no more an imperialist than Melville was a 'blubber capitalist' or Hawthorne a Puritan or Nabokov a pedophile." But he is critical of the ways in which the romantic hunger for development celebrated by Mailer "expunges the feminine symbolic" that is potential in the mythological that Mailer adapts to his purposes. Howley closes with a brief consideration of Mailer's project in relation to Said's critique of the discourse of Orientalism. For Howley, *Ancient Evenings* is a highly reflective spiritual autobiography of sorts, one in which the Mailer who imagines ghosts in a tomb recollecting ancient evenings are a mirror for more than the author himself: "Surely Mailer's egocentric literalizing of himself as an heroic writer of mythic proportions is responsible for the fact that *Ancient Evenings* has been consigned to" what critic Michael Glenday has called "the 'purgatory of neglect'" (Glenday 118).

Tough Guys separates two gargantuan works, the 800-page *Ancient Evenings* that tells the story of Menenhetet's four lives and the 1300-page CIA/Cold War epic *Harlot's Ghost*, that ends (mockingly?) with the words "to be continued." Brian McDonald's "Spooks and Agencies: *Harlot's Ghost* and the Culture of Secrecy" takes up Mailer's epic fiction about the CIA to argue, against Louis Menand's criticism, that the novel is important "not for the contribution of the CIA and its methods to the West's victory in the cold war, but rather for the curious failure of the CIA to provide accurate intelligence." It would seem that the novelist is attempting to accurately represent the world in a way that puts the writer into a losing battle with the historian, but McDonald compares Mailer and DeLillo to elucidate the ways in which their books provide a "'refuge' from the "gloom [...] of unknowing' that perpetually surrounds the Kennedy shooting." This fictional approach to reality, DeLillo avers in his "Author's Note" to *Libra*, is "a way of thinking about the assassination without being constrained by half-facts or overwhelmed by possibilities, by the tide of speculation that widens with the years" (458). McDonald shows the ways in which Mailer, in the last third of his career, incorporated what he learned through his nonfictional experiments into his novels.

Mailer wrote *three* encyclopedic political novels during the third phase of his writing life; Howley's "Imperial Mailer" treats the first, McDonald's "Spooks and Agencies" the second, and historian Heather Wolffram treats the third in "The Nazi Occult and *The Castle in the Forest*: Raw History and Fictional Transformation." This essay compares Mailer's representations of Nazi occult beliefs in *Castle* with the understanding we might expect from an intellectual historian rather than a novelist, though we should keep in mind Mailer's report that the germ of the novel came from his reading of Ron Rosenbaum's book *Explaining Hitler*. Surveying the various hypotheses that have been developed to explain "what made Hitler *Hitler*," Rosenbaum accounts not for the genesis of the Fuehrer, but rather for our fascination. The book is a quest to understand "Hitler explainers" (*Explaining Hitler* xii). "Unconvinced by any of the theories he found here," writes Wolffram, "or perhaps intrigued by the sense of inexplicability that pervades Rosenbaum's book, Mailer says he sought an exceptional explanation for Hitler, one that he found in the occult." After a fascinating review of late-nineteenth and early-twentieth-century German occultism, Wolffram concludes that occultists "cannot in any serious way be seen as an important source for or sinister force behind Hitler's genocidal dream" before asking, "why do so many books (both fictional and crypto-historical), films, games and comics continue to rehearse this theme?" Wolffram argues that the occult solution helps historians evade difficult questions and form an overarching historiographical pattern that historians are beginning to challenge only now. And what does Mailer do with this material? For Wolffram, "Mailer's novel with its conglomeration of theories combines the two historiographical trends," and Mailer's aesthetic aim seems to have been to place the reader between them, to reproduce the unresolvability that served as the engine for Rosenbaum's quest. On the one hand we have the theodicy in which "human history, society and politics are manipulated by two invisible opposing forces," but on the other hand Mailer's youthful history frustrates his Satanic handlers by acting on his own. "Mailer's young Adolf, thus, seems a product of both grand historical forces (diabolic and occult) and his own will," and so "Mailer's use of the historiography on the occult roots and connections of Nazism and his playful nod to the crypto-historiography in this field, can thus be seen as part of this larger project of creating a grand theory."

Mailer has challenged taboos about sexual expression like no other twentieth-century writer, and he combined religious themes with sex like no other writer in the world. By combining these with politics, he somehow managed to seem responsible even when he was more of an intellectual hedonist than most readers would tolerate, and his interest in *Fame*, which brought him to meditate on presidents, starlets, and authors as well, have made his work self-reflexive in ways that have been, in the funhouse days of postmodernism, de rigor. Whether or not everyone else was doing it, the author of *Advertisements for Myself* got there first, and the final three pieces in this volume are roughly about what could be called, to borrow from a famous best seller title from the 1970s, *The Joy of Fame*. My own essay "Late Mailer: His Writing and Reputation since *Ancient Evenings*" is a meditation on the relationship between two reputations, that of Mailer's personality and that of his work. After ten essays on Mailer's fiction, it is perhaps a return of the repressed that discussion of his life arises again in the final chapters. "Late Mailer" considers the possibility that Mailer's reputation will undergo some kind of subsequent regeneration, just as Melville's did decades after his death. Mailer's life and career were both characterized by a series of victories against death, and in works like *Ancient Evenings* he made this struggle into the central, structuring metaphor of reincarnation.

The final essay in the volume is Lawrence Shainberg's "History Looking at Itself: on the Road with the Mailers and George Plimpton," an account of a trip to Vienna in which Plimpton and the Mailers, in a weirdly wonderful postmodern replay, acted out the fraught triangle of F. Scott Fitzgerald, Zelda Fitzgerald, and Ernest Hemingway. Mailer liked saying that all novelists are actors at heart, and Shainberg's essay lovingly restores to memory Mailer's performative predilections and improvisations, all while juggling work, play, and fame while under great pressure. Juggle he did. In a career spanning six decades, in which he wrote three dozen books in a wide variety of genres, participated in politics both as commentator and candidate, gave innumerable interviews—he even acted in *and* directed films—Mailer was a public intellectual like no other, and there is no American author who can succeed him. The essays in *Norman Mailer's Later Fictions* all strive to appreciate Mailer's qualities as a writer in ways appropriate to the author's monumental achievement.

NOTES

1. Scott Sherman compares Jones/Baraka and Mailer in "A Turbulent Life": "Writing in the *New York Herald Tribune*'s Sunday supplement, Jones announced his arrival in an essay that evoked Norman Mailer's *Advertisements for Myself*." Mailer's provocative sentences were, "I write now, full of trepidation because I know the death this society intends for me. I see Jimmy Baldwin almost unable to write about himself anymore...."

2. On Mailer's persistent self-presentation as a *novelist*, see J. Michael Lennon's "Norman Mailer: Novelist, Journalist, or Historian?" *Journal of Modern Literature* 30:1 (Fall 2006): 91–103.

3. The most famous staging of this argument appears in the pages of *Armies of the Night* (1968), when Robert Lowell ruffles Mailer's feathers by complimenting him as the finest journalist in America. Mailer's experiments in nonfiction, starting with *Advertisements for Myself* (1959) and continuing through *Armies* and *Miami and the Siege of Chicago* (1968), in quasifictional biographies such as *Marilyn* (1973), and, most famously, *The Executioner's Song* (1979), liberated energies in American nonfiction generally, linking together writers such as Mailer, Joan Didion, Hunter S. Thompson, Gay Talese, and Tom Wolfe.

WORKS CITED

DeLillo, Don. *Libra.* New York: Viking, 1988.

Glass, Loren. *Authors, Inc.: Literary Celebrity in the Modern United States.* New York: New York University Press, 2004.

Glenday, Michael. *Norman Mailer.* New York: St. Martin's Press, 1995.

Epstein, Jason, quoted in Hillel Italie's "Norman Mailer Embodied a Generation of Literary Ambition." *New York Sun* November 11, 2007, http://www.nysun.com/arts/norman-mailer-embodied-a-generation-of-literary/66250/. Accessed 28 August 2009.

Lennon, J. Michael. "Norman Mailer: Novelist, Journalist, or Historian?" *Journal of Modern Literature* 30:1 (Fall 2006): 91–103.

Mailer, Norman. "Interview with Robert Begiebing," in *Conversations with Norman Mailer,* ed J. Michael Lennon. Jackson: University Press of Mississippi. 306–329.

McDonald, Brian J. "Post-Holocaust Theodicy, American Imperialism, and the 'Very Jewish Jesus' of Norman Mailer's *The Gospel According to the Son.*" *Journal of Modern Literature* 30:1 (Fall 2006): 78–90.

Partridge, Jeffrey F. L. "The Devil in Mr. Mailer: *Gospel According to the Son* and Christian Belief." *Journal of Modern Literature* 30:1 (Fall 2006): 64–77.

Sherman, Scott. "A Turbulent Life." *Dissent* (Spring 2002) http://www.dissentmagazine.org/article/?article=613. Accessed 15 April 2009.

PART I

Sex

From Egypt to Provincetown, By Trump Air: Modernist History and the Return of the Repressed in *Ancient Evenings* and *Tough Guys Don't Dance*

Scott Duguid

Norman Mailer's *Ancient Evenings* (1983) is among the most ambitious, perplexing, and radically imaginative novels of the postwar period. Set during the nineteenth and twentieth dynasties of ancient Egyptian civilization, the novel is a slow, detailed meditation on civilization and its discontents, a project animated by Mailer's predominant obsessions with death, magic, violence, and power. Following the restless activity of his work of the 1960s, in the early 1970s Mailer rededicated himself to novel-writing as an ambitious, epic enterprise with his Egypt book. At the end of *Ancient Evenings'* 700 pages, Mailer includes its dates of composition, 1972–1982, a clear assertion of the labor expended on the novel, and a mark of modernist authorship reminiscent of the *Trieste-Zurich-Paris 1914–1921* at the conclusion of Joyce's *Ulysses* (732). Mailer's Egypt is reconstructed entirely through the consciousness of his "Proustian"[1] narrator Menenhetet II (or rather his Ka, or double) on its journey through the Land of the Dead. While it has major flaws, the novel is a serious and obsessive stylistic achievement in the lineage of other modern exotica of its kind such as Flaubert's *Salammbo* and Thomas Mann's Joseph tetralogy. Mailer sought to surpass Mann (*Conversations* 300–301) in his utter immersion in the otherness of Egypt's ritualistic premodernity, and, as Nigel Leigh observes, went to great pains to "avoid unconsciously modernizing the material" (155).

Ancient Evenings' modernism can be understood in a radically negative sense, through its utter exclusion of what Adorno calls the "empirical world" (1). This exclusion of history can nevertheless be read in direct relation to the politics of 1972–1982—in particular, the aftermath of the failures of the 1960s, the global protests against American power in Vietnam to which Mailer made incisive and activist literary contributions in *Armies of the Night* (1968) and *Miami and the Siege of Chicago* (1968). Leigh, for example, reads *Ancient Evenings* as a "Marcusean refusal" founded on a "nostalgia born of radical pessimism" (176, 173). This reading finds accord with a larger trend that Andreas Huyssens calls "an intense search for viable tradition in the 1970s," a search typified by a spate of Egypt exhibitions, which Huyssens disparages as a "nostalgia for mummies and emperors" (171). In this vein, Richard Godden regards the Egypt book as Mailer's "ur-text for the seventies", an "extended parody" of "liberal creativity" (215). Mailer's familiar themes of biology and identity, Godden suggests, have become here historically arid: in *Ancient Evenings* "the male seed has become the vehicle of much repetition but very little history and absolutely no politics" (215).

Godden's reading of *Ancient Evenings* is doubly suggestive for my argument, since he not only locates *Ancient Evenings* within the 1970s avant-garde's flight from history and politics, but also articulates this in terms of the virility of the post-1960s liberal narrative. And this, I will show, is precisely the theme that Mailer picks up in his next novel *Tough Guys Don't Dance* (1984), a work that also has a reputation for containing "no politics" (Manso, *Norman Mailer* 66). But ought *Ancient Evenings* be read as quite such a radically antihistorical work? Certainly, Harold Bloom has noted in the Egypt book a "relevance to current reality in America" (3), and hints of political allegory have been detected in the novel.[2] However, extrapolating from Leigh's hint that Mailer was at pains to avoid "unconsciously" modernizing the book, any hints of contemporary relevance might be attributed less to conscious allegory, but rather a psychoanalytical return of the repressed. And it is in this dynamic sense that I take *Ancient Evenings* to be also closely related to Mailer's other post-1960s work in general, and *Tough Guys Don't Dance* in particular.

During the intense ten-year writing period of the novel, Mailer took occasional sabbaticals to "immerse myself again in daily matters of American life" (*Pieces* 189), including major projects such as

The Executioner's Song (1979). With the significant exception of the latter, however, Mailer's occasional turns to "daily matters" were of a decidedly minor sort, encompassing works on graffiti, Henry Miller, and Marilyn Monroe. On its face, *Tough Guys Don't Dance* continued this pattern. A drama of mistaken identity, decapitated heads, hasty burials, unlikely coincidences, and drug and real estate deals, the novel's pastiche of the hard-boiled style of the forties reinforces the view that Mailer was swimming with the nostalgic imperatives of the times. This suggestion is further reinforced by the novel's affectionate rendition of Provincetown, a place Mailer has affectionately described as "the Wild West of the East" (*The Presidential Papers* 95–112). A writer and artist's colony since the arrival of the Provincetown Players in the 1910s, Mailer's association with the town, beginning with summer visits in 1945, was even longer than his six-decade writing career.[3] Set in the isolation of a Provincetown winter, *Tough Guys Don't Dance* is removed from the national scene, and according to Mary V. Dearborn, was based on local Provincetown characters (388–389) and events. Author Michael Cunningham, himself a Provincetown resident, has commented on this local sense of otherness: "Provincetown lives at a bemused distance from the rest of the country. It does not quite consider itself American" (*Land's End* 71).

Tough Guys Don't Dance has been considered a quick contract-filler potboiler, "another expression of the author's diverse literary repertoire" (Glenday 126), and an easily consumable literary "hamburger"[4] following the hermetic difficulty of *Ancient Evenings*. Yet there are two senses in which *Tough Guys Don't Dance* carries a clear historical/political subtext. First, the novel can be read as a satire on the machismo of the Reagan 1980s and its concomitant political backlashes against feminism and the "1960s." Second, *Tough Guys Don't Dance*'s scandalous homage/pastiche of Raymond Chandler (*Pieces* 133) participates in the nostalgic rhythms of 1980s postmodernism, a discourse that Frederic Jameson regards as intimately related to Reaganite ideology about America's relation to its own cultural past.[5] Mailer moved rapidly from the sustained and intensive labor of *Ancient Evenings*, to the quick composition of *Tough Guys*; from seriousness to light comic pastiche; and from modernism to its repressed Others, mass culture and history, in classically American style. By reading these works side-by-side, this essay will ultimately want to move beyond a "nostalgia" reading of *Ancient Evenings*, taking up Mailer's retention of a modernist aesthetics and historicity in its own terms. For the present, to the extent that *Tough Guys Don't Dance* represents a return of the repressed, the central metaphor the novel employs for Mailer's return to American themes is that of *addiction* and *withdrawal.* This theme is directly established at the novel's opening. Tim Madden, a Provincetown writer, wakes on the "twenty-fourth drear morning after my wife had decamped" (*TG* 1), having spent the interceding time drinking and smoking heavily and suffering from writer's block. Madden's strenuous efforts to "kick the habit" (4) of his partner is not only correlated with cigarette addiction, but this withdrawal is linked with a libidinal addiction to nation: "She was as insatiable as good old America, and I wanted my country on my cock" (180). Madden's erratic narrative consciousness draws associations between the enervations of cigarette withdrawal and a disruption of assured American consumer confidence: "In the throes of not smoking, I might rent a car and never notice whether it was a Ford or a Chrysler" (3). Immediately, Mailer's first published pages after the long withdrawal of *Ancient Evenings* supply a self-parodic fictional echo of his own most serious writerly ambitions: after the major Egypt book comes a very American work about petty vice and consumption.

The plot proper of *Tough Guys Don't Dance* begins with a flashback to the hazily recollected previous evening. The breakdown in Madden's personal life is reflected in the winter's isolation, which he is spending in solitary drinking in a local bar. This sense of insularity is disturbed by the arrival of strangers, a man and a woman who are "theatrical to the hilt. A set of poses" (17), and "characters in a soap opera" (24). The woman not only represents a pre-feminist vision of womanhood—"the Liberation could go screw itself!"—but, more crucially for the plot, she reminds Madden first of "the porny star, Jennifer Welles" (18), and then of his estranged wife Patty. A first sign of the novel's preoccupation with doubling, this resemblance provokes in Madden an uncanny sense of "outrage" (19). This is not simply a winter resident's aversion to tourist trade. While *Tough Guys Don't Dance* is saturated with a sense of Provincetown's "bemused distance" from the rest of national life, it is the arrival of the Californian strangers that sets in motion the plot's unlikely chain of grisly events. "Republican California" (24) is the implicit correlative to the Provincetown setting: "Perfectly groomed blondes remain as quintessential to such places as mustard on pastrami. Corporate California had moved right into my psyche" (18–19). This penetration of the unconscious is given an exact topography that is mappable onto the female body and the nation both: Madden recalls "the porny star"'s "well-turned promiscuous breasts— one nipple tilted to the east, one stared out to the west" (18). There is a clear echo here of Fitzgerald's East and West Eggs from *The Great Gatsby* (a novel his aspirant wife Patty has evidently read with attention [56]). While the couple pretend a passing interest in Provincetown's real estate, the woman is an "avid map reader" (22) who is drawn to Ptown's phallic geographical irregularity at the "tip of Cape Cod" (23).

The novel opens the following morning. Madden rises with a hangover, the aforementioned "withdrawal" symptoms, a fresh tattoo, and little recollection of the night's events. He has also found blood on the front seat of his wife's Porsche. Following a tip off from the mysterious new Acting Chief of Police, Alvin Luther Regency, Madden goes to check his marijuana stash in the woods of nearby Truro. There he finds a decapitated blonde female head. It is, however, uncertain whether it belongs to his wife Patty or the California stranger, Jessica Pond, or if Madden himself is the killer. The novel's sleuth-work is driven as much by Madden's repressed guilt as by the conventional lines of enquiry of detective fiction. When a second blonde head in the stash is discovered, Madden is assured of his literal innocence, but his behavior continues to be determined by anxieties concerning identity that the narrative has unleashed. These anxieties, as the title suggests, are closely related to a crisis of masculinity. Madden is primarily locked in oedipal struggle with his father Dougy, a comically tough Irish ex-docker, who retains his tough guy nickname Big Mac "in defiance of all MacDonald hamburgers" (77).

In its preoccupation with masculinity, *Tough Guys Don't Dance* clearly has a lot of fun with Mailer's own macho image and reputation as scourge of feminist critics. Yet, reading the novel, one is often reminded of Kate Millett's early feminist assertion that "he always seems to understand what's the matter with masculine arrogance, but he can't give it up" (qtd. in Manso, *Norman Mailer* 525). Millett identifies a dominant tension in Mailer's work, with her arresting implication that masculinity is a habit; more precisely, an *addiction*. The themes of addiction to nation and masculinity are intertwined in the novel, which explores the seriocomic potential of maleness, balancing an affectionate wry nostalgia for macho excesses, with a forensic comprehension of masculinity's toxicity and violence.

Tough Guys Don't Dance plays the addiction of masculinity as high comedy. Mailer took his title from Roger Donoghue's comic anecdote about the mobster Frank Costello. This anecdote evokes the mythology of the mob and a lost golden age of masculinity, closely associated in the novel with Tim's legendary but undemonstrative father. The anecdote is the macho unit of exchange. Tim recalls Dougy's "filthy-minded" drinking buddies, who "rolled around in sex like it was stuck to their pants," and whose basic means of social exchange is to tell dirty stories to and about each other: "Every one of these old friends [. . .] had a quirk and the rule of the game was to kick your old buddy on the quirk" (95). This is an exercise in emotional control that reveals a masculinity comfortably and easily taking pleasure in its own absurdity, and this is mirrored in *Tough Guys Don't Dance*'s own narrative excesses, its predilection for yarns, jokes, one-liners, hearsay, rumor, scandal, storytelling, and slander. This is self-parody of a kind that conforms to one aspect of masculine aggression, the gratuitous offense of liberal good taste, what James Ellroy calls "dog language" ("James Ellroy"). This variety of language game, which is rather more about a certain kind of masculine testing than politics as such, exults in its own capacity to offend—although it is a mode of speech with its own addictive qualities.

The novel's enjoyment of Dougy's masculinity is also a function of his link to America's labor past. But like the unionism that he represents, in the world of *Tough Guys Don't Dance* Dougy is an anachronism. His appearance half way through the novel is as a ghostly, cancer-stricken presence, the family specter that haunts not only Madden's sense of self but also the cultural imagination. Dougy has been supplanted by postindustrial consumer society as well as identity politics and political correctness. Dougy, however, is relatively sanguine about his cultural obsolescence, and while one suspects he will never give up "dog language," he makes progressive noises about gay rights. Dougy's "illness" makes him "less of a bigot," hinting at a parallel between his own physical emaciation and the emergence of AIDS (yet another specter that haunts this novel). This is not a tolerance, however. Dougy will extend to his own son, "You were supposed to be a man, Tim. You came from me. You had advantages" (255). Manliness in *Tough Guys* implies a form of public display where vulnerability and weakness are either refused or their visible signs rigorously eliminated. David Savran makes the claim that "taking it like a man" implies the "contradictions connected with a masculine identification":

> It implies that masculinity is not an achieved state but a process, a trial through which one passes. But at the same time, this phrase ironically suggests the precariousness and fragility—even perhaps the femininity—of a gender identity that must be fought for again and again and again. (Savran 38)

Dougy Madden would be unlikely to use this kind of language. Nevertheless, Dougy, a "tough guy" by anyone's standards, attributes his cancer as a *failure* of masculinity, a failure he attributes to an incident where he reluctantly sought hospital treatment for bullet wounds rather than doggedly pursue his assailant. *Tough Guys Don't Dance* doesn't, however, simply invite us to find Dougy's stoicism and stony unforgivingness as comic. Mailer also invites a certain nostalgic respect for its heroism. Tim Madden's personal history, by contrast, is one of continuing failure to perform this inheritance. The novel presents this quest seriocomically, and is explicit about its homoerotic undertones. Madden directly cites Freud's theory of "homosexual panic" (*TG* 100) when he recounts his failed attempt to climb the phallic Provincetown monument. This memory brings on an attack of throbbing in his tattoo (significantly, a form of bodily penetration). Madden's period of memory loss implicates him not only in murder, but his drunkenly acquired tattoo also acts as a displaced reminder of latent impulses that equally require an alibi.

Like many a Mailer hero from as early as *The Naked and the Dead*, Madden's determination to keep "a tight asshole" (*Naked* 34) is not simply to maintain masculine integrity (although his father does applaud Tim for his abstinence in his spell in prison), but rather to avoid compromise with systems of power; in this case, to maintain liberal idealism in an essentially corrupt world. Fredric Jameson notes that in Mailer's writing "sex...always stands for power relationships, for imposing your own ego" (qtd. in Fetterley 155). Madden's interrogations by Acting Police Chief Regency are not simply homosocial studies in how power exercises itself but also ideological struggles between conservatism and liberalism that echo the struggles between General Cummings and Lieutenant Hearn in Mailer's first novel. Where Dougy Madden represents a nostalgic masculinity, Regency's masculinity embodies the spirit of Reagan's America: "He was large enough to play professional football, and there was no mistaking the competitive gleam in his eye: God, the spirit of competition, and crazy mayhem had come together. Regency looked like one Christian athlete who hated to lose" (48). A reference to a former partner, a Randy Reagan, reinforces the lexical echo of "Reagan" in Regency. Regency's core personal animus toward Madden, which is the driving force of *Tough Guys'* detective plot, is crucially determined by this political subtext.

Tough Guys Don't Dance revolves around Regency's murderous plot to frame Madden, his wife Madeleine's former lover, for the deaths of Patty Lareine and Jessica Pond. Ostensibly, this is a revenge motivated by sexual jealousy and compounded by what Regency sees as Madden's responsibility for a car accident that left Madeleine infertile. This revenge plot is also motivated by the desire to "frame"

1960s liberalism in the round, and it is this spirit of retribution that is at the heart of this drama of buried heads in the marijuana patch. This spirit of retributive machismo ("Vengeance is mine, saith the lord" [*TG* 147]) deriving from the legacies of Vietnam is entrenched in 1980s popular culture. As a self-confessed "enforcer" and "maniac" (347), Regency embodies what Savran describes as "the homicidal potential of paranoid white men" (Savran 5) in the post-Vietnam period, which stretches culturally from the Manson murders, through Rambo in the 1980s, and on to Timothy McVeigh and the Patriot movement. Regency's misogyny and violence thereby encompasses the 1980s twin backlashes against 1960s liberalism and against feminism.

Regency represents a somewhat less recoupable form of masculinity than that of Dougy and his drinking buddies, especially in contrast with their relatively playful use of "dog language." Madden assesses Regency's form of coercive language games as follows: "There was much to be said for Regency as a cop. Pressure came off him and it was constant. Soon, you made a mistake" (138). This constant pressure aims to expose not just practical inconsistencies in Madden's testimony, but also any signs of effeminate liberal softness. For Regency, what constitutes machismo is a certain kind of practical intellect, the ability to assess people and situations with unequivocal and righteous judgment, a quality he calls "acumen." To display "acumen" is not only to assess whether someone is "swish" or a "faggot" (139, 140) but also to operate as an entrepreneur in the business world. For Wardley Meeks III,[6] if one lacks "acumen," one way to reassert the "property rights to [one's] rectum" (29) is to take on a sexually aggressive and duplicitous blonde and to engage in the atavistic world of free enterprise, in this case real estate and drug-dealing. In this world, masculinity and femininity are functions of whether one takes the active or passive role in sex and business alike. Patty Lareine's body, "as pneumatic as a nineteen-year old model in *Playboy*" (158) echoes the 1980s cultural predilection for "hardbodies," which is mirrored in her display of stereotypically masculine aggressive traits.

The novel encodes Regency's combination of soft and hard sell in terms of this cultural narrative. Madden's description of him as a "big-breasted mother with an enormous phallus" (52) is not only a vivid example of the novel's bawdy humor, but more tellingly a concise summation of Reaganite ideology. Reagan's proclamation of "morning in America" (McCabe) in the 1980s resided on a nostalgic return of the 1950s, culturally imagined as a comforting time of tranquil domesticity and family values, but to be used in service of domestic law and order and cultural conservatism on the one hand, and supply-side economics, unprecedented budget deficits, and corporate junk bond raiding on the other. *Tough Guys Don't Dance* satirizes that nostalgia, with Madden and Madeleine Falco living happily in picket fence domesticity after the bloody conclusion of the novel. It also, like postmodern cinema such as *Blue Velvet*, points murderously to the latent violent and dark side of that cultural imaginary.

Yet *Tough Guys Don't Dance* is no less alert to the failures of 1960s liberalism. The countercultural heroism Mailer had given political form to in his notorious essay "The White Negro" (1957) translates in Mailer's 1980s novel into a decidedly apolitical sleaziness exhibited by the book's stooges, Stoodie and Hank "Spider" Nissen. Contrasting with Madden's cultural proclivity for mystical experience and marijuana, Nissen's preference is for consumer technology and cocaine, a drug associated with 1980s excess and an uncomplicated relationship to pleasure: "Don't give me that mystical sauce. It went out with LSD [...] Cut yourself a little coke" (116). Madden is finally as anachronistic as his father, and without the culturally validating masculine achievement, personally or politically. In accordance with Godden's reading of *Ancient Evenings*, the narrative of the failure of 1960s idealism is effortlessly read here as a deficit in liberal virility. The right-wing backlash that Regency represents, however, wasn't simply a settling of old scores against an obsolescent hip counterculture; there were new ones to settle, and crucial cultural battlegrounds developed by way of hysterias over drugs and sex. Regency justifies his predilection for pot with the punning remark that "Conservatives aren't right in every last item in the inventory" (53), implying a libertarian logic where consumer goods and political/social stances alike are selected from the catalogue.

Completely lacking in these exchanges is any sense of intersubjective political communication; instead, there are entrenched stances, legacies of America's enervating culture wars. Madden confronts Regency with the remark: "Count your plagues. I'll count mine [...] nuclear pollution for your side, herpes for mine" (141). This is the best that the novel can do in terms of meaningful political debate. The choice of "plagues" is suggestive, however, for although there was a public hysteria about herpes in the early 1980s, this has since been seen as a "trial run" for AIDS hysteria (Sontag, *Illness* 158). It is here that Regency's rhetoric of revenge has a specific reference, and why Provincetown in particular, and its large gay community, supplies a relevant dramatic locus for the revenge plot.[7] A few months before Mailer wrote *Tough Guys*, Provincetown had been the subject of major media interest after a period of panic that all but shut down tourism in the summer of 1983. Provincetown witnessed a thousand AIDS deaths at the height of the epidemic, and, according to Peter Manso, at one stage funerals and memorial services were taking place in the small town at the rate of about one a week (*Ptown* 258). Regency's references to the gay "plague" and "Kaposi's" sarcoma (141) introduce into Mailer's writing this new divisive factor in political discourse.[8]

How the AIDS epidemic modified Mailer's own much-maligned sexual politics, including his distaste for contraception, is not a question that *Tough Guys Don't Dance* invites us to ponder.[9] Nevertheless, 1980s Provincetown is an arresting location for Mailer's drama of masculine crisis and homosexual panic because its pastiche of the detective novel and its bawdy humor frequently segues into the registers of camp. The Mailer-directed film version of the novel in particular resembles fellow Provincetown resident John Waters as much as it does Raymond Chandler. The novel itself has a definite relationship with camp, both in its themes of performativity, and in respect of its attitude to cultural forms. Performatively, the objective correlative to Madden's paranoid quest for a "gender identity that must be fought for again and again and again" is a burlesque pantomime of gender confusion, of effete and ineffectual lawyers hooking up with avaricious and androgynous broads, of closets vacated and reentered. While Mailer has expressed wariness about describing *Tough Guys Don't Dance* as a work of camp irony ("Karma of Words" 13), a critical cultural index to this sensibility are a number of references to the English novelist Ronald Firbank, whose novels were part of Susan Sontag's original "canon of Camp" (Sontag, *Against Interpretation* 277–278). Mailer's own relationship to camp extends as far back as his collection *Cannibal and Christians* (1966), a book whose "Argument" is in part a response (*Cannibals* 15) to Sontag's "Notes on Camp" (1964). Sharing Sontag's ethical reservations about camp, at the time of *Cannibals and Christians* Mailer saw in some camp forms (from Warhol to Genet to Terry Southern) an avant-garde impulse. In terms of Mailer's own fictional practice, the "moral surrealism" (*Cannibals* 62) of contemporary works such as *An American Dream* (1965) were in part attempts to forge what we might call a kind of "serious camp" out of some of the same forms, notably the detective novel, as *Tough Guys Don't Dance*. Yet by and large, Mailer associates camp with an inauthentic and nihilistic visual mass culture.

For Sontag, camp is essentially a matter of performance: "To perceive Camp in objects and persons is to understand Being-as-Playing-a-Role. It is the farthest extension, in sensibility, of the metaphor of life as theatre" (*Against Interpretation* 278). Madden's own failed masculine postures (he frequently thinks of himself as an actor) chime with the theatricality of the California strangers, and indeed most of the novel's protagonists are to some degree involved in gender performance. This is a theme consistently dramatized in the novel's bad taste, ribald humor, especially in its playing with notions of female authenticity. Patty Lareine and her double Jessica Pond share with the porn actress Jennifer Welles an uncertain status as genuine blondes. Madden claims that Welles' appeal lay in the discrepancy between her blonde hair and her "*dark* pubic hair [...] Any lady who chooses to become a blonde is truly a blonde" (18). By contrast, Madden vouches for Madeleine's version of authentic womanhood with a detailed (and Updikean) description of her "cunt" (151–155). This is, of course, both a provocation of Mailer's feminist critics and an aspect of the novel's special pleading for the irony of male language at its most charmless. Whatever one makes of this literary gamesmanship, however, one can see in the novel's humor/anxiety about female authenticity a vital connection with the wider theme of the return of the repressed. In his essay on "The Uncanny," Freud observed that the exposed female genitalia are uncanny precisely because of an association with the "homely" and "unhomely" (*heimleich, unheimleich*) feelings associated with maternity (947). It is with Madeleine that Madden finds a successful domesticity and "home," and conveniently succeeds in resolving the "panic" plot. Madeleine Falco's authenticity is vouched for by her Brooklyn-Italian (i.e., East Coast and European) "roots," contrasting with the inauthenticity of Lareine and Pond, whose interchangeability evokes the uncanny theme of the double. Lareine and Pond's inauthenticity suggests not only the duplicity of the *femme fatale* (a classic *noir* theme), but also the avarice that they represent (Hollywood; the porn industry; "corporate California"; the "West"; Reaganite self-interest). The novel's decapitations (and their symbolic repetition through the mutilation of polaroids of Pond and Lareine) are a grisly and blackly humorous elaboration of the themes of simulation and dissimulation; the severed blonde heads act as a signifier of femininity literally torn from its referent, the body.

The duplicity of the *femme fatale* in *Tough Guys Don't Dance* is, through this macabre twist, planted onto the novel's evocation of the lifeworld of postmodern simulation. Patty Lareine, for example, has been trained by her lawyer to simulate in court using video performance (20). *Tough Guys'* appropriation of a style of writing and filmmaking of the forties is alive to more contemporary and technologized forms such as video, and in particular genres of the period such as the porn video and the video nasty (the film version explicitly refers to *Texas Chainsaw Massacre*). The detective tradition, once seen as a pulp commercial form, had by the 1980s a certain literary and filmic respectability. *Tough Guys* rewrites this tradition with its sense of the trash aesthetics of modern and commercial forms, which Mailer links to a distrust of the mediating technological eye of the "Sony video camera" (107). Allusions to visual forms such as photography, film, video, and TV commercials abound throughout the novel. There are three things to note here. First, these forms are implicitly inimical to the kind of anecdotal storytelling the novel valorizes, as embodied in Tim's father Dougy (who in this sense stands in for the disrupted "story" of unionism). Macho storytelling is contrasted with these "feminine" trash forms, following an association between mass culture and the feminine Mailer had made as early as 1959 in "A Note on Comparative Pornography."[10] Second, it is clear that for Mailer the promise of an avant-garde impulse in camp has seemingly dissipated with the rise of these postmodern forms. Third, this is of interest because of the novel's representation of violence:

> The suspicion creeps in that much of what the author knows about violence does not come from the imagination (which in a great writer can need no more than the suspicion of real experience to give us the whole beast) but out of what he has picked up from *Son* and *Grandson of Texas Chainsaw Massacre* and the rest of the filmic Jukes and Kallikaks. We are being given horror-shop plastic. ("Children" 1075)

This is not a comment on *Tough Guys Don't Dance,* but a quotation from Mailer's own review of Bret Easton Ellis' *American Psycho* (1991). Mailer's remarks apply in large part to his own earlier novel, however, and this is not the only parallel between the two works. Both are satires of the manners and the rapacious greed of the Reaganite 1980s. Both novels illustrate this narrative with the dismemberment of female bodies (which in Ellis' case provoked a hostile response from women's groups). *American Psycho* most definitely conforms to Savran's narrative of white male psychopathy. And, in post-AIDS and postmodernist terms, *American Psycho* reprises Mailer-esque themes such as the relationship between sex and technology, and the desensitization of bodily experience in a mediated, prophylactic world.[11]

American Psycho's initial reception was marked not only by moral outrage but also by a great deal of confusion as to the precise quality of its aesthetics. Mailer's review echoes this early confusion. Given the themes of masculinity and paternity we have already observed in *Tough Guys*, however, Mailer's review is strongly marked by virile oedipal struggle. He writes that "the first novel to come along in years that takes on deep and Dostoyevskian themes is written by only a half-competent and narcissistic young pen" ("Children" 1076). The phallic tussling here is obvious, but what is more suggestive about the piece is that the ethical reservations Mailer expresses about *American Psycho* reflect, largely unconsciously, the aesthetic and critical reception of Mailer's own fiction. He regards *American Psycho* an "ugly" and "deranging" ("Children" 1077) work, and even expresses concerns as to the novel's representation of violence toward women. This is quite startling coming from the author of *An American Dream* and *Tough Guys Don't Dance*. The review, written just after the end of the Cold War and the beginning of the discourse of the "end of history," provides a useful gloss on Mailer's own fictional practice. But it is also a retrospective comment on the 1980s and on the spiritual function of art at a time of the apparent abandonment of political or religious faiths. He writes of this "book of horrors":

> *American Psycho* is saying that the eighties were spiritually disgusting and the author's presentation is the crystallization of such horror. When an entire new class thrives on the ability to make money out of the manipulation of money, and becomes altogether obsessed with the surface of things—that is, with luxury commodities, food, and appearance—then, in effect, says Ellis, we have entered a period of the absolute manipulation of humans by humans: The objective correlative of total manipulation is coldcock murder. ("Children" 1073)

While Mailer praises Ellis because "he has forced us to look at intolerable material" ("Children" 1077), Mailer contends that Ellis' book finally fails as art because "by the end we know no more about Bateman's need to dismember others than we know about the inner workings in the mind of a wooden-faced actor who swings a broadax in an exploitation film" ("Children" 1076). This is a misreading of Ellis' work, but it is a strong one that offers a fascinating glimpse into the terms of Mailer's own aesthetic practice. Mailer bases his criticism on the novel's lack of affect, depth psychology, and insight into "extreme acts of violence" ("Children" 1074), the "inner life of the murderer" ("Children" 1073), or "real experience." Because of his insistence on the real as a core aesthetic principle, however, Mailer distances himself from Ellis' aesthetic strategies for grasping the manners and workings of a "society altogether obsessed with the surface of things"—that is, postmodern society's free uninterrupted flow of consumable images and signs.

At its core, Mailer's objection to *American Psycho* is principally an objection to the novel's subjectivity. What confused many readers of *American Psycho*, in addition to its fractured narrative, was the sheer tedium of reading pages and pages of lists of commodities. There is a trace of this listing in *Tough Guys*, where Madden notes "Spider" Nissen's "Honda 1200CC, his Trinitron TV, his Sony video camera, his Betamax recorder and his Apple computer" (107). *American Psycho* is an extreme and maximal form of this "postmodern" impulse to inventorise (Frow 27–28), and it is this extremity that qualitatively distinguishes it from Mailer's contract whodunit. Paradoxically, the Mailer text that most closely provides an aesthetic analogue to *American Psycho* is the modernism of *Ancient Evenings*. Mailer's description of *American Psycho* as "a species of dream where one is inhaling not quite enough air and the narrative never stirs because there is no narrative […] One would like to throw the book away. It is boring and intolerable" ("Children" 1070) echoes quite eerily the hostile early reviews of his own Egypt novel.[12] *American Psycho*'s endless lists of commodities aren't so far away from *Ancient Evenings*' endless accumulations of sense impressions.

If *Ancient Evenings* and *American Psycho* both display a compulsion to inventorise the object world, can these compulsions be meaningfully distinguished? *American Psycho* represents an extreme case of commodity fetishism since his habits of consumption alienate the narrator, Patrick Bateman, not only from the system of global exchange that he, as a stockbroker, is materially involved in (expressed in the complicit contradiction between his faux-empathy for third-world suffering and the occasional racist murder), but also the very subjective coherence the products are expected to sustain. The cumulative effect of the torrent of blank names is not that desire is induced; in fact, the residual glamor effect of Bateman's status objects is nullified by their repetition (Mailer accurately notes that "we are being asphyxiated with state-of-the-art commodities" ["Children" 1070]). The commodity name here fails to signify not only the objects themselves, but also through pulverizing excess and repetition the stable status identity Bateman would appear to covet. Ellis does not invite one to covet what Patrick Bateman has, because they constitute what he repellently is.

Mailer's ambitions for *Ancient Evenings*, by contrast, are perhaps suggested by his claim that the Egyptian world was "one of the places where magic was being converted into social equivalence" (qtd. in Leigh 168). The narrator's immersion in the object world, and telepathic capacity to inhabit other consciousnesses, is the means by which Menenhetet II mediates the breadth of Egyptian civilization. *Ancient Evenings* is a tactile novel written in tactile, synaesthetic language ("A story not told was equal to food not eaten" [*AE* 466]). Menenhetet's consciousness is absorbed in the sensual world of the Nile: the power of the scent of the river, as that of the book's lists of exotic spices, evokes not only polymorphous desire ("Her desire for me looked ready to rise with the river beyond the Palace walls" [*AE* 519]) but also the interconnectedness of the Egyptian lifeworld: its palaces, brothels, slave quarters, temples, and markets. The libidinal rhythms of the body reflect the inflows and outflows of commodities and armies along the Nile, connecting Egyptian experience to neighboring cultures and races (Hittite, Nubian) within the reach of its empire (just as the river Liffey in Joyce's Dublin reflects that city's colonial position).

In his review of *American Psycho*, Mailer urges Ellis that the "abstract ought to meet the particular" ("Children" 1075) in his representation of Bateman's consciousness and psychopathic violence. And it is through particularity that Mailer in *Ancient Evenings* attempts to "re-create a society unaffected by Western culture's ruling beliefs" (qtd. in Lennon 18). By turning to the preconceptual world, *Ancient Evenings* renders in fiction an imaginative space of radical nonidentity. For Adorno, the categorical impulses of Enlightenment operate to gather the particular, nonidentical elements of the natural world into concepts. The name Adorno gives to this process of identification is domination (a notion that fits with Mailer's long-held insistence on the "totalitarian" cancer of modernity and its aesthetic forms). However, in a radical "postmodern" (more properly, Marxist) rereading of Adorno, published about the same time as *American Psycho*, Frederic Jameson reconfigured Adorno's notion of identity with an interesting twist. Once one works through the problem of "levels," Jameson concludes that what Adorno means by identity is at root exchange value (*Late Marxism* 23), or capital itself. In the alternative economy of Mailer's Egypt, transactions both libidinal and financial are detected in their particularity in contradistinction to the interchangeable commodity signs of *American Psycho*. *Ancient Evenings'* emphasis on the natural world, on the body and its waste products, on the magical and erotic, corresponds to this nonidentical world that Jameson calls "heterogeneity, otherness, the qualitative, the radically new, the corporeal" (23).

It is in this notion of alternative economy that the theme of the return of the repressed finds it ultimate purchase, and signals *Ancient*

Evenings's clear relationship to the aesthetics of modernism. A critique of Mailer's primitivist modernism might be launched on any number of grounds: its fetishization of sense experience; its exoticism; even its Orientalism ("Karma of Words" 2–3). And, yes, it is subject to a certain "nostalgia," but if so this is clearly distinguishable aesthetically from the impulses underlying the nostalgia of postmodern cinema, or of other 1980s cultural forms such as neoexpressionist painting. The returns of the repressed I've tried to outline here closely resemble what the art historian Hal Foster has called the return of the Real, the persistence of a modernist aesthetics within the dominant hyperreality of postmodernism at large. Moreover, the irreducibly detailed narrative consciousness of *Ancient Evenings* might be analogous in fiction with Robert Hughes' call a few years ago for "slow art" (offering perception distinct from "fast" information society). On the other hand, where does that leave us with *Tough Guys Don't Dance*? Adorno famously described modernism and mass culture as "torn halves of an integral freedom, to which however they do not add up" (qtd. in Bernstein 2), and it has indeed been useful to see *Ancient Evenings* and *Tough Guys Don't Dance* as a late, postmodern variation on that theme. This is in line with what Jameson calls in his Adorno book the "persistence of the dialectic." Taken as an imperfect whole, Mailer's works of the 1980s do help us to trace the moves in the game that are involved in these cyclical, "addictive" movements.

NOTES

1. The biographer Mary V. Dearborn calls *Ancient Evenings* a "meticulously realized modernist text" (365, 369)
2. In conversation with John Whalen-Bridge, Mailer conceded that he did have President Carter in mind for his characterization of Ramses IX. John Whalen-Bridge, personal e-mail, 2 July 2004.
3. See Marquard: "Mailer began spending summers in Provincetown in 1945, and had lived there year-round since the 1990s."
4. Quoted from *People* review, dust jacket of *Tough Guys Don't Dance*.
5. *Ancient Evenings* and *Tough Guys Don't Dance* make an interesting case history of Jameson's identification of a transition to modernist authorship (individual style open to parody) to postmodern pastiche (*Postmodernism* 16–19). For Jameson on 1980s cinema and its relation to the historical imagination, see *Postmodernism* pp. 293–296.
6. The resemblance to Reagan's adviser Edwin Meese III is likely too close to be coincidental.
7. In the early 2000s, Michael Cunningham and Peter Manso both published books on Provincetown, igniting a literary controversy that on

its face looked like a spat between "old" Bohemian Provincetown, and gay Provincetown. Mailer's contribution was to publicly criticize Manso's book, although this may have been largely because of his displeasure at Manso's 1986 biography.

8. See Mailer's account of the 1992 U.S. election, "By Heaven Inspired" (*The Time of Our Time* 1092–1113).

9. See, for example, "Mailer Meets Madonna," *Esquire* September 1994: 46–59.

10. See *Advertisements for Myself* 350–353. For further discussion of Mailer's association of mass culture with the feminine (and its relation to the postmodern), see chapter 2 of Cohen, and my own essay on *The Naked and the Dead*.

11. The scene in Mailer's *An American Dream* in which Stephen Rojack removes his lover's diaphragm has a post-AIDS counterpoint in *American Psycho*. For a discussion of contraception and technology in *An American Dream* see Joseph Tabbi, 58–59.

12. In the most quoted of these negative reviews, Benjamin DeMott called *Ancient Evenings* a "disaster." Benjamin DeMott, review of *Ancient Evenings, New York Times Book Review*, 10 April 1983.

WORKS CITED

Adorno, Theodor. *Aesthetic Theory,* trans. Robert Hullot-Kentor. London: Athlone Press, 1999.

Bernstein, J.M. "Introduction," in *The Culture Industry: Selected Essays on Mass Culture,* Ed. Theodor W. Adorno and J.M. Bernstein. London: Routledge, 1991.

Bloom, Harold. "Norman in Egypt." *New York Review of Books* 28 April 1983.

Cohen, Josh. *Spectacular Allegories: Postmodern American Writing and the Politics of Seeing.* London: Pluto Press, 1998.

Conversations with Norman Mailer, ed. J. Michael Lennon. Jackson and London: University Press of Mississippi, 1988.

Cunningham, Michael. *Land's End: A Walk through Provincetown.* London: Vintage, 2004.

Dearborn, Mary V. *Mailer: A Biography.* Boston, New York: Houghton Mifflin, 1999.

DeMott, Benjamin. "Norman Mailer's Egyptian Novel." *New York Times Book Review* 10 April 1983. http://query.nytimes.com/gst/fullpage.html?res=9F03E6D71E39F933A25757C0A965948260. Accessed 31 July 2009.

Duguid, Scott. "Norman Mailer and Pop: Totalitarianism and Mass Culture in *The Naked and the Dead*". *US Studies Online* 3 (2003). http://www.baas.ac.uk/resources/usstudiesonline/article.asp?us=3&id=8. Accessed 31 July 2009.

Ellis, Bret Easton. *American Psycho.* London: Picador, 1991.

Fetterley, Judith. *The Resisting Reader: A Feminist Approach to American Fiction.* Bloomington and London: Indiana University Press, 1978.

Foster, Hal. *The Return of the Real: The Avant-Garde at the End of the Century.* Cambridge, MA and London: MIT Press, 1996.

Freud, Sigmund. "The Uncanny," in *The Norton Anthology of Theory and Criticism,* trans. Alix Strachey, ed. Vincent B. Leitch, William E. Cain, Laurie A. Finke, Barbara E. Johnson, John McGowan and Jeffrey J. Williams. New York, London: W.W. Norton, 2001. 929–952.

Frow, John. *Time and Commodity Culture: Essays in Cultural Theory and Postmodernity.* Oxford: Clarendon Press, 1997.

Glenday, Michael K. *Norman Mailer.* London: Macmillan, 1995.

Godden, Richard. *Fictions of Capital: The American Novel from James to Mailer.* Cambridge: Cambridge University Press, 1990.

Hughes, Robert, writ. and narr. "The New Shock of the New." BBC 4, 30 July 2004.

Huyssens, Andreas. *After the Great Divide: Modernism, Mass Culture and Postmodernism.* Macmillan, 1988.

"James Ellroy's Feast of Death." *Arena.* Dir. Vikram Jayanti. BBC2, 6 May 2001.

Jameson, Frederic. *Late Marxism: Adorno, or, the Persistence of the Dialectic.* London: Verso, 1990.

Jameson, Frederic. *Postmodernism, or, the Cultural Logic of Late Capitalism.* London, New York: Verso, 1991.

Joyce, James. *Ulysses,* ed. Jeri Johnson. Oxford: Oxford University Press, 1993.

Leigh, Nigel. *Radical Fictions and the Novels of Norman Mailer.* Basingstoke: Macmillan, 1990.

Lennon, J. Michael, ed. *Critical Essays on Norman Mailer.* Boston Mass.: G.K. Hall, 1986.

McCabe, Colin. "Midnight in America." Dir. Steven Spielberg, 2005. *The Independent.* 1 July 2005.

Mailer, Norman. *Ancient Evenings.* London: Picador, 1984.

———. *Cannibals and Christians.* 1966. London: Sphere, 1969.

———. "Children of the Pied Piper: A Review of *American Psycho.*" *The Time of Our Time* 1065–1077.

———. "The Karma of Words." Interview with John Whalen-Bridge. *Journal of Modern Literature* 30 (2006): 1–16.

———. *Pieces and Pontifications.* London: New English Library, 1985.

———. *The Naked and the Dead.* London: Wingate, 1952.

———. *The Presidential Papers.* Harmondsworth: Penguin, 1964.

———. *The Time of Our Time.* London: Abacus, 1998.

———. *Tough Guys Don't Dance.* New York: Ballantine, 1985.

Manso, Peter. *Norman Mailer: His Life and Times.* Harmondsworth: Penguin, 1986.

Manso, Peter. *Ptown: Art, Sex, and Money on the Outer Cape*. New York: Scribner, 2002.

Marquard, Bryan. "A Literary Lion's Quiet Coda in Provincetown," *The Boston Globe*, 14 November 2007, http://www.boston.com/ae/books/articles/2007/11/14 /a_literary_lions_quiet_coda_in_provincetown/. Accessed 23 August 2009.

Savran, David. *Taking It Like A Man: White Masculinity, Masochism, and Contemporary American Culture*. Princeton, NJ: Princeton University Press, 1998.

Sontag, Susan. *Against Interpretation and Other Essays*. New York: Picador, 2001.

Sontag, Susan. *Illness as Metaphor and Aids and Its Metaphors*. London: Penguin, 2002.

Tabbi, Joseph. *Postmodern Sublime: Technology and American Writing from Mailer to Cyberpunk*. Ithaca, London: Cornell University Press, 1995.

Tough Guys Don't Dance. Dir. Norman Mailer. Perf. Ryan O'Neal, Isabella Rossellini, and Wings Hauser. Cannon, 1987.

CHAPTER 3

Mailer and the "Diet of Reality": *Tough Guys Don't Dance* and American Values

James Emmett Ryan

The denial of lower, coarse, vulgar, venal, servile—in a word, natural—enjoyment, which constitutes the sacred sphere of culture, implies an affirmation of the superiority of those who can be satisfied with the sublimated, refined, disinterested, gratuitous, distinguished pleasures forever closed to the profane. That is why art and cultural consumption are predisposed, consciously and deliberately or not, to fulfill a social function of legitimating social differences.

Bourdieu 7

The rise to cultural prominence of American New Journalism in the 1960s and 1970s, when the movement was popularized by talented celebrity-journalists like Tom Wolfe, Truman Capote, Joan Didion, and Hunter S. Thompson, followed in many respects the earlier example of Norman Mailer's highly public self-fashioning after the success of his first novel. Beginning with his critically acclaimed—and autobiographical—early fiction, most notably *The Naked and the Dead* (1948) and *The Deer Park* (1955), and continuing soon after with iconoclastic provocations in early collections such as *The White Negro* (1958) and *Advertisements for Myself* (1959), Mailer had already set in place a template for a postmodern form of creative non-fiction in which the journalist/novelist could become a legitimate actor in his own narratives, while the boundary lines between the previously discrete genres of journalism, fiction, and autobiography became increasingly blurred if not entirely discarded. Eventually, the rubric New Journalism was assigned by Tom Wolfe to this new literary method in 1973, although it is less frequently remembered that Mailer had been at work setting out its principles for nearly twenty years by that time.[1] Mailer's trailblazing work in the 1950s and early 1960s had undoubtedly struck a chord with a rising generation of new writers.

As Wolfe summed up his own affinity for this brand of literary composition,

> [w]hat interested me was not simply the discovery that it was possible to write accurate non-fiction with techniques usually associated with novels and short stories. It was that—plus. It was the discovery that it was possible in non-fiction, in journalism, to use any literary device, from the traditional dialogisms of the essay to stream-of-consciousness, and to use many different kinds of simultaneously, or within a relatively short space...to excite the reader both intellectually and emotionally. (15)

Apart from spawning a generation of writers who would continue to challenge the importance of these literary boundaries, Mailer's own successful turn from relatively traditional realistic fiction to what would eventually be described as the New Journalism served as an indication of his finely tuned instincts not only as a mass media celebrity but also as a tough-minded reporter alert to contemporary events, issues, and ideas. Reflecting on his ambivalences concerning literary genre in his essay collection *A Spooky Art: Some Thoughts on Writing* (2003), Mailer admitted readily to the significance of his work in journalism:

> I discovered [the peculiar advantage of being a reporter] at the beginning of the Sixties, when I started doing journalism and realized it was a marvelous way for me to work. It was vastly easier than trying to write novels, and I was discouraged with the difficulty of writing fiction at that point. I had run into the business of trying to tell a good story and yet say exceptional things about the nature of the world and society, touch all the ultimates, and still have it read like speed. I always had a terrible time finding my story in the novel.... Then I discovered that this was the horror of it. Audiences liked it better. They'd all been following the same events you'd been seeing up close, and they wanted interpretation. It was those critical faculties that were

being called for rather than one's novelistic gifts. I must say I suc-
cumbed, and spent a good few years working at the edge of journalism
because it was so much easier. (186)

The extent to which its specific literary techniques were "New" is a
matter beyond the scope of this essay, but it is nonetheless apparent
that Mailer's seminal work as a journalist forms a crucial part of the
legacy of late-twentieth-century American social commentary.
Mailer's ambitions and importance as a novelist, then, ought to be
measured alongside his substantial—and in many ways superior—
accomplishments as a journalist, even if his unique form of journalism
is understood as in some ways a new type of literary enterprise. In the
discussion that follows, I briefly survey Mailer's career as a writer of
important fiction and journalism, before turning to a discussion of
his novel *Tough Guys Don't Dance* (1984) as an instance where his
distinctive journalistic sensibilities are fused to a pulp fiction criminal
narrative with a resulting cultural commentary that charts a path of
evolving morals in American popular culture.

In terms of broad public recognition of Mailer's work as a journalist,
one could point for example to *The Executioner's Song* (1979). An
extraordinary piece of journalism that not only earned Mailer a Pulitzer
Prize for fiction (he previously had been awarded the Pulitzer Prize for
nonfiction for *Miami and the Siege of Chicago*)—*The Executioner's Song*
also reached a large popular audience with its unique blend of shrewd
character analysis combined with a searing look into the social world of
the murderer Gary Gilmore, a brutally original manifestation of the
American criminal mind. Indeed, surveying the major works in Mailer's
career since he emerged on the American literary scene with his tour de
force novel, *The Naked and the Dead* (1948), suggests that the larger
part of his legacy will be measured in terms of his contribution to work
that includes at least a substantial amount of journalistic reportage.
While it is true that his accomplishments in fiction have been recognized by critics, particularly the novels that appeared in the years following the publication of *The Naked and the Dead*: *The Barbary Shore*
(1951), *The Deer Park* (1955), *An American Dream* (1966), and *Why
Are We in Vietnam?* (1967), most of Mailer's important work between
1950 and 1980 appeared in the form of journalism of one kind or
another. In any case, a fair evaluation of Mailer's impact during these
years must take into account such major journalistic and critical interventions as *Advertisements for Myself* (1959), *The Armies of the Night*
(1968), and *Miami and the Siege of Chicago* (1968), and *Of a Fire on the
Moon* (1970).[2]

Indeed, most of Mailer's mid-career celebrity came not through his work as a novelist but as a highly visible reporter; his novels (notably the ones written after 1980) testified to his great narrative power and imagination, but they frequently veered toward the self-serving and narcissistic. Alluding to the way Mailer the reporter emerged as a major public figure during the Vietnam era, the critic Louis Menand has recently suggested that the turmoil of the 1960s enlisted Mailer's affinity for the "anything goes" ethos of that decade, and that his literary adventures paralleled his tendency to seek publicity for himself. It was a decade during which, writes Menand, "anyone who seemed sufficiently far out held an appeal. And Mailer was a performer, a kind of celebrity the sixties loved" (151). The journalism that made Mailer famous during these years, though, was also a prelude to his return to serious fiction in the late 1970s, first with what he called his "true-life novel," *The Executioner's Song,* and eventually with the major novels of his later career: the merely lengthy *Ancient Evenings* followed a decade later by his gargantuan novel about the CIA, *Harlot's Ghost* (1991).[3] Critical judgments of these longer works aside, most students of Mailer's already lengthy career would agree that by the early 1980s, his real strength was expressed in experimental journalism, not fiction.

Still, as the preceding discussion is meant to indicate, Mailer must be credited with ushering in the New Journalism, a heady brew of fiction and reportage that through its popularity with readers and its adoption by major writers of the 1960s and 1970s implied that the traditional realist novel—and perhaps even the already-old-fashioned modern novel—was moribund, and was ineluctably giving way to a new model of contemporary nonfiction writing that could supply for a new generation of readers something like the shock of naturalist authenticity and psychological complexity that had been associated with modernist fiction in earlier decades of the twentieth century. Traditional popular genres could, from this point of view, speak only to and for the moral and aesthetic world of previous generations; the brave new world of literary postmodernity that the New Journalism exemplified would insist upon radically new literary forms able to come nearer to documenting the new aesthetic and moral complexities of the media-saturated late twentieth century in America. The dominance of the New Journalism, with Mailer's work in its vanguard, had made it possible to think that the American "novel" had entered a new and important period of bold experimentation and reconfiguration. And so there was a good deal of surprise associated with the speedy publication of Mailer's hard-boiled crime novel *Tough*

Guy's Don't Dance (1984) so soon after the decidedly mixed critical reception given to his long novel *Ancient Evenings* (1983). After decades of literary experimentation, what was at stake in Mailer's decision to try his hand at a rather conventional crime story?

An unapologetically formulaic tale whose events unfolded on the Massachusetts peninsula of Cape Cod, the cleverness of *Tough Guys Don't Dance* lay partially in its ability to invert so many assumptions about what many outsiders had presumed to be the Cape's Yankee gentility and picturesque charms. What is missing from the Provincetown of *Tough Guys* is precisely that aspect of tourism that many year-round residents on the Cape were happy to bid farewell each winter season:

> So if you wanted to look for some little splash of money, you waited for summer when enclaves of psychoanalysts and art-oriented well-to-do members of the liberal establishment came up from New York to be flanked by a wide panorama of gay society plus the narcs and dope dealers, and half of Greenwich village and SoHo. Painters, presumptive painters, motorcycle gangs, fuckups, hippies, beatniks and all their children came in, plus tens of thousands of tourists a day driving in from every state in the Union to see for a few hours what Provincetown looked like, because there it was—on the extremity of the map. People have a tropism for the end of the road. (37)

As any Cape Cod year-rounder could confirm, Provincetown's winter is no time to find its tourist-season glitz and glamour. True to the off-season realities of the warm-weather resort, and rather than emphasizing the scenic splendors of Cape Cod in its crowded mid-summer glory, *Tough Guys* discloses all too well the decidedly bleak and more mysterious off-season subculture of Provincetown and a good deal of the Cape Cod peninsula. With summer tourists having returned to the mainland, the Cape Cod that Mailer describes instead emphasizes its qualities of isolation and loneliness: a place whose social scene—undiluted by the summer wave of well-heeled tourists—comprises a motley assortment of drifters, struggling artists, literary eccentrics, drug-runners, and other modern pirates.[4] The Cape Cod off-season doldrums, amid the grey-clouded chill of Massachusetts winter—this is Mailer's chosen locus for his crime novel. And as we shall see, however, the Provincetown winter-world Mailer describes is indeed riddled with criminality and moral collapse, but it is not a "subculture" at all. To the contrary, the deep and radical irony of Mailer's hard-boiled American tale of the early 1980s is that bohemia has been mainstreamed, criminality has been popularized, and the old idea of "vice" has morphed into a daily and unavoidable commonplace.

It has often been said that Mailer's intellectual powers make the writing of a potboiler such as *Tough Guys Don't Dance* something of an insult to his considerable creative abilities.[5] Not to mention a nearly subliterary affront to the loyal readers who had followed him through the serious existential days of the 1950s through the difficulties of his entanglements with the galvanizing social movements of the 1960s: feminism, civil rights, and resistance to the American war in Southeast Asia. His choice to write in the pulp fiction mode, though, and his decision to serve up such rich helpings of what used to be thought of as coarse or prurient, shows a kind of adjustment on his part to the tastes of his audience and not simply an urge to sensationalize or go slumming. Put another way, the Mailer who once had earned his daily bread through attacks (carried out through fiction or journalism) on normative morality and centrist politics displays in *Tough Guys Don't Dance* nothing so much as the observation that popular criminality has been mainstreamed. No longer especially shocking or even surprisingly deviant, Mailer's pulp fiction novel registers the banality of American vice.

It should be remembered, though, that *Tough Guys Don't Dance* is certainly not a complete departure for Mailer, particularly given its concern for homicide and crime more generally. Thematically, it is a bit like his true-crime accounts of murder in *The Executioner's Song* and, some years after *Tough Guys*, his lengthy examination of the John F. Kennedy assassin in *Oswald's Tale: An American Mystery* (1996). It also returns to Mailer's controversial fictionalization of the murdered wife in *An American Dream* (1966), with the key difference that for a good deal of *Tough Guys* we don't know if the protagonist killed his wife or not—or even if it was the wife who was killed. *An American Dream* laid everything out in chronological order, so that the only thing to keep us turning pages was the question, Would Rojack get away with murder? Here, there are other reasons to turn pages. Did Tim Madden kill his wife? Whose head was buried in his marijuana patch? Who removed it? Is Tim crazy? Is someone driving him crazy? All of these "whodunit" questions, of course, readily—if surprisingly—demonstrated within the opening pages of the novel that Mailer had turned to crime fiction, that formulaic and often-sensationalized popular form.

Using narrative techniques and themes borrowed from hard-boiled detective fiction writers such as Raymond Chandler, Dashiell Hammett, and Elmore Leonard, Mailer surprised his readers and reviewers by conjuring up a nether world of criminality and vice that churned beneath the calm social surfaces of a resort community. Murder, violent retributions, cuckolding, pornography, alcoholism, séances, casual marijuana use, drug-running, sexual obsessions (both straight and gay), casual wife-swapping, and financial greed are only the most prominent social fascinations in *Tough Guys Don't Dance*. Elements like these had to a certain degree been present in his earlier writings, but in his later contribution to America's pulp fiction canon, Mailer slyly demonstrates the way these American "vices" are inescapably a vital and increasingly manifest part of the nation's contemporary culture. And Mailer's most deeply ironic gesture comes into sharp focus with the recognition that Provincetown itself—the first Massachusetts landing point for the seventeenth-century Puritans who would define so much of America's religious and moral legacy—also serves as the site for remembering America's seldom-admitted love affair with misbehavior. In my remaining discussion, I will adumbrate some of Mailer's deft approaches to staging, in *Tough Guys Don't Dance*, the insatiable character and manifold satisfactions of American criminality. The effect of these dramatizations—analogous in some ways to Mailer's earlier revelations about the murderer Gary Gilmore in *Executioner's Song* and his later ruminations about the extralegal maneuverings of the CIA in *Harlot's Ghost*—is to suggest in vivid ways the colonization of American culture by what had once been understood as criminal impulses. Just as importantly, Mailer aligns American criminality—in the case of *Tough Guys*, grisly murders and mutilations—with aspects of its sexual culture, a phenomenon he had described in provocative ways many years earlier: "[m]urder, after all, has exhilaration in it.... Besides, murder offers the promise of vast relief. It is never unsexual" (Mailer, *American Dream* 15).

For the uninitiated, Cape Cod itself might seem an unlikely place for staging a grisly crime story like the one narrated in *Tough Guys Don't Dance*. With its saltbox-and-shingled neighborhoods, lofty real estate prices, and reliable herds of summer tourists from the heartland of America, the tourist's Cape Cod is in some ways difficult to imagine as a place where a protagonist like Mailer's Tim Madden awakens in a state of alcohol-induced amnesia. Hungover and shaky from an apparently long night of drink and debauchery, he soon discovers not one, but two severed female heads nestling atop his large hidden stash of marijuana. But just as Key West has long been notorious as Florida's "mile zero"[6] destination for writers, dreamers, artists, smugglers, drifters, and misfits, so too with Cape Cod's Provincetown—the novel's primary setting where Mailer himself spends his summers. For example, and as Mailer reminds us frequently in his novel, Provincetown served as the very first seventeenth-century landing point for the dour, black-hatted pilgrims, who camped briefly on the sands of Race Point beach in what would become the village of Provincetown before making their settlement at Plymouth Plantation. He emphasizes as well that the Cape Cod peninsula might just as easily been seen as a province of religious piety along the lines of the historic Massachusetts Bay Colony as a whole, but that instead Provincetown itself always had retained a dual identity. On the one hand, a glamorous summer-time playground for the rich, famous, and creative; and on the other hand, a Wild West of the East Coast: a gay/queer sexual paradise, a drug-runner's hideout, a pirate's refuge, and a winter ghost town inhabited by the evil spirits of Hell-Town (Provincetown's alternate identity).

A regular at Provincetown's Widow's Walk Tavern, Tim Madden (who, we later learn, is not only a small-time drug-dealer but also a writer, thereby merging the idioms of art and crime) is introduced as an addict to nicotine, alcohol, cannabis, danger, and sex with his recently estranged wife. As the novel opens, however, Madden is viciously hungover from a memory-erasing bender the night before. All of these traits Mailer introduces casually in the first several pages of the novel, as though there were no need to provide any particular explanation for such matters as Madden's off-handed criminality, nor for his activities of wife-swapping and attendance at bizarre séances (of all things). Much of this rather lurid detail conforms to the traditions of crime fiction by writers like Elmore Leonard, in which the criminality of the protagonist often tends to provide him with the requisite street-smarts to prevail over his enemies. But apparently even more is at stake for Mailer in *Tough Guys*, in which he produces not only a clever piece of genre fiction but also a good deal of trenchant cultural commentary. The opening pages provide a telling example of the way Mailer deftly enlists our complicity with the practice of—and knowledge about—the underworlds of American vice. The title of Tim Madden's book, albeit barely in progress because of his drinking, suggests something of the same naturalistic theme: *In Our Wild—Studies Among the Sane*.

When describing the soon-to-be-murdered Jessica Pond, though, Mailer calls upon American popular culture as a way of describing the appearance of the beautiful woman from California whom he encountered first in the Widow's Walk Tavern. Tim Madden is instantly drawn to her sexually and thinks immediately of her resemblance to an extremely popular American adult film star from the 1970s: "There used to be a porn star named Jennifer Welles who had the same appearance. She had large, well-turned promiscuous breasts—one nipple tilted to the east, one stared out to the west—a deep navel, a woman's round belly, a sweet buoyant spread of buttocks, and *dark* pubic hair. That was what encouraged the prurience to stir in those who bought a ticket to watch Jennifer Welles. Any lady who chooses to become blonde is truly blonde" (13).

Craftily, then, as Mailer's narrator describes the charms of the fictional Jessica Pond, his comparison of her to an adult movie star familiar to millions of his readers—albeit a film star somewhat less well known than the other blonde film icon to whom he had devoted *Marilyn* (1973) only a decade earlier—he uses the increasingly commonplace American indulgence in pornography for descriptive leverage.[7] For literary novelists of earlier generations, it would have been impossible to expect that readers would have been awash in a tide of pornography, literary or cinematic. But by the time Mailer introduces himself into the world of crime fiction, it is possible not only that a large part of his readership would partake of pornography, but also that—thanks to an increasingly pervasive visual mass media—plenty of his readers would be aware of the *same* pornographic icons from viewings on videocassette recorders, which became ubiquitous in American homes in the late 1970s and early 1980s. All of which appears to be a phenomenon related to what Steven Marcus has called a sign that "pornography has lost its old danger, its old power—negative sanctions and outlawry being the most reliable indicators of how much a society is frightened of anything, how deeply it fears its power, how subversive to its settled order it conceives an idea, or work or act to be" (286).[8] To observe, as Mailer does, that his readers have undergone a transformation of moral sensibility through their exposure to mass-produced erotica is another way of concurring with Menand's suggestion that "[e]ven Mailer cannot be obscene any longer. Everyone has heard it all." There is this possibility, of course, but at the same time the cultural analysis that seeps from the pages of Mailer's crime novel suggests a good deal more than the mere fact of Americans awash in prurient materials (154).[9]

One way to understand Mailer's turn to crime fiction is to trace his suggestions that the very dichotomies that once had been used to render American culture understandable: upper-class/lower-class, morality/criminality, conservatism/liberalism, sobriety/intoxication, and so on had been irreversibly blurred. The streets of Provincetown, the locus of the author's own residence as well as the setting for *Tough Guys Don't Dance*, provide a living theater for the collapse of moral and social categories that Mailer implicitly suggests. The bustling summer streets openly display some versions of America's popular criminality, whereas the winter streets and sparse off-season population of the novel's action depict scenes of vice enacted by a skeleton crew of misfits who startle only to the extent that one recognizes the banality of their actions and desires in modern America. There are many other hints of these collapsed dichotomies of taste and behavior in the novel, such as the Philips Exeter–educated Tim Madden waking up with a tattoo—a once-notorious signifier worn mostly by criminals, common sailors, and other social outsiders but that these days (even more so than in 1985) amounts to nothing more than commonplace inscriptions for decorating the hides of the upper- and middle-class millions.

Even more sharply portrayed is Madden's adversary, the bizarre Alvin Luther Regency, police chief of Provincetown and sometime lover of both of Madden's estranged wives. During a conversation with an amnesiac Madden soon after the murders, Regency excuses Madden's lesser crime of marijuana farming with this paean to cannabis: "See, I don't care whether you're a Left-Winger or a Right-Winger. I don't care what kind of fucking wing you fly. I love pot. Conservatives aren't right in every last item of the inventory. They miss the point here. They think marijuana destroys souls, but I don't believe that—I believe the Lord gets in and wrestles the devil" (34). Just as Mailer's fictional inventory of the criminality lurking beneath Cape Cod's benign surfaces distorts (and corrects) the popular view of the resort community, so too does his pot-smoking police chief subvert, once and for all, any remaining notion we might have about the rectitude of American law enforcement officials. In Chief Regency, we are invited to consider the paradox of two perennial American battles that were so prominently headlined during the Reagan 1980s, during which *Tough Guys Don't Dance* appeared: the "war on crime" and the "war on drugs."

The thematic evidence of the *Tough Guys* narrative in some ways brings home certain points that Mailer had been making for some time about obscenity as it relates to literary art, an issue that many of his novels confront in one way or another. As he had written in a 1969 essay, "The End of Obscenity," the primary stakes in the contest of free expression versus censorship have to do with a vexing conflict in human values:

> Back of the ogres of censorship and the comedies of community hypocrisy, there still rests the last defense of the censor, a sophisticated argument which might urge that sex is a mystery and men explore it

and detail it and define it and examine it and eventually disembowel it of privacy at their peril. It is the argument of tradition against the power of reason. (*Existential Errands* 193–194)

In keeping with this remark, *Tough Guys* appears to indicate a retreat from the proposition of sexuality as a realm of the mysterious and profound, or as an unknowably transcendent component of the human experience. At the very least, and as Mailer had demonstrated to a relentless and comical degree in *Why Are We in Vietnam* (1967)— which featured profanity in nearly every sentence of its narrative— obscene or vulgar language itself was no longer much of an issue in postmodern America. Twenty years after wrangling with issues of censorship in publishing *The Naked and the Dead* (in which he retreated to the expletive "fug" rather than its more familiar cognate version), "profane" language had already become banal, having lost almost entirely its ability to shock American readers.[10]

So too, instead of mystery or transcendence, Mailer shows Tim Madden sorting out the banality of human secrets (which turn out not to be mysteries at all). Amateur pornography, for example, is the instance of demystification to which the otherwise-baffled Madden returns time and again. Himself a sometime erotic photographer of his salacious lover, the murdered Patty Lareine, Madden learns of more nude polaroids of Lareine when they are discovered by Madeleine Falco (his ex-wife, now married to police chief Alvin Regency). At this juncture, it is Madeleine whose reaction appears most quaint and oblivious to the pervasive criminality in which the community and her own husband are immersed. Her hysterical reaction betrays the irony of her situation, not to mention the pervasiveness of what an earlier generation of Mailer's readers might have identified as "vice." Mailer narrates her shock of horror in a flatly deadpan tone: "She had found some photographs. That was clear at last. She had been putting fresh laundry in his drawers and came across a locked box she had not seen before. It had enraged her that he kept a locked box in their bedroom. If he had secrets, why didn't he hide them in the cellar? So she smashed the box." Madeleine's horror, though, might apply equally well to her own participation in the casual trafficking in overtly sexual images, what once might simply have been named pornography. Stunned at the image of another woman posing for the camera of her own husband, Madeleine bitterly describes them this way: "They're of Patty Lareine. They're nude. They're obscene." More revealingly, she continues that "[t]hey're worse than the ones you took of me. I don't know if I can bear it" (175).

Earlier in the novel, the exchanges between the estranged lovers Madeleine Falco and Tim Madden create a somewhat different perspective on obscenity. Reunited for a conversation with his ex-wife, Madden trades barbs with her over drinks of bourbon, and learns for the first time of her marriage to Chief Regency. Almost immediately in that exchange, Madden proclaims his renewed love for her, asking why she had married Regency in the first place. To this query, Madeleine (the same Madeleine who would later complain of sexually explicit polaroids) bluntly tells him of her new "taste for good old boys with mammoth dicks" and goes on to detail their lovemaking sessions. When Madden imagines the same kind of question directed at himself, he attributes his preference for Patty Lareine to "a question of Comparative Fellatio," and allows that he chose her over Madeleine because "She was as insatiable as good old America, and I wanted my country on my cock" (110). And although Madden's response to this never-voiced question remains unspoken, Mailer makes it obvious that these characters are communicating on a purely visceral, sexual level, even as he makes clear that these characters are enacting scenes symbolic of a new American ethos.

Because they are fashioned almost entirely in bleakly deterministic terms, the characters in *Tough Guys Don't Dance* seem to be drawn according to the contours of figures from Theodore Dreiser or Frank Norris, or from the other early twentieth-century naturalists who had so influenced Mailer during his student years at Harvard: John Dos Passos, James T. Farrell, and Ernest Hemingway. They differ from earlier naturalistic characters, though, in that whereas Dreiser's incipiently famous Sister Carrie and her adulterous, middle-aged lover George Hurstwood are impelled by desires that they can scarcely articulate and which Dreiser's Victorian proprieties barely allow him to reveal, Mailer creates his own novel around characters who communicate primarily in the coarse language of base motives. Vice and criminality become the vital substances for ordinary Americans and for ordinary writers with a writer's block (like Tim Madden), while propriety of any kind comes to appear quaintly passé and perhaps even unpatriotic. Madden's thoughts about his two wives exemplify this alienation from the world of conventional morality and this new patriotism of vulgarity. From the tough-talking Madeleine Falco, Madden turns to the beautiful, greedy, but ill-fated Patty Lareine. As Madden somberly reflects, however, their relationship was grounded in sexual adventure, which Mailer once again describes in terms of national cultural identity. Discovering a new lover, for Madden, is not so different from establishing a national identity, for he formed a "romantic point of reference with Patty Lareine, their first night together—during a wife-swapping escapade in North Carolina—when they were as happy as Christopher Columbus, for we each discovered America, our country forever divided into two bodies" (205). To reinforce his idea about the ironies of American moralizing in tension with its practice of vice, Mailer points to Patty Lareine's soon-to-be ex-husband who joined them for the tryst in North Carolina—the brutally nicknamed "Big Stoop." A chiropractor, preacher, and sexual adventurer, "Big Stoop" stands in Mailer's view as a classic national type, "one of our fundamental American madmen: he could orgy on Saturday and baptize on Sunday" (205).

Soon after the publication of *Tough Guys Don't Dance*, I and my fellow Cape Codders were treated to a mass media invasion—during the winter, fittingly enough—by a large film crew led by director Norman Mailer. Alas, in the opinion of most critics, the film fared about as well as had the novel, which is to say disastrously. The *Washington Post* opined that the film version was "hysterical, incoherent, and blasphemously original.... You never know if you're laughing with, or at, the movie" (Qtd. in Singer 30). To make matters worse, the film was nominated in several categories at the 1987 Razzie Awards: Norman Mailer for worst director and screenplay (he tied for worst director with *Ishtar* director Elaine May); Ryan O'Neal (as Tim Madden) for worst actor; Debra Sandlund (as Madden's ex-wife Patti Lareine) for worst actress and worst new star, and Isabella Rossellini (as first ex-wife Madeleine Falco for worst supporting actress). Altogether, an embarrassment of critical insults.

Nevertheless, the lack of critical acceptance of novel and film should not obscure the nature of Mailer's achievement, an achievement produced through a rather slight novel written (by his own admission) in haste and ostensibly to pay some tax bills. By enlisting his imagination in the service of the popular crime novel, Mailer in *Tough Guys Don't Dance* not only demonstrated his creative flexibility and adaptability to a genre that he (along with other artistically ambitious writers) had previously avoided, but also enacted and promoted an important form of "cultural work." This notion of cultural work, in the specific sense used here, draws upon Philip Fisher's ideas about the way culture engages popular literary forms as means of explaining "what the present does in the face of itself, for itself, and not for any possible future." In fact, that this cultural work was being performed can be measured by registering the very repetitiousness and formulaic quality of the crime novel as a popular literary form. Fisher's observations about setting and form in early American novels can be applied to the formulaic (and thus repetitive) gestures of Mailer's crime novel as well: "Popular forms are frequently repetitive, and they are frequently read almost obsessively, as detective novels, westerns, romances, and pornography are, becoming part of what might be called a diet of reality that returns again and again to the same few motifs so that they might not slip away" (7). In the case of Mailer's novel, the most pressing "diet of reality" involves a "criminal" turn in American popular culture that at the same time has the effect of "decriminalizing" a good deal of what formerly had been understood as "vice." For this reason, Mailer's *Tough Guys Don't Dance* can be evaluated (and has been evaluated) in negative or even pejorative terms because of its failure to achieve the formal brilliance and narrative depth of books like *The Executioner's Song* and *The Naked and the Dead*, and for its reliance on an exhausted popular genre. But the novel can also be understood as an extremely revealing sort of cultural barometer, one that has the capacity for providing an index to the transformation of popular taste and a vivid registry of national morals. Whether these transformations of taste and morality have been in the direction of nihilism or freedom—or both—only future generations will be able to judge.

NOTES

1. Although Wolfe, along with Hunter S. Thompson, has been credited with much of the stylistic innovation in the New Journalism, it is less commonly observed that their characteristically energetic, even mercurial journalistic styles owe much to the example of the rock critic Lester Bangs, whose writings began in 1969 to appear in *Rolling Stone* magazine, where much of Thompson and Wolfe's work would appear over the years. A useful selection of criticism by Lester Bangs is *Psychotic Reactions and Carburetor Dung: The Work of a Legendary Critic* (1988).
2. For a useful bibliography and overview of Mailer's key works, see Whalen-Bridge 217–220.
3. In a memorable review of *Harlot's Ghost* (1991), John Leonard wrote in *The Nation* that Mailer's 1,310 pp. sprawling novel included "every narrative form known to the modern Russian novel: picaresque and epistolary; Bildungsroman and roman a clef; the historical, the gothic, the pornographic; the thriller and the western. There are also journal jottings, cable traffic, interoffice memorandums and transcripts of wiretaps. For so many species of story, there are as many tics of prose; seizures and afflatus. When his battery's charged, Mailer windmills from one paragraph to the next-baroque, anal, Talmudic, olfactory,

portentous, loopy, coy, Egyptian; down and dirty in the cancer, the aspirin or the plastic; shooting moons on sheer vapor; blitzed by paranoia and retreating for a screen pass, as if bitten in the pineal gland by a deranged Swinburne, with metaphors so meaning-moistened that they stick to our thumbs, with 'intellections' (as he once put it) slapped on 'like adhesive plasters' " (623).

4. Robert Merrill observes that while *Tough Guys Don't Dance* turned out to be a much different project than what Mailer had begun pondering as early as 1967, Provincetown had long been a fascination for Mailer, who "[wrote] at length in *Of a Fire on the Moon* (1970) about his experiences in Provincetown and describes a novel that he planned in 1967 'about a gang of illumined and drug-accelerated American guerrillas who lived in the wilds of a dune or a range and descended on Provincetown to kill' " (Merrill 232). Scott Duguid's view of *Tough Guys Don't Dance* is close to my own when he argues that after the composition of the lengthy Egyptian-themed *Ancient Evenings*, the novel that preceded it, Mailer turned to composing "a very American work about petty vice and consumption" (Duguid 24).

5. In a recent survey of Mailer's fiction, Barry Leeds takes the conventional view of *Tough Guys Don't Dance* as a relatively trifling production compared with some of his earlier novels, remarking that "unlike *An American Dream*, *Tough Guys Don't Dance* remains merely an entertaining potboiler" and that it "collapses in its last hundred pages and never recovers" (76). Robert Merrill, however, sees Mailer's foray into the crime novel as more successful, despite the haste with which it was written. Merrill argues that while Mailer admitted to having finished the novel in only two months (rather than the ten years it would require to complete *Ancient Evenings* (1983), "Certainly there has been little correlation between the time Mailer spends writing something and the quality of the finished product" (232).

6. For another excellent novel about America's furthest continental reaches, see Thomas Sanchez, *Mile Zero* (1989), which focuses on the complexities and mystery of Key West.

7. In a 1965 essay, Leslie Fiedler singled out *An American Dream* as the novel that best exemplified Mailer's conflation of pornographic tropes and avant-garde aesthetics, calling his new sensibility "porno-esthetics" (197).

8. Marcus is generally skeptical of any claims to subversion that pornography might claim, especially in the modern period. Writing of the Victorian period, he argues that "[a]t best, pornography may be subversive in the sense that it reveals the discrepancy which exists in society between openly professed ideals and secretly harbored wishes or secretly practiced vices—it may act indirectly to 'unmask' society's official version of itself. It never, to my knowledge, is capable of taking the next step of subversion: it cannot supply a vision that either

transcends or transvalues what passes for current reality. On the contrary, pornography is perfectly and happily at home with hypocrisy,
cant, injustice, and all kinds of social malevolence; it may even be
regarded as dependent upon them for its existence" (Marcus 230).

9. Although his recent review-essay on Mailer's work makes no mention
of *Tough Guys Don't Dance*, Menand argues that, in general, Mailer's
use of sexually explicit scenarios in his fiction is part of his complaint
against technology's damaging effect on the modern spirit: "He is
sympathetic to the use of grossly offensive imagery to shock audi-
ences into some awareness of the technological horror of their spiritual condition. He has always relied heavily on obscenity in his won
fiction with that end in mind" (154). My argument differs from
Menand's in its assertion that Mailer's use of "obscenity" is in fact
journalism—documentation of American reality—rather than a
warning about what eventually may happen to American life.

10. Reflecting on obscenity and the writing, Mailer wrote in *The Armies
of the Night* that "he had kicked good-bye in his novel *Why Are We in
Vietnam?* to the old literary corset of good taste, letting his sense of
language play on obscenity as freely as it wished...—it was the first
time his style seemed as once very American to him and very literary
in the best way" (45–46).

WORKS CITED

Bangs, Lester. *Psychotic Reactions and Carburetor Dung: The Work of a Legendary Critic,* ed. Greil Marcus. New York: Anchor Press, 1988.

Bourdieu, Pierre. *Distinction: A Social Critique of the Judgment of Taste,* trans. Richard Nice. Cambridge, MA: Harvard University Press, 1984.

Bromwich, David. "The Adjuster." *American Studies. The New Republic* 13 January 2003, 26–29.

Duguid, Scott. "The Addiction of Masculinity: Norman Mailer's *Tough Guys Don't Dance* and the Cultural Politics of Reaganism." *Journal of Modern Literature* 30:1 (Fall 2006): 23–30.

Fiedler, Leslie. "The New Mutants," in *A New Fiedler Reader.* Amherst, NY: Prometheus Books, 1999 (1965). 178–188.

Fisher, Philip. *Hard Facts: Setting and Form in the American Novel.* New York: Oxford University Press, 1985.

Leonard, John. "Don Quixote at Eighty." *New York Review of Books* 50:4 (13 March 2003): 10–12.

Mailer, Norman. *An American Dream.* New York: Dell, 1966.
———. *Ancient Evenings.* Boston: Little, Brown, 1983.
———. *The Armies of the Night.* New York: Penguin, 1968.
———. *The Barbary Shore.* New York: Holt, Rinehart, 1951.
———. *Existential Errands.* Boston: Little, Brown, 1972.
———. *Harlot's Ghost.* New York: Random House, 1991.

————. *Miami and the Siege of Chicago: An Informal History of the Republican and Democratic Conventions of 1968.* New York: World, 1968.

————. *The Naked and the Dead.* New York: Rinehart, 1948.

————. *Of a Fire on the Moon.* Boston: Little, Brown, 1970.

————. *The Spooky Art: Some Thoughts on Writing.* New York: Random House, 2003.

————. *Tough Guys Don't Dance.* New York: Random House, 1984.

————. *Why Are We in Vietnam?* New York: G.P. Putnam's Sons, 1967.

Leeds, Barry H. *The Enduring Vision of Norman Mailer.* Bainbridge Island, WA: Pleasure Boat Studio, 2002.

Leonard, John. "Don Quixote at Eighty." *New York Review of Books* 50 (13 March 2004): 10–12.

————. "Review of *Harlot's Ghost.*" *The Nation* 253 (18 November 1991): 622–629.

Marcus, Steven. *The Other Victorians: A Study of Sexuality and Pornography in Mid-Nineteenth-Century England.* New York: Basic Books, 1966.

Menand, Louis. "Norman Mailer in His Time," in *American Studies.* New York: Farrar, Straus and Giroux, 2002.

Merrill, Robert. "*Tough Guys Don't Dance* and the Detective Traditions." *Critique: Studies in Contemporary Fiction* 34:4 (1993): 232–247.

Sanchez, Thomas. *Mile Zero.* New York: Vintage Books, 1990.

Singer, Mark. "Tough Guy." *New Yorker* 21 May 2007, 30–31.

Whalen-Bridge, John. "Norman Mailer." *Dictionary of Literary Biography: American Novelists since WW II* 278 (2003): 217–232 Detroit: Gale. [Online]. Available: http://galenet.galegroup.com.

Wolfe, Tom. *The New Journalism.* New York: Harper and Row, 1973.

PART II

God

CHAPTER 4

Mailer's "Gnostic" *Gospel*

Ashton Howley

Wise men of old gave the soul a feminine name. Indeed she is female in her nature as well.

Robinson, The Exegesis on the Soul *192*

The Christian puts his Church and his Bible between himself and his unconscious.

Carl Jung, Man and His Symbols *92*

For where the truth is with us in one place, it is buried in another.

Mailer's Jesus *4[1]*

Mailer's favorite religious idea, one that he usually incorporated into his literary characters' speech and into his own, is that "there is a God and a Devil at war with one another, neither of whom is invincible" (*Time* 1223). Mailer found this Manichean doctrine attractive for at least three reasons. Given the "philosophical vertigo" (1224) induced by the concept of a benevolent deity, "capable of doing everything and anything at any given moment" (*Conversations* 29), but continuously allowing war, genocide, torture, rape, disease, poverty, and starvation to occur, Manicheanism dissolves theodicy's cognitive dissonance. Based on the premise that God cannot be omnipotent, Manicheanism "diminishes the absurdity," in Camus' words, "of an intimate relationship between suffering humanity and an implacable god'" (qtd. in Smith 545). Another reason that Mailer was drawn to this Manichean doctrine is that it restores substance to evil; that is, evil is not the perversion or absence of the good but an active force embodied by the world's Archon and his minions. Third, Manicheanism, inherently existentialist, grants free will to human beings, whom Mailer regarded as microagents of benevolence or malevolence, existing on "some mediating level" (*Time* 1224) between "a Creator" and "an opposite Presence (to be called Satan, for short)" (qtd. in Levenda 1). Since there is "the most lively possibility of a variety of major and minor angels, devils and demons, good spirits and evil, working away more or less invisibly in our lives" (1), Mailer thought, the responsibility for those who claim to be working on God's side is to ensure that they are not deluded. Insisting that today's denizens of the global community are "alienated" from their "capacity to decide [their] moral worth" (*Time* 956), Mailer felt that "[u]nless our concept of spirituality deepens immensely in the next century," there is no "certain[ty] that we're going to make it" (Abbot 3). Without the "inner coherence" (1224) necessary to fathom the depths of one's own motives, "consciousness alienated from instinct begins to construct its intellectual formulations over a void" (1235).

Yet to call Mailer's religious ideas "Manichean" without disclaimers is to attribute a looming irony to his syncretism. Although the Manicheans were "obsessed with duality" (Walker 125), they sought to resolve "this dualism" by placing "great emphasis on self-control and asceticism," and by "oppos[ing] marriage, sensual indulgence, the eating of animal food and the drinking of wine." Mailer is everywhere dualistic, but he is nothing like ascetic. No litany of Manichean's antimaterialist doctrines could accurately describe his exuberant verbal-formalizings of the phenomena of lived experience in his novels. Confirming his readers' awareness of his status as one of the twentieth century's most prolific littérateur-celebrants of the body's pleasures and pains, its pits and pitfalls, highly influenced by such literary aficionados of the flesh as Hemingway, Lawrence, and Miller, the nuances, both physical and psychic, of Promethean Ali's rising-from-the-ropes defeat of George Foreman, in *The Fight*, of Menenhetet's remembrances of his feats in love and war during Egypt's long Night of the Pig, in *Ancient Evenings*, and of Picasso's gestalt-revisitings of the autopsies he observed, in surfaces of faces spookily blurred-asunder, in *Portrait of Picasso as a Young Man*—Mailer's commentaries on the muscular, sexual, and aesthetic performances of just these three titans alone reveal how prodigal a Manichean he is—how dissimilar to the body- and world-despising founder of Manicheanism, who conceived of human beings as reluctant spirits, trapped, for a time, in the corporeal world, the "preserve of Satan" (Walker 189).

Mailer is better labelled a "gnostic" writer, a term that conveys his allegiances to the immanent world of nature and of the body, and that he himself embraces in *On God: An Uncommon Conversation* (195). His syncretic ideas and "Gnosticism" have both been assigned, inaccurately, in my opinion, an antiphysical bias that would "satisfy any characterization" of them "as world-denying and body-hating" (King 194).[2] Because "Gnosticism has come to have significant application in a variety of…areas, including philosophy, literary studies, politics, and psychology" (5), the meaning of this term is as tattered as the scrolls themselves, many of which were unearthed in the late 1940s in Nag Hammadi, Egypt, and placed under the rubric "gnostic," the Greek ancestor of "know" whose latinate form is *scire*, the root of "science" (Harris 64). As these papyri entered the light of unbiased textual analysis, conventional generalizations about the world-shunning impulse allegedly inherent in the term gave way to their assessors' open-minded willingness to think anew about its meaning. But not without controversy. On one hand, Catholic apologist Philip Jenkins complains that the "gnostic" papyri, which "depict a world of individualistic mystics and magi whose unfettered speculations are unconstrained by ecclesiastical structures," have "acquired an importance far beyond their real historical value" ("Hidden Gospels"). Jenkins regards the canonical gospels as authoritative because the Nicean bishops did so. On the other, Elaine Pagels, for whom orthodoxy has always "tend[ed] to distrust our capacity to make such discriminations and insist on making them for us" (184), argues that "exploring…the history of Christianity in the light of the Nag Hammadi discoveries" (29) is necessary to stem the prevailing "tendency to identify Christianity with a single, authorized set of beliefs—however these actually vary from church to church." This tendency, Pagels claims, "decisively shaped—and inevitably limited—what would become Western Christianity" (29). Similarly, Karen King contends that the "strategies devised by early Christians to define orthodoxy and heresy are alive and well in the politics of religious normativity in the modern world.... [c]laims to be true to tradition, charges that opponents are contaminating the original, pure form of the tradition…or eschewal of intellectual or moral questioning as an unnecessary confusion of faith—such practices effectively replicate the pattern of ancient polemics" (24). Mailer was contemptuous of the "Judeo-Christian enterprise" (*On God* 191) for posturing as the "absolute arbiter over the more mysterious elements of existence." In his opinion, because ours is an era in which "Fundamentalist notions of absolute authority" (194) have become "a manic faith machine capable of inspiring world disasters," it is crucial for everyone to let themselves "wander through the forests of theology" (196). "Theologians," he continues, "no matter at what high level they cerebrate—are trapped...by their already-received religious systems" (144); "obliged to do their thinking with ideas they are not all that free to change," they unconsciously "avoid many questions they cannot begin to confront."

Radically revisioning "normative Christianity" (King 2), Mailer's *Gospel* is germane to discussions about the meaning of "gnosticism." In his humanizing portrayal, a feature of many of the Nag Hammadi papyri, Jesus validates the symbiosis between the realms of nature and of the spirit while striving to reconcile his two main ideological inheritances, paganism and Essenic Judaism. Another common element is the mentoring role that Mailer's Satan assumes. That *Gospel* illustrates Mailer's Manichean idea, that God is not all powerful, has been noted by its few commentators, but that it restores psychological, theological, and dramatic balance to the story of Jesus, by rendering the trinity as a "quaternity" (de Franz, qtd. in Jung, *Man* 246), a term that reflects what many of the Nag Hammadi codices do, the "four-cornered divine person: father, son, holy ghost, and Satan," has not. The "fourth principle" (Matton 168) that both the Nag Hammadi gospels and Mailer's include emphasizes the importance of Satan and of other elements denigrated in Christian ontology—"evil, the earth, matter, the body and the feminine" (de Franz, qtd. in Jung, *Man* 246). Although Mailer makes Satan a Manichean missionary who shows Jesus just how far from perfect and omnipotent his heavenly father is, in the fact that this unlikely spokesman chooses to focus on Jehovah's misogynism, Mailer makes way for the most remarkable feature of *Gospel*, one that provides the third link between it and "gnostic" literature—Mailer's Jesus reiterates all but *verbatim* an esoteric passage deriving from *The Gospel of Mary*, one of the Nag Hammadi scriptures that renders evil/sin as an imbalance attaining between "the material and the spiritual" (King, qtd. in Robinson 523). Devoted to resolving the imbalances in human beings that lead them to bring evil into the world of experience, Mary's gospel presents its thematic concerns in terms of gender, linking the feminine with the unconscious and making esotericism an inherent component of spirituality.[3] The esoteric passage attributed to Mary and appearing in *Gospel* facilitates Mailer's revival of an "essential aspect" (Smith 540) of the Nag Hammadi papyri, the "the vessel of spiritual transformation, a feminine principle."[4]

This essay examines *Gospel* less as Mailer's Manichean narrative and more as his "gnostic" Christology. I begin by exploring Jesus' efforts to reconcile the paganism he inherits from his mother and the

Essenic beliefs he derives from Jehovah. Since his ideological inheritances, representing the different "forms of belief and practice" (King 21) that those who assembled the New Testament texts pitted against one another, "notably Judaism and paganism," encode their divergent bases, respectively, in Plato and in Aristotle, I will discuss Mailer's reference to himself as a "left-medievalist" ("World Empire"). I then consider how Mailer's rationalized presentation of Jesus' miracles compensates for the Plato-inspired "avoidance of the humanity of Jesus" (Jeffrey, *Dictionary* 344) implicit in the canonical writers' stressing of his supernaturalism. My comments on the "left" side of medieval iconography provide the framework in which Satan's role and the passage that Mailer borrows from *The Gospel of Mary* can both be understood. These features of Mailer's gospel constitute his method of conveying his "gnostic" doctrine, that evil is the result of psychic disequilibrium, even as Jesus' efforts to hold in balance a series of dualisms make him Mailer's *exemplum* for those who would more clearly discern which side of the cosmological war they serve by understanding themselves in greater depth. Since Mailer's ideas about people's struggle to achieve a balanced awareness of the dualistic forces operative in the psyche reveal his clear affinities with Jung, I will occasionally invoke him in what follows. Although Mailer studied Jung when organizing his material for *Castle in the Forest,* according to J. Michael Lennon,[5] he had not done so when composing *Gospel.* In *On God,* Mailer writes: "[h]aving a view of the universe that makes sense to oneself, is, I think, Jung's finest prescription for mental health.... [o]ne of his conclusions was that nobody could be cured of their neurosis until they found their own vision of God" (26). Dramatizing his own unique vision, Mailer's *Gospel* invites his readers to recognize the incongruities defining mainstream religions. Among these are the emphasizing of transcendence over immanence, the irrational nature of theodicy, the assigning to women the role of the scapegoat, and the avoidance of both esotericism and depth-psychology, as if the unconscious, intuition, speculation, and hypothesis had little to do with, and even threatened the stability of one's spiritual life.[6] As I shall show, *Gospel* represents his endeavor to balance metaphysics and psychology in a manner that Christianity and Islam, "two essentially inauthentic unbalanced theologies" ("World Empire"), in his opinion, do not inspire.

Consider how Mailer's Jesus, recounting his early experiences as carpenter, "ponders on the substances of His Kingdom that we worked upon with our hands" (6), "find[s] communion with the wood" (5), and deepens his awareness of the fact that "apples from the tree in Eden had possessed knowledge of good and evil" (6), before claiming that "sometimes it would seem that good and evil were still in the wood" (6). He goes on sermonizing about the fact that "a crude plank could act with knowledge of good and evil" (6) and that he "could feel a fine spirit between grain and my hand," as if he were a medieval alchemist communing with objective correlatives to interior states of being. He is projecting, as he later learns from Satan, his own inner nature wherein good and evil, his equivalent propensities for all that is symbolized by light and by shadow, reside. For this reason, during his youth, when he is still unconscious of the roots of his identity, he is endlessly distracted by his appreciation of what effectively serves as a mirror for himself, the natural world, in all of its beautiful physicality. His inherent pagan sensibility incites his awareness of the spiritual forces embodied in wood and of spells cast by fish hauled in by fishermen who cast stronger spells (68). However, like Herod and Manasseh (17, 46), pagans beneath the surface, Jesus must conceal his unorthodox affinities. "Being Essenes," he says, "we were, of all Jews, strictest in our worship of the one God and were full of scorn for Roman religions with their belief in many deities.... [s]o I could hardly talk to my family of a spirit in the wood. That was pagan" (6).

To appreciate the subtle manner in which Jesus becomes Mailer's vehicle for balancing paganism and Judaism, the reasons that Mailer referred to himself as a "left-medievalist," must be noted. As someone who could sound like a Platonic theologian when speculating about God and the Devil as transcendent personalities, but who could also sound like a proponent of Aristotelian naturalism when elaborating on his commitment to the immanent world, Mailer engaged the major tension that Western philosophers and theologians of the medieval period inherited from their counterparts in the ancient world. This tension, the result of the endemic differences between "Platonic theology and Aristotelian logic" (Jeffrey, *By Things Seen* 227), finds succinct embodiment in Raphael's visual metaphor of it, *The School of Athens*. Raphael's painting shows Plato and Aristotle engaged in conversation, with Plato holding his *Timæus* in his left hand and pointing, with his right hand, toward heaven, and with Aristotle clutching his *Ethics* in his right hand, while gesturing, with his left hand, toward earth. Here Plato directs their attention beyond the "reality line" (243) that separates the immanent and the transcendent worlds, his pursuit of the question of what reality is elevating his mind beyond this line. This question brings Plato into "the intelligible world of forms, the realm of the One, the universal" (233). However, the "young and swarthy" Aristotle directs their attention to "the realm of nature, the many, the tangible particulars of creation" (240, 243). Scientifically, but not theologically, the Scholastics' findings in Aristotle eclipsed the attractiveness that Plato had held for the Western imagination for more than a millennium. Aristotle's insistence that only the "measurable, physical world" (235) is real, and that "all practicable questions" rightly belong in "the immanent and objective realm of philosophy," gradually persuaded the medieval writers— Pecham, for example—to develop the "logical, dialectical techniques" that would help them "carry the values of the classical and biblical past into an increasingly 'tangible'...world" (251).

The narrator of Mailer's *Gospel*, rendering many features of his narrative Aristotelian, challenges his readers' willingness to accept as veritable truth the New Testament's allegedly supernatural events. Conforming to Aldous Huxley's notion of "empirical theology" (qtd. in Surette 26), a notion that accounts for the ways in which naturalistic accounts "strip myth and ritual of...transcendental or religious significance" (29), Mailer's Jesus enacts the inductive process of Aristotelian logic, a process that, beginning with what his senses take in and proceeding as he forms speculative thoughts about what is occurring in his environment, is premised on what Aristotle saw as the basis of "human rationality" (Stumpf 89, 102): for Aristotle, the fact that there is "no life...without body" meant that all reasoning must first be grounded in one's sensory responses to nature. During the wedding in Cana, for instance, Mailer's Jesus pays homage to the organic unity of the natural world, of the "Spirit who resided" within "one red grape" (61). Later, he conjectures that coincidence alone suggests a causal relation between his spoken command and the becalming of the storm-tossed Sea of Galilee (93). Later still, he accounts for his ability to feed a large crowd with only a small amount of bread and fish, when he observes that "[t]he morsel became enlarged within [each person's] thoughts" (116), here revealing the medieval alchemists' tendency to regard nature's "prima materia" as "the unknown substance embodying or carrying the projection of psychic content" (Jung, *Abstracts* 152). While, typically, Mailer's Jesus restrains his self-projecting tendencies, the author here speaking directly through him when he says that "[e]ven as waste will exist in all matters, so in the working of miracles, extravagance is best avoided" (117), he mostly describes his performances of miracles skeptically, prefacing them with a series of tentative evasions. "I had to hope that the daughter was not dead but resting in the long shadow of sleep that is near death" (96), he remarks, "[f]or then I might save her," referring to the first person he does or does not raise from the dead. As he implores his disciples, "[e]at of me, for this is my body'" (223), he reasons with himself, saying, "[a]nd what I said was true.... [i]n death our flesh returns to the earth and from that earth will come grain" [223]), again veering away from supernaturalism. These are just some of the miraculous-turned-rhetorical performances of Jesus, whom Mailer imagined as "an exhausted...magician after a long night of performance" (Busa 29), doing "the best that can be done under the circumstances" and requiring what magicians do, "collaboration between the artist and his public" (E.M. Butler, qtd. in Sagan 170). The "miracle of faith would be present or would not" (126), Mailer's Jesus says. But his efforts in rendering his miracles explainable, through logical appeals from the sensory to the rational, reify Siger of Brabant's observation, that "'[w]e have nothing to do with the miracles of God, since we treat natural things in a natural way'" (Jeffrey, By Things Seen 230). As Lawrence Eldredge comments, philosophers and theologians susceptible to Aristotle tended to glorify the immanent creation of the transcendent creator. By "diminishing divine control," Eldredge claims, the "shadow of determinism" (By Things Seen 212–213) was cast upon Platonic speculation and removed from pagan philosophy, which "stresses nature and natural processes rather than the God of nature and his ways."

Mailer's Jesus reveals his skepticism toward the New Testament's supernatural content also in his penchant for validating his persistent misgivings. Readers of Gospel opening it randomly can observe him winding an endless thread of entangling questions that make tactical evasiveness a virtue. "Was the Holiest descending toward us in the form of a dove?" (33), he asks John the Baptist. "Is it not death and destruction to see him?" (35), he again queries, prompting his cousin to wonder, "[d]id the light of the Lord appear when you were immersed?" (37). Thus Mailer, rendering many of the gospel texts in the interrogative mood, and hoping to inspire some commonsense hypotheses about the story of Jesus, aims to complicate conventional interpretations of the gospels. To compel readers of the Bible to ask questions about what they take in, in effect, he turns Jesus into a novelist like himself. Such novelists, Mailer says, form "suppositions about the nature of reality" ("World Empire"), in order to "enrich" their "minds and—it is always a hope—some readers' minds as well." For Mailer, the doors of intuitive perception, swinging on the hinges of hypotheses, "open the mind to thought, to comparison, to doubt, to the elusiveness of truth" ("Invisible Kingdom"); however, in the minds of people loyal to their "frozen hypotheses," "[s]erious questions are answered by declaration and will not be reopened."

Satan's role and the esoteric passage from *The Gospel of Mary* show less subtly Mailer's ambition in writing *Gospel*, to effect a balancing of a myriad of elements in the story of Jesus. Here the significance of Mailer's calling himself a *left*-medievalist must be understood as his way of gesturing to his Aristotelian affinities for all that is symbolized by left-handedness in medieval iconography, as his gospel reflects—immanence, evil, darkness, and the female principle (Cf. Jung, *Psyche* 54). Mailer's sinister source of dark enlightenment, helping Jesus "comprehend that one must enter the darkness that lives beneath every radiance of spirit" (126), establishes three main points with him, the first of which is directly Manichean, that Jehovah is not omnipotent. Foremost among His limitations, Satan insists, is his lack of empathy for human beings and especially for women. Persuading Jesus that human limitations mirror divine ones, that Jehovah, too, is fraught with imperfections, misogynism foremost among them, Satan's counsel announces storms of confusion in Jesus. Feeling himself coming "closer to the light" by getting "nearer to the darkness," Jesus recognizes, "[b]y the light in [Satan's] dark eyes" (54), that good and evil are forces of agency, both human and divine. Satan comes to the discussion armed with the most damning evidence against Jehovah, the latter's own words as recorded in the Old Testament. Making the fact that Jehovah "has no inkling of women" (50) and always speaks "only to men" (51) his primary target-issues, he tells Jesus about God's failure to "comprehend that women are creatures different from men and live with separate understanding" (50). Reluctantly, Jesus realizes that he has not yet drawn lines of distinction between himself and Jehovah, that his attitudes, too, are just as antifemale, as when he recalls himself saying that "the mouth of a strange woman is a deep pit .... [a]nd a great city is like a strange woman" (148). These comments reveal merely his own estrangement from the feminine. Wistfully reflecting on the fact that he typically traces the causes of his shortcomings—his timidity, for instance—to his mother, he realizes that, for most of his youth, he felt like "a man enclosing another man within" (26), needing the self-protective "[v]irtue" with which his mother "had built a fence around the first fence in order to guard her" (12), to hide his inmost feelings. As the erudite Satan goes on citing passages from the Old Testament, the evidence he conjures of Jehovah's cruel misogynism depicts Jehovah's sadistic reveling at its worst. Although Jesus is too naive to offer much of a defense against Satan's sincere remarks about Yahweh's fetishized bloodlust, he becomes aware of his own stance toward the feminine while also admitting that Jehovah is neither all-loving nor all-powerful.

The consequence of Jesus' conversation with Satan is his rejecting the notion of Jehovah *de potentia absoluta* and of himself as a vessel of perfection. The fact that it is Satan who awakens Jesus to Jehovah's limitations and imperfections is significant both dramatically and theologically. As a source of wisdom for Jesus, who helps him to modify his idealizing of Jehovah, Mailer's Satan restores balance to the gospel story. A dramatic reflection of the Platonic emphasis on transcendence, the biblical imago of the triune divinity made it impossible for the leaders of the early Christian Church to attribute substance to evil, creating the millenia-running "paradox" of theodicy. Satan articulates Mailer's "gnostic" idea that evil is present in the psyches of all creatures, both human and divine, Jesus and Jehovah alike. This doctrine, frequently appearing in the Nag Hammadi scriptures, reflects "the gnostic insistence on evil as an active principle" (Smith 541) operative in the unconscious and running counter to the "incomplete Christian view of evil as the *privatio boni*, the absence of good." The writers of the New Testament gospels, such as John's, where Satan vaguely exists as the "tempter," rendered as drama what the Church Fathers rendered as doctrine, namely, the "main prejudice of the Christian tradition" (Robinson 538), the "apparent circumventing" of evil, originating in the idea, Summum Bonum, that evil is no more than the absence or distortion of the good.[7] The result is the theological equivalent of an unfortunate psychic feature of our unconscious existence: the "primitive tendency in us...to shut our eyes to evil and drive it over some frontier or other, like the Old Testament scapegoat, which was supposed to carry the evil into the wilderness" (Jung, *Undiscovered* 109–110).

Mailer's Satan prepares Jesus for his encounter with another of the canonical writers' scapegoats. In Mary Magdalene's presence, Jesus must mentally subdue the misogynistic passages from the Old Testament that flood his mind (176, 177), as he struggles against his inherited tendency to project his misogynistic attitudes onto Mary: one side of him hears "the soft voice of the spirit" compelling his recognition that she is "a creature of God" and perhaps "near the Lord in ways I could not see" (177); the other side wishes to project onto her his "own evil...rich and dark and begging to be cast forth from me" (179). "It is written," he tells her, "I will raise up thy lovers, and they shall come against thee...shall take away thy nose and ears and thy residue shall be devoured by fire." To which she responds, "I do not wish to lose my nose," undercutting his threatening rhetoric and drawing attention to the positive valence she gives to Jesus' initially negative, because fearful, response to her physical beauty: "[a]s

I feared, she was beautiful" (177). Undergoing another shift in perspective, Jesus comes to recognize the fact that the health of the body and that of the soul depend upon a balancing of warring principles, a fact that affirms Aristotle's insistence that the soul and body share the same substance, and that leads Jesus to moderate his Manichean despising of the body as the vehicle of the soul's progress through the vale of confusion, sickness, pain, and death.

Jesus then cites the esoteric passage from *The Gospel of Mary* that documents her vision of "the seven forms" (Robinson 526) of "the fourth power." To glean the significance of its appearance in Mailer's gospel, a brief foray into Mary's is necessary. The "seven-powers narrative" (Robinson 524) begins after she asks Jesus, "[w]hat is the sin of the world?" In response, he reveals that "[t]here is no sin, but it is you who make sin" (525). By sin, he refers to an imbalance between the spirit, the soul, and the mind. Between the spirit, which communes with nature, and the soul, the means of entering into visionary states of being, is the mind, the seat of "the Son of Man" (525). Jesus then urges her to go inward to embrace that which "is within you," saying, "[f]ollow after him" (525). Confused by his elusive meanings, Mary asks, "Lord, now does he who sees the vision see it through the soul or through the spirit?"—to which he responds, "[h]e does not see through the soul nor through the spirit, but the mind which is between the two....[f]or where the mind is, there is the treasure" (525–526). Then Mary has her vision, which, in the surviving fragments, takes up with these words: the "soul answered and said, 'I saw you.... [y]ou did not see me nor recognize me.... I served you as a garment, and you did not know me'" (526). As this embattled dialogue between her spirit and her soul intensifies, her vision is born, one that expunges from the depths of her being all the hindrances in her causing their conflict. The first of the seven forms, appearing in her vision, is "darkness," the "second [is] desire, the third ignorance, the fourth is excitement of death, the fifth is the kingdom of the flesh, the sixth is the foolish wisdom of the flesh, the seventh is the wrathful wisdom" (526).

The esoteric passages in *The Gospel of Mary* work to remove the negative valences attributed to the feminine by patriarchal religious traditions, which typically reveal the "ambiguous rift of disturbing estrangement evident in the politics of exclusion" (King 25). To Mary's esoteric vision, Mailer adds the term "wed" (181), a salient term that invokes the "gnostic" trope of psychological balance as a marriage between warring masculine / conscious and feminine/ unconscious sides of self, and that instills the male-female syzygy in his version of Jesus' narrative, bringing the symbolic feminine into the light of his consciousness and out of the shadow of denial cast by Jehovah's misogynism. Similarly, the "gnostic" scriptures, in their depictions of Jesus' relationship with Mary, are based on the dyadic relation between masculine and feminine components, the "mysterium coniunctionis," in Jungian terms that describe the psychological wholeness attained by "the self" as its "nuptial union of opposite halves" (*Psyche* 64): "the body comes from the female, who is characterized by emotionality; the spirit comes from the male, who stands for rationality" (55).[8] Nor does the "gnostic" writers' gender psychology constitute "sexist rigidity" (Jung, *Aspects* xiv), for, accordingly, everyone is "a compound of two mixtures, the female and the male" (*Psyche* 55).

Given the lack of commentary on the appearance in Mailer's *Gospel* of this bizarre passage from Mary's, doubtless many readers wonder what Mailer is doing here. Doubtless, too, interpreting the reasons for its appearance as his way of making Jesus veer Christianity into alignment with psychologically balanced "gnostic" traditions might strike some readers as so much hermeneutical overstatement. However, this interpretation finds support in the fact that this "gnostic" concept of the psyche as a martial battlefield is one of his stock ideas, second only to his Manichean notion about the cosmic war between God and Satan. Even before *The Prisoner of Sex* (1971), his lengthiest treatment of this theme, the self-styled "Doctor of Dialects" (*Prisoner* 20) incorporated the "gnostic" dialogue as a forum for discussing these embattled principles in "The Metaphysics of the Belly" (*The Presidential Papers* 277–302). His dialectical conversation between himself and his fictional interlocutor elaborates on the soul's relation to its physical embodiment, a conversation he felt was worth including also in *Cannibals and Christians* (206–243). He writes, "when the soul enters a particular tangible existence, it weds itself to that existence" (*TPP* 297); in the body, the "meeting of opposites takes place ... between a male principle ... and something female in the soul of the man." "Being is first the body we see before us" (*TPP* 295), he argues, here sounding like his fictional version of Mary Magdalene, when she makes the same Aristotelian point to Jesus, urging him to embrace the fact that "without the flesh there is no life" (180). In Mailer's terms, between the masculine and feminine components, "agreement with a balance ... would offer men vision and women 'the power of the soul'" (*Prisoner* 181).

The terms that Mailer uses in "The Metaphysics of the Belly," and the presence that he bestows to Satan and to Mary in his gospel, align him not only with the "gnostic" literature but also with the latter's twentieth-century counterpart, archetypal psychology. One of its basic axioms, Aristotle's "notion of soul as life" (Hillman, *Archetypal* 17, 5), makes the psyche "indistinguishable from bodily life." By contrast, the masculine principle is allied with mind. When Mailer claims that psychological equilibrium grants women "the power of the soul" (*Prisoner* 181) and "offer[s] men vision," he reflects precisely the same "gnostic" psychologizing of gender that Jung does when he claims that spirit is "characteristically masculine, in contrast to soul, which he conceived of as feminine" (Beebe, *Aspects* xii). Both "spirit and soul…figure in the development of both men and women" (*Aspects* xiv), increasingly, as they form the "*syzygy* or conjunction" in their psyches of these gendered components of their unconscious.

In "The Metaphysics of the Belly," Mailer discourses on these principles, but in his gospel, he renders them dramatically. In his version, Jesus and Mary represent the balanced psyche that Mailer, reflecting these traditions in "The Metaphysics of the Belly," *Prisoner* and *Gospel*, upholds as the optimum state of being, a state that contemporary psychologists and neuroscientists have also put forward as integral to balanced human perception. As these scientific domains have established over the past century, the unconscious, the seat of intuition and of repression (the right-brain, in right-handed people, and vice versa), and, contrastively, the cortex-dominated left-hemisphere wherein the faculties of logic and of reason operate, are continuously engaged in a struggle for dominance. Old associations—for instance, the associating of left-handedness and the feminine—appear in current psychological and therapeutic discourse as methods of developing right-hemispheric awareness (journal-writing and painting with the nondominant hand, for example).[9] While human beings' hemispheric duality naturally entails a degree of bipolarity, stereotypical standards for men and women further polarize the masculine and feminine sides of their psyche. Men's suppression of their feminine nature cuts them off from their emotions, hinders their intuition, and blocks their memories— this is the crippled state in which many of Mailer's male characters find themselves, Dougy Madden, for instance, in *Tough Guys Don't Dance*. Leonard Shlain, commenting on the fact that cultural biases often favor masculine orientation, argues that, "when a critical mass of people within a society acquire literacy…left-hemispheric modes of thought are reinforced at the expense of right-hemispheric ones, which manifests as a decline in the status of images, women's rights, and goddess worship" (qtd. in Ackerman 156), a decline that has been apparent for millenia in "left-brained, misogynistic cultures dominated by a male god" (156).

Interpreting, in Mailer's gospel, Jesus' encounter with Mary in this psychological fashion requires regarding the story of Jesus as symbolic language designed to transmit information about human psychology. Uninterested in "search[ing] out the real story" (Abbott 54),[10] Mailer preferred to enliven the myth of Jesus by probing the depths of his own responses to the gospels. If "the act of soul-making is imagining" (*Re-Visioning* 27), writes James Hillman, "since images are the psyche, its stuff," then "[c]rafting images" becomes "an equivalent of soul-making," a crafting that "can take place in the concrete modes of the artisan, a work of the hands," and "it can take place in sophisticated elaborations of reflection, religion, relationships... [and] social action." *Gospel* is par excellence a matter of religious reflection on Mailer's part, his partaking of the "soul's first habitual activity" (*Re-Visioning* 117), to borrow once more from Hillman, one that "belongs to the essence of consciousness as wetness to water, as motion to wind." Mailer espouses a similar agenda for himself as a writer of fiction, which he considers a synergy of "possibility, mystery, confusions and evocations" (Lennon, *Provincetown* 44) wherein the "waters" are never "clear."

The term "Gnosticos," as Lennon describes in his interview with Mailer, refers to "someone who seeks knowledge by searching the depths of the self, looking at the self as the available ground for enlightenment" (*On God* 188). It is only out of "the depth" in one-self, Mailer's Jesus says in the final line of *Gospel*, where "sorrow wells up an immutable compassion," that one generates the awareness that he, at least, considers definitive of the authentic spiritual life. "The kingdom of God is within you" (*Jerusalem* 17:20), Luke's gospel records: "the kingdom of God...is within and everywhere" (18:36), states John's. The principle with which Jesus made the locus of spirituality not a literal temple appears throughout the "gnostic" papyri; for instance, in the fragments of Oxyrhynchus: "[t]he kingdom of heaven is within you, and whosoever knoweth himself shall find it.... [k]now yourselves" (qtd. in Jung 37). These scriptures demonstrate that the recorded sayings of Jesus circulating in the ancient world fostered "a belief in the efficacy of individual revelation and individual knowledge" (Smith 538). Such a belief requires no hierarchy, no doctrines, no churches. As the Jesus of *The Gospel of Mary* puts it, "[d]o not lay down any rules beyond what I appointed for you, and do not give a law like the lawgiver lest you be constrained by it" (Robinson 525). However, as the ending of *Gospel* makes clear, Mailer observed that today's adherents of Christianity have institutionalized their religious practices in ways that make them resemble, not the Jesus of the New Testament, but the Pharisees.

When Mailer's Jesus laments the fact that "[i]n the last century of this second millennium were holocausts, conflagrations, and plagues worse than any that had come before" (240), making it clear to him that "the contest" between God and Satan remains so equal, that neither of them "can triumph" (240), some readers will assume that Mailer refers to transcendent personalities warring against each other, like the two gods in Lowry's *Under the Volcano* (347), "engaged in an endlessly indecisive and wildly swinging game of bumblepuppy with a Burmese gong." But they also must regard these terms as metaphors for human behavior, if they would remain true to Mailer's Aristotelian allegiances. Admitting that he is "like trees, bear[ing] a fruit of good and evil" (124), Mailer's Jesus perpetuates this mainstay of the "gnostic" scriptures, that good and evil in the human psyche, codependent like shadow and light, "predicate one another" (Jung, *Psyche* 54). It was Mailer's ambition in his *Gospel*, then, to impart the "real secret" (Robinson 540) of the "gnostic scrolls," that the psyche is "a source of knowledge," even as "many of the Gnostics were nothing other than psychologists."

NOTES

1. All citations are taken from the hardcover edition of *The Gospel According to the Son*.
2. Harold Bloom claims that Mailer's "gnosis" is based on a "doctrine insisting upon a divine spark in each adept that cannot die because it never was any part of creation anyway" (38).
3. As I argue later in this essay, many ancient "gnostic" ideas about spirituality and gender receive corroboration in contemporary neuroscience. As Diane Ackerman writes, a "woman's brain has a larger corpus callosum, the sparkling bridge between the hemispheres, and also has a larger anterior commisure, which links the unconscious realms of the hemispheres" (154).
4. This passage is also included in the selections from *Gospel* in *The Time of Our Time* (1264–1268).
5. Professor J. Michael Lennon, personal communication, 26 August 2008.
6. Here I am paraphrasing James Hillman's comment that "[m]etaphysics and theology so easily become ways of avoiding psychologizing" (*Archetypal* 136).
7. Jettisoning substance from evil, Augustine insisted that goodness and the "God-image [are] within, not in the body," and that evil is "nothing but the privation of the good" (Jung, *Psyche* 38, 41, 46–51). Alienating evil from tangibility, Origen claims that "evil is characterized as a mere diminution of good and thus deprived of substance";

Basil, that "evil has no "subsistence in itself.... [it] is not a living and animated entity"; Titus of Bostra, that "there is no such thing as evil"; Dionysius the Areopagite, that "evil does not exist at all." Inheriting their ideas, Thomas Aquinas insisted that "it cannot be that evil signifies a being, or any form or nature."

8. Among the textual sources, collected in the Nag Hammadi library, of the concept of God as a syzygy of masculine and feminine components are the Clementine Homilies, *The Tripartite Tractate* (1,5), *The Gospel of Truth* (I, 3 and XII, 2), *A Valentinian Exposition* (XI, 2) *with On the Anointing, On Baptism A and B and On the Eucharist A and B, The Gospel of Philip, Authoritative Teaching* (VI, 3), *The Thunder, Perfect Mind* (VI, 2), *The Thought of Norea* (IX, 2), *Trimorphic Protennoia* (XIII, 1), *The Exegesis on the Soul* (II, 6) and *Eugnostos The Blessed* (III, 3 and V, 1).

9. For example, see Lucia Capacchione (Recovery, 37–39) and Diane Ackerman. (12–18, 27–33, 47–53, 151–158).

10. Walker, drawing on New Testament scholar Burnett Hillman, comments that the "known facts of [Jesus'] life are meager in the extreme.... [a]part from the forty days and nights in the wilderness, of which we are told virtually nothing, all that is reported to have been said and done by Jesus in all the four gospels, could not have occupied more than three weeks....[t]he teachings of Christ are not even preserved in the Aramaic language in which they were proclaimed" (70–71). Nonetheless, Walker writes, "what is important is not so much whether his mission took place, as whether it took effect" (71), as a "cosmic, archetypal [and] apocalyptic" myth of tremendous staying-power, constructed out of innumerable cultural mythologies whose far-back origins were primarily Egyptian. Cf. Gerard Massey's comparison of hundreds of biblical elements with their origins in Egypt's *Book of the Dead* (*Ancient Egypt* 226–243, 398–469).

WORKS CITED

Abbott, Sean. "Mailer Goes to the Mountain." *At Random* Spring/Summer (1997): 48–55.

Ackerman, Diane. *An Alchemy of Mind: The Marvel and Mystery of the Brain.* New York: Scribner, 2004, 154, 156.

Bloom, Harold, ed. *Modern Critical Views: Norman Mailer.* New York: Random House, 2003 (1986): 33–40.

Busa, Christopher, ed. "Interview with Norman Mailer." *Provincetown Arts* 14 (1999): 24–32.

Capacchione, Lucia. *The Power of Your Other Hand.* Hollywood: Newcastle, 1988, 37–39.

Eldredge, Lawrence. "The Concept of God's Absolute Power at Oxford in the Later Fourteenth-Century," in *By Things Seen: Reference and*

Recognition in Medieval Thought, ed. David Lyle Jeffrey. Ottawa: University of Ottawa Press, 1979, 211–226.

Harris, Sam. *Letter to a Christian Nation.* New York: Vintage Books, 2008 (2006), 64.

Hillman, James. *Archetypal Psychology.* Dallas, TX: Spring, 1985, 5, 17,136.

———. *Re-Visioning Psychology.* New York: Harper and Row, 1977 (1975): 117, 27.

Jeffrey, David Lyle. "Breaking Up the Synthesis: From Plato's Academy to the 'School of Athens,'" in *By Things Seen: Reference and Recognition in Medieval Thought,* ed David Lyle Jeffrey. Ottawa: University of Ottawa Press (1979): 227–252.

———. "Heresy," in *The Dictionary of Biblical Tradition in English Literature,* David Lyle Jeffrey. Grand Rapids, MI: William B. Eerdmans (1992): 344–346.

Jenkins, Philip. "Hidden Gospels." 2008 http://www.bibleinterp.com/articles/hiddengospel.htm.

Jung, Carl Gustav. *Abstracts of The Collected Works of C.G. Jung: A Guide to the Collected Works, Volumes I–XVII.* Maryland: Information Planning Associates, 1976, 152.

———. *Aspects of the Masculine,* trans. R.F.C. Hull. Introduction and Headnotes by John Beebe. New Jersey: Princeton University Press, 1991 (1989), xii, xiv.

———. *Psyche and Symbol: A Selection from the Writings of C.G. Jung.* Trans. R.F.C. Hull. Selected and introduced by Violet S. de Lazlo. New Jersey: Princeton University Press,1991 (1958), 38, 41, 46–51, 54, 55, 64.

———. *The Undiscovered Self.* 1957. New York: Mentor Books, 1958, 109–110.

King, Karen L. *What Is Gnosticism?* Cambridge: Harvard University Press, 2003, 2, 21, 24, 25, 194.

Levenda, Peter. *Unholy Alliance: A History of Nazi Involvement with the Occult.* New York, London: Continuum, 2003 (1995), 1.

Lowry, Malcolm *Under the Volcano.* New York: Penguin Books, 1971. 347.

Mailer, Norman with Michael Lennon. "America and Its War with the Invisible Kingdom of Satan." 22 January, 2005.http://www.commondreams.org/views05/0123-10.htm.

———. *Conversations with Norman Mailer,* ed J. Michael Lennon. Jackson: University Press of Mississippi, 1988, 29.

———. *The Gospel According to the Son.* New York: Random House, 1997.

———."I Am Not For World Empire." *American Conservative* 2 December, 2005. http://www.amconmag.com/12_2/ mailer.html.

———. *On God: An Uncommon Conversation.* New York: Random House, 2007, 26, 188, 191, 194, 195.

———. *The Presidential Papers.* London: Corgi Books, 1965 (1963), 277–302.

Mailer, Norman with Michael Lennon. *The Prisoner of Sex*. New York: Donald I. Fine, 1971, 20, 181.

———. *The Time of Our Time*. New York: Random House, 1998, 956, 1223, 1224, 1235.

Massey, Gerald. *Ancient Egypt, The Light of the World: A Work of Restitution and Reclamation in Twelve Books,* vol. 1. New York: Samuel Weisner, 1970 (1907), 226–243, 398–469.

Matton, Mary Ann. *Jung and the Human Psyche: An Understandable Introduction*. London and New York: Routledge, 2005, 168.

Pagels, Elaine. *Beyond Belief: The Secret Gospel of Thomas*. New York: Random House, 2003, 29, 184.

Robinson, James M., ed. *The Nag Hammadi Library,* rev. ed. New York: HarperCollins, 1990 (1978, 1988), 192, 523–526, 538, 540.

Sagan, Carl. *The Demon-Haunted World: Science as a Candle in the Dark*. New York:Ballentine Books, 1996, 170.

Smith, Richard. "Afterword: The Modern Relevance of Gnosticism," in *The Nag Hammadi Library,,* ed. James M. Robinson, rev. ed. New York: HarperCollins, 1990 (1978, 1988): 532–549.

Stumpf, Samuel Enoch. *Socrates to Sartre: A History of Philosophy,* 2nd ed. New York: McGraw-Hill, 1975 (1966), 89, 102.

Surette, Léon. *The Birth of Modernism*. Montreal, Québec, and Kingston, ON: McGill-Queen's University Press, 1993, 26, 29.

Von Franz, Marie-Louise. "Science and the Unconscious," in *Man and His Symbols,* eds. Carl Jung and Marie-Louise von Franz. New York: Bantam Doubleday, 1968 (1964), 241–246.

Walker, Benjamin. *Gnosticism: Its History and Influence*. Great Britain: Aquarian Press, 1985 (1983), 70–71, 125, 189.

Wansbrough, Henry, ed. *The New Jerusalem Bible: Reader's Edition*. New York: Doubleday, 1990.

CHAPTER 5

A Jew for Jesus? A Jewish Reading of Norman Mailer's *The Gospel According to the Son*

Mashey Bernstein

A number of years ago, when I was at a party in Norman Mailer's house, I asked him about his latest novel. He told me that it was a reworking of the Gospels. I warned him that the last Jew to do that, Sholem Asch, was almost excommunicated for attempting such an endeavor." While no such fate awaited Mailer on the publication of *The Gospel According to the Son* in 1997, its critical reception shows that the problems for Jews who write on or who use Christian iconography has not abated since that earlier text, *The Nazarene*, was published in 1939. Nonetheless, Mailer's novel follows a long tradition in American Literature, developing directly out of his lifelong literary and theological concerns.

There are specific literary problems for someone who wants to rewrite the Gospels. One cannot approach these texts "cold" as they come with such heavy baggage. Not surprisingly, theologians and critics, it turns out, are diametrically opposed on what method works best. And Mailer was not immune from attacks from both camps. In his review of Mailer's novel in the *New Republic*, James Wood argues that

> [i]n a sense, the four gospels of the New Testament are enemies of the novel. They are not narratives; they are witnessing that occasionally fall into narrative... Jesus did not live the life of a character in a modern novel....The whole machine of persuasion that is the secular, modern novel—verisimilitude, a believable character, an uncertainty

about meanings and endings, the pacing of time, the description of place—is irrelevant. (30)

But according to John Ashton in *Understanding the Fourth Gospel*, to read the Gospels as history and, therefore, as primary texts is to misread them. They belong closer to literature and use many of the same principles of that genre:

> Folk literature for the most part but literature all the same.... The Epistles, the New Testament as a whole, occurs in the context of myth, of story, of story-world and plot.... If they are literature, what is the purpose of rewriting them? Why bother? Furthermore, given the changes in time and expectations, we cannot write like them. For one thing, it has been done before and for another it cannot be done again. (430)

It would be as futile a gesture as Gus Van Sant's 1998 shot-by-shot remaking of Alfred Hitchcock's 1960 *Psycho*.

Despite these hazards, Mailer took a literal approach, which led to the novel receiving some of its harshest criticism. His original desire to rewrite the Gospels came from a literary rather than a religious impulse. As he recounts in *The Spooky Art*, he was stuck in a hotel room in Paris and took out a Gideon's Bible, "a text he hadn't read in over thirty years," and soon became appalled at the literary quality of the writing. "Sayings popped out...that were worthy of Shakespeare, but much in the double columns were poorly described. An ungainly prose pronged with golden nuggets." He became inspired. "There have got to be a hundred novelists in the world who can do a better job. I'm one of them" (87).

Ironically, the style of his book was the aspect that concerned most of its initial reviewers. Mailer was the butt of many for choosing a style that to them was neither fish nor fowl. J. Bottum, writing in *A Monthly Journal of Religion and Public Life*, echoes what many reviewers felt: it reads like "a translation committee draft from midway through the process that turned the Authorized Version into the Revised Standard." Most critics were expecting a style more in keeping with previous Mailer work, orotund complex sentences loaded with quasimystical utterances that bordered on the arcane. On the contrary, what they got was simple prose, almost to the point of naiveté. Had another writer presented the material in this way, I am sure that the style would not have merited the attention it received— but since this was *Mailer,* many were knocked askew.

Yet the deliberate attempt to capture the imagined voice of Jesus was, according to Mailer, a result of "seven variations of style" and a search for the "balance between a biblical rhythm and a contemporary one." The prose does not make Jesus sound like a typical Mailer character, but it accommodates the demands of the original when necessary.

> While I would not say that Mark's gospel is false, it has much exaggeration. And I would offer less for Matthew, and for Luke and John who gave me words I never uttered and described me as gentle when I was pale with rage. Their words were written many years after I was gone and only repeat what old men told them. Very old men. Such tales are to be leaned upon no more than a bush that tears from its roots and blows about in the wind.
>
> So I will give my own account. For those who would ask how my words have come upon this page, I would tell them to look upon it as a small miracle. (*Gospel* 3–4)

So to take this example as paradigm, in a few short lines, Jesus dispenses with the veracity of the Gospels, makes an interesting analogy, and cracks a joke. The table is set for the banquet to follow.

Criticism of the novel carried an undercurrent of suspicion and cynicism that went beyond what one might expect when dealing with a literary work. Let me use a comment by the Catholic writer Mary Gordon in *The Nation* as a segue from the purely literary to the more theological: "Most of these faults are failures of voice. And failures of voice stem from failures of hearing. Mailer may have read the New Testament, but he hasn't heard its voice" (27).

One cannot help but feel that the fact that Mailer is Jewish played a large part in the way that the text has been received. Other authors have rewritten the Gospels without being taken to task so severely. (Jack Miles in *Commonweal* lists books that used a similar device to Mailer but were not the subject of such critical "outrage.") It seems that when Jews get involved, non-Jews feel that there is something unsavory or even downright suspicious about the intentions. There is no doubt that given the historically tenuous feelings between the two religions the problem of rewriting the Gospels whether from a theological or literary impulse is different when undertaken by a Jew than by a Christian. Both Christian and Jew may ask whether the Jewish writer can or should treat the Gospels as history or as literature, as truth or, most significantly, as falsehood. From the Jewish point of view, as we shall see with Asch, the Jew also runs the risk of being considered a blasphemer or, from the Christian, as a desecrator.

Gordon does not use words like "blasphemer," but her supposedly formalist criticism carries within it a subtle current. Even though Mailer has never been an observant Jew he must have been aware of the treacherous theological waters into which he was about to wade.

Asch and Mailer respond to the original text in diametrically opposing ways: Asch by creating a romantic sort of Gospel full of highly realized scenes such as the dance of Salome and with a tripartite plot line that deals with the Pharisees and the politics of the period; Mailer goes in the opposite direction by almost slavishly following the Gospels with little added in terms of fictional coloring. Neither author, it should be added, ever calls into doubt the veracity of the original story.

When he published the novel in 1939, Asch encountered three main problems, ones that interestingly are almost identical to the ones later encountered by Mailer: an accusation of heresy, a castigation for what was perceived as his lack of knowledge of both the Christian and Hebrew testaments in their original language, and finally criticism of the purely literary kind. Asch encountered a further problem: one of timing. The year 1939 when the Nazi were consolidating their actions against Jews was not a good time to publish a tract with a somewhat sympathetic anti-Semite as its protagonist. Jews were also sensitive to the loss not only of actual members of their faith on the physical plane with pogroms—and worse on the horizon—but also to the many intellectuals who had deserted Judaism by converting to Christianity or to apostasy that was a result of the Haskala, or enlightenment movement. Conversion to Christianity by intellectuals was, therefore, a real and not an imagined threat. In light of these facts, Asch's book became a sore point. As Samuel Niger, a frequent defender of Asch, said, "It is natural in view of Jewish suffering at the hands of those who turned Jesus into a God, that his name should be taboo" (as quoted in Madison 221).

But more than the temporal issues, the issues hinged on the nature of religion. Asch was attacked as an apostate, a missionizing Jew and worse. He is accused of knowing "little Judaism and less Christianity." According to a Professor Tchernowitz, Asch could only read the New Testament in Yiddish and "had scarcely any workable knowledge of any other tongue." His supposed attraction to Christianity made him act like a country bumpkin encountering a "city department store" for the first time (as quoted in Lieberman 24), leading him to distort the real and fundamental differences between Judaism and Christianity, in favor of the latter. Asch in his defense could only argue, in his book, *What I Believe* (1941) that he was a devout Jew, dedicated to the welfare of his people. (Nonetheless, his career was ruined and he never recovered his previous popularity among Jews or even Yiddish readers.)

As an artist, Asch maintained his right to express himself according to his ability and his conscience. Asch's philo-Christianity had its rationale. According to Charles Madison, Asch "persuaded himself that by retelling the story of Jesus he would expose the enemies of the Jews as defilers of Christianity as conceived by its founders...By depicting Jesus as a pious Jew, he hoped to demonstrate the falseness of the anti-Jewish position taken by later followers of Christ" (248).

Part of the problem, as Madison points out, is that Asch creates such a wholly successful narrative that clearly embraces the ideas of its main characters. His literary powers are so strong and his evocation of time and people so potent that he has become them. He captures not only the physical realities of the time such as the court of the High Priest but also, on the theological level, the mystical yearning of the contemporary Jew for a Messiah. Jesus is exposed as a righteous Jew and extremely sensitive youth who feels this yearning and comes to see himself as the Son of God.

Tellingly, the critical reaction to Asch and Mailer shows that the tension between Judaism and Christianity, especially around the role of the Jews in the Crucifixion, has not quieted in the sixty intervening years, the brouhaha over Mel Gibson's *The Passion of the Christ* (2004) being an obvious case in point. The concerns are not without validity, even in modern times such as recent pronouncements of the current Pope to return to the liturgy of the Mass statements about converting Jews. In their purest forms, these two faiths, while closely connected in many ways, have a troubled history, one marked by hatred, animosity, and distrust, fueled in part by the reported (and disputed) role of the Jews in the Crucifixion of the Christian Messiah as depicted in Matthew 23 and the refusal of Jews to convert to Christianity. So bitter was this animosity that it makes one question why Jewish writers of whatever ilk would want to use Christian motifs and ideas in their works. The Orthodox Rabbi-author Chaim Potok explores this theme in his novel *My Name Is Asher Lev*. In this novel, a young Jewish painter raised in an Orthodox home becomes notorious for a painting entitled *The Brooklyn Crucifixion* in which he uses his family as stand-ins for Jesus, Mary, and Joseph of the Christian Gospels. Lev embodies the real life conflicts that face all Jewish artists, be they in art or literature, who use Christian imagery in anything more than the most cursory fashion: he stands accused of being a "traitor, an apostate, a self-hater, an inflictor of shame upon my family, my friends, my people..." Also he is a "mocker of ideas sacred to Christians, a blasphemous manipulator of modes and forms revered by Gentiles for two thousand years" (3). These words echo those of Asch's most vociferous critic, Chaim Lieberman:

> This Christianity is sworn to war with Judaism from generation to generation until it is ultimately submerged. It may tolerate any other religion under the sun, but Judaism must be blotted out. This doctrine is, rehearsed in the ears of Christendom from century to century, has generated an enmity 'which may be felt' and which has become a part of normal Christian living. (18)

Nonetheless, Jewish writers have not shied away from using the Gospels or the image of Jesus in their text. I am thinking in particular of Henry Roth's *Call It Sleep*, Philip Roth's short story, "Conversion of the Jews," Edward Lewis Wallant's *The Pawnbroker* and *Children at the Gate*, J.D. Salinger's *Franny and Zooey*, as well as Malamud's *The Assistant*.

There have been a number of responses offered for the attraction of Christianity for Jewish writers. The image of Jesus can be used to discuss martyrdom or the irony of the fact that Jesus was a Jew and that this aspect of his upbringing had been ignored by Christian anti-Semites. Perhaps they had a desire to escape from Jewish parochialism. A desire for universalism—the idea that we are all the same and not parochial entities—drove the Jewish writer to what Irving Howe in his study of Jewish life in the first half of the twentieth century, *The World of Our Fathers,* terms an "unexpected interest" in Christian symbolism (587). Howe suggests that writers emerging from a mindset bred in the isolated ghetto or *shteitl* would not only have found in modern society a more humane form of Christianity but also, once they began to study outside of the ghetto, would have discovered how inseparable Christianity was from Western Culture, an idea caught in all its ambiguity and ambivalence by Cynthia Ozick: "English is a Christian language. When I write English, I live in Christendom" (9).

In some ways, the writer Edward Lewis Wallant captures this Jewish issue when in his last novel *Children at the Gate* his protagonist Sammy Abel Kahn—who will die Christ-like impaled on a fence—says trenchantly, "we are all sons of God, bubi" (120). In his unpublished papers Wallant makes the following interesting observation that might apply to Jewish writers who are attracted to the figure of Jesus:

> Whether Christ ever lived is really not important. The fact of man's invention of him is reality enough. That is might well be a myth

explodes no barrier of logic for the very necessity that led to the creation and perpetuity of a carpenter capable of perfect love shows that
wistful Nazarene, watered down and blurry from self-abuse in each
man who ever looked upward to do his pleading.

It is not surprising, therefore, that certain writers have transmuted
their religious impulses in other directions, especially a fascination
with Christianity, viewing its mythos, with, if not favor, at least with
some degree of benign tolerance. True, not all of these writers are
consistent in their viewpoints nor do they advocate a conversion from
their birth-faith (although some have married out of the faith), but at
the same time they present an interesting perspective on Jewish identity. Such an "attraction" has echoed the trend of Jewish-American
life as a whole, especially a tendency to assimilation and a conversion
to other ideologies, for example, communism. The figure and myth
of Jesus Christ lends itself not only to the martyrdom that befell Jews
but also to messianism that attracted many disgruntled Jews who
became socialists and writers in that vein. Michael Gold's novel *Jews
without Money* ends with an almost Christ-like paean to the masses:

> O, workers' revolution...you are the true Messiah. You will destroy
> the East Side when you come and build there a garden for the human
> spirit. O revolution, that forced me to think to struggle and to live, O
> great beginning. (224)

Bernard Sherman applies the term "prophecy" to writers who share this
response—Mailer among them—to the problems of modern man:

> Each found that the distinctively Jewish element was the demand—
> very often in fervid, prophetic, even mystical terms—that man fulfill
> his highest possibilities, that he achieves a Messianic release in a world
> in which mind and justice were triumphant. The locus of this spirit of
> social compassion is the prophetic vision of Isaiah. (16)

(Ironically, Isaiah emerges as an important figure in the dispute
with the Devil in *Gospel*.) It is a well-known connection, and
Nathan Glazer points out in this vein that "the Jewish religious
tradition probably does dispose Jews...towards liberalism and
radicalism" (13).

Mailer emerges from this Jewish tradition, the strong Left-wing
liberal side that while eschewing ritual and rabbis took to heart the
other strand: its strong social concerns. Even though Mailer has never
been considered a major figure in the canon of American-Jewish

writers like Bellow, Malamud, or Philip Roth, he has never disavowed his religious affiliations. Nearly all his central characters claim some sort of Jewish parentage or ancestry, from Rojack to Harlot and, of course, Jesus. In many ways, Jesus is a natural evolution from Mailer's early work and those issues that have concerned him over his career.

At the same time, Mailer theology is close to a traditional form of Judaism as described by Rabbi Abraham Joshua Heschel who in his eponymous work argued that "God was in Search of Man." Without Man, God's plans are rendered void. Heschel uses the term "prophet" to describe this connection and it is a term that helps explain Mailer's ideology, its basis in his Jewishness. Richard Poirier in describing Mailer can also be describing the Jew who has no Jesus to turn to. Mailer is "dependent on a past which is essentially mythic and he prefers to think of himself as someone living within the perils of time while knowing he is the carrier of life which is not wholly his own to waste" (105). This description seems appropriate to describe Jesus, another Jew concerned with the state of man's soul. Ironically, I realize that by comparing the Jew Jesus and the Jew Mailer I am in danger of fulfilling Mailer's own sense of prophecy in which the critics would be only too happy to pounce on him: "That egomaniac. Does Mailer now think he's Jesus Christ?" (SA 87)

Mailer (and Asch) differ from all the other writers mentioned in their direct retelling of the story of the Gospels. There is a distinct difference in using the imagery in a universal form and a retelling of the story of Jesus in a way that might be perceived as embracing a Christian point of view. The Jesus in *Gospel*, while still close to the figure portrayed in the original Gospels, has been transformed in a way that makes him share many of the ideas of Mailer's earlier characters and certainly their theology.

His Jesus is full of doubt, not quite sure of his role, questioning his sayings and more importantly his actions.

> I decided my character had to be more of a man than a god, an existential man, dominated by the huge cloud that he is the Son of God. Jesus, as the protagonist, doesn't feel worthy, but he is ready nonetheless to do his best every step of the way. Not in command of the situation, but will do his best. And he does have startling successes. (SA 87)

This stance has been the role of many a Mailer hero, each of whom has been concerned with the spiritual value of man in a corrupt or fallen world. From Rojack (who fights against a Devil-like character in *An American Dream*) to a neat dissertation on the existential aspects of God in *Tough Guys Don't Dance*, as well as diversions in *Harlot's Ghost*,

Mailer's world is one in which flawed though good men try to make sense of a world where evil or the forces of darkness seem to prevail.

Mailer's concerns—and those of his heroes—are at once human and divine. In the face of a threat against the integrity of the self, the individual finds that he cannot shirk his awesome responsibility. Within him burns the "mystery" of human existence; it feeds his "rage, his anguish and his frustration" and he knows what would satisfy it. These phrases from Mailer's seminal statement *"The White Negro"* define the dynamism that motivates the Mailer hero and the Son of *Gospel*. The "impulse to action" expresses the need to live with the demands of life and not to succumb to the void: "A life...directed by one's faith in the necessity of action is a life committed to the notion that the substratum of existence is the search, *the end meaningful but mysterious"* (Advertisements 341, my italics). Mailer's great characters, his "hipsters," live through action. In this way, the "hipster" activates his whole being, not merely his intellect or his physical body but also his spirit and soul. In his novels, Mailer reverts to a time when an essential unity existed between the spirit of man and the expression of that spirit. Because of this religious framework, the terms God, Devil, Good, and Evil have a vibrancy and personality for Mailer just as they did in "more primitive" religious times and, therefore, make Mailer at home in the times of Jesus.

In *Of a Fire on the Moon* Mailer makes the following comment that turns out to be a "prophetic" indication of the later concerns: "The real heroism, he thought, was to understand and because one understood, be even more full of fear at the enormity of what one understood. Yet at that moment continue to be ready for the feat one had decided it was essential to perform" (101). There is an echo of those words in the final understanding of Jesus in *Gospel:*

> I did not dare to wonder whether I had failed in the larger part of my mission. Instead I lifted my eyes and prayed, "Father, give back to me the glory that I had with You before the world was"...I could feel that love of God. Such love was like an animal of heavenly beauty. Its eyes glowed in my heart. As these prayers echoed within my chest, so did I know that I must go the Temple...and I must go with these questions in my heart. If they were heavy, so must I carry them as my burden. (206f.)

In the face of a threat against the integrity of the self, the individual cannot shirk his responsibility to discover his own set of values. Only by this discovery can he reclaim himself from the surrounding chaos. Mailer's concerns are totally spiritual: Man, he believes, is God's agent, fighting His battles. Human activity becomes a symbolic drama, where, as Charles Feidelson notes in his text *Symbolism and American Literature*, "every passage of life, enmeshed in the vast context of God's plan, possesses a delegated meaning" (79). Every action that man performs has a significance that detracts or adds to the sum of all meaning, ordering chaos, inventing form, and flowing into the flux of Time, and every action individually realized and existentially self-defining is a dance over the hot coals of life. In this (unchristian) scenario, there is no Jesus to save one, no afterlife that will reward one. Since Jesus cannot call on Jesus to save himself, ironically Jesus in Mailer's world is the ultimate (Jewish) hero. No scene in *Gospel* brings this out more than Jesus' encounter with the Devil, the most admired section of the novel. Here, the naive Jesus tackles a being of infinite seductiveness, power, and wit.

Like Milton, Mailer finds himself giving some of the best lines to the Devil. The Devil uses every trick in the book from the physical to the spiritual, from hallucinations to lying to undermine Jesus, but the Son is up to the task; if anything, by fighting the Devil he enlarges his own powers and confidence in his own destiny: "If I could increase in my powers...perhaps the world of men might multiply in virtue with me. So I had begun to believe in my Father...I had been tested, had proved loyal, and now my tongue began to feel clean" (Gospel 57). The scene is in many ways reminiscent of Stephen Rojack's final battle on the parapet with Barney Oswald Kelly, the Devil figure of *An American Dream*. While Jesus knows who his father is, he still has to learn who he is and make the connection between the two so that God's plans can be fulfilled. Whereas Rojack only has time to react, Mailer's Jesus has the narrative space to reflect: "I was obliged to wonder. Why has the Lord left me alone with Satan? Was it to scourge me of an excess of piety? Before long I would learn that there might be truth in this. There was work to do, and it could not be accomplished on one's knees" (57). Like Rojack in the earlier novel, the Jesus of *Gospels* must take gambles of a sort in order to work out his path in ways that better his chances.

Mailer has long argued this point: if man is made in God's image, then perhaps God too is an existential Being: "God is not all powerful but existential, discovering the possibilities and limitations of His creative powers in the form of the history which is made by his creatures" (Presidential 632). As Mailer noted in one of his last interviews, "God wants to do more and gave us free will precisely because we're God's children...I see God as a creative artist...but not all powerful. And not all-good. And so, as an artist, God wants us to go further than God went." (Shaikh 3). Man, therefore, has a life that is not his to waste, as Cherry explains in *An American Dream*: "I believe God is just doing His best to learn from what happens to some of us" (185). While Jesus and his Father have a somewhat distant relationship, one in which God "does not speak" often to his son, Mailer imagines Jesus closing the gap in this way: "it is believed that God gained a great victory through me." Mailer's Jesus, like Asch's and the biographical original, can be understood as Jewish to the core.

I did not find any Jewish magazines from the conservative *Commentary* to the liberal *Tikkun* commenting on the novel which can be seen as indicative of the argument that Jewish critics as well as readers are still uncomfortable about Jews reworking Christian texts. One of the few, David Gelertner gets it, in the *National Review*, only partially right when he argues that Mailer doesn't tell the "story like a Christian." Gelertner then goes on to argue:

> Don't conclude that...he tells it like a Jew. Jewish scholars have long rejected as impossible the Gospel account of the legal proceedings culminating in the Crucifixion, and Mailer is scrupulously faithful to the Gospels. The Gospels and the Jews disagree radically on the Pharisees: Jews see them as heroes and martyrs struggling to uphold the legal framework of Torah under the killing pressure of Rome. Mailer of course lines up with the Gospels, and it isn't clear that he understands what the normative Jewish view is. (55)

With a strange literalness, Gelertner is blind-sided by theological pedantry, but Mailer does know a lot about the basic impulses of Judaism. His Jesus does not rely on the powers of a superhuman Son of God for self-redemption. He only has his own truths by which he can live or achieve salvation. In his first novel *The Naked and the Dead* Mailer quotes Yehudah Halevy, the Spanish mystic a.k.a. the Kuzari (1075–1141) to introduce a similar notion. The character Joey Goldstein calls the Jew "the heart of all nations." In fact, the Kuzari calls the Jew "the heart" because he is "Endowed...with the most perfect soul and with the loftiest intellect which it is possible for a human being to possess and...with...immanence enabling him to enter into communication with God...and to comprehend great truths without instruction after slight reflection" (Philosophers 65). While one can read this as religious chauvinism, it also is a perfect description of Jesus. If Jews believes that they are all "sons of God," then Mailer's Jesus is the perfect example of such a person. His Jesus, therefore, is neither a romanticized version nor a cynical one. Mailer's character is an honest portrayal of a flawed man who is the Son of God, a Jew, and an existential hero—the perfect Mailer creation. No wonder Mailer found him attractive.

WORKS CITED

Asch, Sholem. *The Nazarene.* New York: G.P. Putnam's Sons, 1939.

Ashton, John. *Understanding the Fourth Gospel.* Oxford: Oxford University Press, 1991.

Bottum, J. "The Gospel According to the Son." *First Things: A Monthly Journal of Religion and Public Life* 75 (1997): 53–54.

Feidelson, Charles Jr. *Symbolism and American Literature.* Chicago: University of Chicago Press, 1953.

Gelernter, David. "The Gospel According to the Son." *National Review* 49:14 (28 July 1997): 55.

Gold, Michael. *Jews without Money.* New York: Avon Books, 1965.

Gordon, Mary. "Jesus Christ, Superstar." *The Nation.* 264:24 (June 23, 1997). 7.

Heinemann, Isaak, ed., *Three Jewish Philosophers.* New York: Atheneum, 1969.

Howe, Irving. *World of Our Fathers.* New York: Harcourt Brace Jovanovich, 1976.

Lieberman, Chaim. *The Christianity of Sholem Asch.* New York: Philosophical Library, 1953.

Madison, Charles. *Yiddish Literature: Its Scope and Major Writers.* New York: Schocken Books, 1971.

Mailer, Norman. *Advertisements for Myself.* New York: G.P. Putnam's Sons, 1959.

———. *An American Dream.* New York: Dell, 1970.

———. *The Gospel According to the Son.* New York: Random House, 1997.

———. *The Naked and the Dead.* London: Hamilton and Co., 1964.

———. *Of a Fire on the Moon.* New York: New American Library, 1971.

———. *Presidential Papers.* New York: Berkley Medallion Books, 1970.

———. *The Spooky Art.* New York: Random House, 2003.

Miles, Jack. *Commonweal* 124:13 (18 July 1997): 21.

Ozick, Cynthia. *Bloodshed and Three Novellas.* New York: New American Library, 1977.

Poirier, Richard. *Mailer.* London: Wm. Collins Sons, 1972.

Potok, Chaim. *My Name Is Asher Lev.* New York: Alfred A. Knopf, 1972.

Shaikh, Nermeen. "Interview with Norman Mailer." *Nextbook Reader* 4 (Spring 2007): 3.

Sherman, Bernard: *The Invention of the Jew: Jewish-American Education Novels (1916–1964).* Cranbury: N.J. Thomas Yoseloff, 1969.

Wallant, Edward Lewis. *Children at the Gate.* New York: Harcourt Brace Jovanovich, 1964.

———. Unpublished Papers: Wallant Collection. Beinecke Library, New Haven, CN.

Wood, James. *The New Republic* 216:21 (May 1997): 30.

CHAPTER 6

Augustinian Evil in *The Gospel According to the Son* and *The Castle in the Forest*: A Case for Non-Dualism

Jeffrey F.L. Partridge

A Major Novel on God and the Devil

And I sought "whence is evil."

Augustine

There is more resemblance between Norman Mailer and Saint Augustine than one might suspect at first blush. Both were intensely serious in their love of wisdom, sensitive to spirit and carnality in their being, unswerving in their belief in a Creator-God, and were faced with the same existential enigma: "whence is evil?" (Augustine 102). This question led both men to the same conclusion: if God is good and He created everything good, then evil must be an opposing force of similar if not equal power and of different origin. There were, as Augustine put it, "two substances" at work in the cosmos (112). Or, as Mailer has expounded in numerous interviews and works, God "is not all-powerful; He exists as a warring element in a divided universe.... It's the only thing that explains to me the problem of evil" (Pontifications, 2). The question led Augustine to Manichaeism, the syncretist blend of Christian, Buddhist, and Persian philosophy named after its Persian founder Mani (c. 215–276) that proposes that our universe is animated by the opposing principles of Goodness (light, or God) and Evil (darkness, or the Devil). While Mailer did not count himself an adherent to Manichaeism per se, as Augustine did for nine years of his life, his self-styled religious beliefs can be described as Manichaean (and when his beliefs were labeled Manichaean in interviews, he never disputed the term). Of course, the major difference between the two men is that Augustine came to reject Manichaeism as an errant and heretical philosophy (this rejection being a key pillar of his *Confessions*); whereas Mailer embraced a Manichaean-type Dualism to the end—unless one considers, as this essay does, the non-Dualist representation of evil in Mailer's final novels, *The Gospel According to the Son* and *The Castle in the Forest*. What this essay will argue is that Mailer, following the whisperings of the unconscious rather than the logic of his theological pronouncements, came to understand evil in his final novels in a way that unwittingly cancels out Manichaean Dualism and embraces the Augustinian notion of evil as the privation and perversion of good.

When describing his philosophical/theological beliefs, Mailer was unswervingly an existential dualist. In his words, "I am an existentialist who believes there is a God and a Devil at war with one another" (Pontifications 84). To Mailer's mind, his beliefs were existentialist, and the notion of an ever-expanding universe presided over by an "existentialist God" who was "doing His best" to win the good cosmic fight was the moral center of his fiction. A closed story, small and structurally claustrophobic—one decided in advance, one whose ends were no mystery and whose unfolding merely a means to that end—was Mailer's idea not only of a bad novel, but also of an immoral one. An ever-unfolding universe, organic and dynamic, was to Mailer the supreme novel; and a great work of fiction was likewise organic, dynamic, and, at its very center, existential. Hence the sprawling storyline and (for some readers) exasperating, unpredictable structure of novels such as *Harlot's Ghost* and *Ancient Evenings*. Hence, I would argue, the exploration of the life of Jesus (the supreme good man) and the life of Hitler (the supreme evil man) in the final two novels of his career despite his intentions of writing a sequel to *Harlot's Ghost*. In discussing his views on God and the Devil and the future of mankind, Mailer once stated: "all this is too endlessly and chronically paranoid to try to get into in the form of an interview. I think you can dramatize these notions in a major novel, but only a major novel" (Pontifications 78). I would like to suggest that despite Mailer's conscious efforts and plans to write *Harlot's Grave* or to extend *Ancient Evenings* into a trilogy, his unconscious led him in the final decade of his life to write that major novel on God and the Devil. In a way, we can conceive of *The Gospel According to the Son* and *The Castle in the Forest* as a two-volume exploration of what to Mailer was the superlative drama of existence.

For all the research that went into his novels (nearly 130 works are listed in the bibliography of *The Castle in the Forest*) and all the planning that went into his novels (he spent six months planning his sequel to *Harlot's Ghost*, which he set aside to write *Castle*), Mailer was religiously committed to an organic, unplanned process of writing. In writing, Mailer claimed to eschew plot and structure in order to concentrate on character: "I'm a great believer in organic novels, in that you don't decide in advance where you're going. You let the characters point the way" (Lee 205). The question must be asked, then, why an author so committed to the open, organic, existential novel would choose to center the efforts of his twilight years on two of the best known figures of human history. Who, after all, doesn't know that a novel about Jesus will end with his death on the cross and his resurrection from the dead? Who doesn't expect little "Adi" Hitler to become a fascist monster responsible for the most terrifyingly evil event of the twentieth century? But according to Mailer, knowing the end point of his characters did not make them any less organic. In regard to *The Castle in the Forest*, Mailer said, "I wasn't trying to make this a railroad track as to how Hitler became a monster" (Lee 208). Bringing a devil in as a narrator, according to Mailer, is what rescued his task from a humdrum determinism: "The unforeseen would be the devil's interpretation of what was going on and what he must do...And that made it absolutely organic for me because even though I knew where I was going in terms of the narrative, the interpretations now became the part I would not determine in advance. I would let the events and the devil's interpretation of these events dictate where I'd head next. And it worked" (205). Thus, even with a Gary Gilmore, a Hitler, or a Jesus as his subject, Mailer's experience as a novelist bore out his belief that in fiction "nothing's automatic; it's existential" (208).

Importantly for my argument, this process of following character was made possible by Mailer's sense of the unconscious, which he understood not only as the topography of his own psyche, but as a Jungian-type realm of shared human psyche or primordial remembrance. Mailer said, "I have this theory that the unconscious is not entirely our own...but it's as if the unconscious taps into a deeper realm of knowledge that we possess" (Lee 210). Tapping into that "deeper realm" was a matter of routine practice for Mailer: "You can't betray the unconscious. Since my unconscious doesn't trust me altogether, I literally had to go through this routine of getting up in the morning with an empty mind, waste an hour in the office once I got there, and then it would begin to come. It was almost like the unconscious said, 'All right, you're here. I can trust you; you're not going to leave now, I can tell'" (211). This "empty hour" (210) became necessary to his process because it allowed him to write *with* his characters rather than *for* them, to write not as a Calvinist Author-God whose characters were predestined to particular ends, but as an existential god bidding his characters to act on their own free will. When discussing what came to be his final novel, Mailer expressed a sense of what might be called divine inspiration, or, again, a tapping into the unconscious. "I was going to do the second volume of *Harlot's Ghost*, that I've been promising for years, and as I sat down to write it, it was almost as if this whisper came into my brain and said, 'No, no, that's not the book you're going to do next, it's this one [*The Castle in the Forest*]'" (204). Mailer even felt a sense of bewilderment at this turn of events, as though it were some kind of supernatural appointment: "Sometimes I wonder, why am I writing this book? It doesn't have a hell of a lot to do with me...It's almost as if I've been assigned to do this book" (212).

I would like to take seriously three particular points raised by the above discussion as I proceed. One, that Mailer's experience of tapping into the unconscious leaves open the possibility of discovery in his writing. In other words, despite his stated views on theology, his organic process of writing would naturally allow for the development of unforeseen representations and discoveries in the novel that would expand and perhaps even contradict his stated views. Two, that Mailer knows what he's talking about when he says that large ideas like God and the Devil and the future of mankind are not the stuff of interviews but can be adequately explored in the organic environment of the novel (that Bakhtinian dialogic playing field). Three, that respect for Mailer's craft and his working process requires that we not pigeon-hole his novelistic world into even his own stated theological views. Mailer, I believe, would not be offended to learn that the unconscious led him down a path he had not foreseen. Indeed, I believe he would approve.

Augustine and Non-Dualism

der Geist, der stets verneint

Goethe

Augustine was initially attracted to Manichaeism because its doctrine of Dualism seemed to satisfy his questions regarding the nature and origin of evil. "Because a piety, such as it was, constrained me to believe that the good God never created any evil nature, I conceived of two masses, contrary to one another, both unbounded, but the evil narrower, the good more expansive" (74). This answer, however, seemed to simply put off still other issues: Could God be unbounded, impervious, and incorruptible if another mass existed outside His power? In Augustine's words, "That said nation of darkness, which the Manichees are wont to set as an opposing mass over against Thee, what could it have done unto Thee, hadst Thou refused to fight with it? For, if they answered, 'it would have done Thee some hurt,' then shouldest Thou be subject to injury and corruption: but if 'it could do Thee no hurt,' then was no reason brought for Thy fighting with it" (100). Of course, the question that plagued him the most is the one stated repeatedly throughout his *Confessions*: "Whence is evil?"

The Catholic answer that "freewill was the cause of our doing ill" seemed for many years inadequate to Augustine (101).

> But again I said, Who made me? Did not my God, who is not only good, but goodness itself? Whence then came I to will evil and nill good, so that I am thus justly punished? Who set this in me, and ingrafted into me this plant of bitterness, seeing I was wholly formed by my most sweet God? If the devil were the author, whence is that same devil? And if he also by his own perverse will, of a good angel became a devil, whence, again, came in him that evil will whereby he became a devil, seeing the whole nature of angels was made by that most good Creator? By these thoughts I was again sunk down and choked. (101)

According to Augustine, he "wallowed in the mire of that deep pit" (43) for nine years before he came to a truly satisfying answer. He came to this understanding much as Mailer saw himself directed toward the subject of *The Castle in the Forest*: not by his own natural powers, but by a "sight...not derived from the flesh" (112).

Through a closer study of Christian doctrine and of Platonist and Neo-Platonist thought, Augustine arrived at an answer that not only satisfied his own intellectual and existential thirst, but has had a profound impact on Western philosophy, Christian doctrine, and literature. (Harold Bloom has called Augustine "a frontier concep-tualizer, poised between the ancient works of Greek thought and of biblical religion" [274].) "Evil," wrote Augustine, "was nothing but a privation of good" (37). Everything created by God was created good, but men and angels used their free will to twist and corrupt the good gifts of the Creator. Thus, evil is nongood; it is "no substance" (113); it is lack. Falsehood, likewise, is lack: "all things are true so far as they be; nor is there any falsehood unless when that is thought to be which is not" (112). Sin, also, is a lack, a perversion of the will for God: "And I enquired what iniquity was, and found it to be no substance, but the perversion of the will, turned aside from Thee, O God, the Supreme, towards these lower things, and casting out its bowels, and puffed up outwardly" (113). In *The City of God*, Augustine wrote that "the enemies of God are so, not by nature but by will" (382); that is, God did not create beings who were by nature evil, but he gave them a will by which to make their choices.

Many representations of evil in literature are expressions of Augustine's theory of evil as privation and perversion of that which is originally good. Goethe's Mephistopheles calls himself "der Geist, der stets verneint," the spirit who always negates (or denies) (63). Milton's Satan is a majestic and glorious angel who seeks his own glory and thus becomes the "Apostate Angel"(I, 125). His power is derived from the good characteristics endowed upon him by God. He and his rebellious minions are cast into a place of light-less fire, itself an image of power through negation: "a Dungeon horrible, on all sides round / As one great Furnace flam'd, yet from those flames/ No light, but rather darkness visible" (I, 61–63). Elrond, J.R.R. Tolkien's elf lord in *Lord of the Rings*, says, "for nothing is evil in the beginning. Even Sauron [the novel's Satan figure] was not so" (261). The great wizard Saruman the White, in accounting for his embrace of a "new Power" to Gandalf, explains that white "serves as a beginning. White cloth may be dyed. The white page can be overwritten; and the white light can be broken" (252). Mordor, like the dungeon of Milton's Satan, is marked by a murky darkness despite its flames, a barren land of dust and ash; and the ringwraiths sit shadowy and phantom-like inside their dark hoods. All of these representations illustrate Augustine's idea of evil as deprived good.

When asked if he believed in the Devil, C.S. Lewis, whose *The Screwtape Letters* has a great deal in common with *The Castle in the Forest*, responded with a distillation of Augustine's theory:

> If by "the Devil" you mean a power opposite to God and, like God, self-existent from all eternity, the answer is certainly No. There is no uncreated being except God. God has no opposite. No being could attain a "perfect badness" opposite to the perfect goodness of God;

for when you have taken away every kind of good thing (intelligence, will, memory, energy, and existence itself) there would be none of him left. The proper question is whether I believe in devils. I do. That is to say, I believe in angels, and I believe that some of these, by the abuse of their free will, have become enemies to God and, as a corollary, to us. These we may call devils. They do not differ in nature from good angels, but their nature is depraved . . . Satan, the leader or dictator of devils, is the opposite, not of God, but of Michael. (vii)

It bears noting that these expressions of Augustinian evil are non-Dualist because they do not conceive of two "substances" or two "masses," as Augustine called them, at work in the universe. In Augustine's conception, everything ultimately derived from One source, and, therefore, the universe is not Dualist in nature even though it may appear to be so.

Throughout his literary oeuvre, Mailer showed no such debt to Augustine, agreeing only with the young Augustine in his Manichaean years prior to his embrace of Christianity. However, with the publication of his final major work, *The Gospel According to the Son* and *The Castle in the Forest*, Mailer may have unwittingly joined ranks with this latter Augustine.

GOSPEL ACCORDING TO THE SON—A TENUOUS DUALISM

The Devil is the most beautiful creature God ever made.

Jesus, The Gospel According to the Son 45

Ostensibly, *The Gospel According to the Son*—which we might call the first volume of Mailer's major novel on God and the Devil—is a novel with a philosophically dualist framework. Satan claims to be God's "equal" (154), which we may want to dismiss as another one of Satan's exaggerations ("Exaggeration," says Mailer's Jesus, "is the language of the Devil" 117). However, Jesus corroborates Satan's claim—not while bungling through life with his identity crisis (as Mailer imagined it), but while he "sat at the father's right hand" (240) in the heavenly realms after his death, resurrection, and ascension. That is, while we may have cause in this novel to doubt Jesus' theological statements on earth, we should reasonably expect his statements from heaven to be reliable. "As yet," says Jesus from heaven, "since the contest remains so equal, neither the Lord nor Satan can triumph" (240).

Jesus characterizes the Lord as preoccupied with Satan, and thereby limited in his power and his ability to love: "My Father...does not often speak to me.... Surely He sends forth as much love as He can offer, but His love is not without limit. For His wars with the Devil grow worse" (240). God's limitations are exposed and exacerbated by his struggle with Satan. This only confirms what Jesus intuits in his moments of agony on the cross: "Even as I asked if the Lord was all-powerful, I heard my own answer: God, my father, was one god. But there were others" (232). Jesus' conclusion that the Lord is but one god among many strains the limits of Dualism, suggesting perhaps that the cosmos is animated by a panoply of gods as in Hinduism or Greek and Roman mythology. However, because the novel portrays only two gods—the Lord and Satan—at war with one another, Jesus' statement remains only a conjecture.

In terms of its stated theology, then, *The Gospel According to the Son* is decidedly Manichaean. The Lord is locked in an existential struggle against the Devil, a foe of equal or near-equal power. Even so, by examining the novel's representation of the Devil through an Augustinian lens, we can detect a small fissure in the walls of the theological dam that will finally burst open in volume two, *The Castle in the Forest*. It begins with the first appearance of Satan in the novel. After fasting for forty days, Jesus encounters a "visitor" who was "as handsome as a prince" (45). Jesus is so impressed by his regal appearance that he says to himself: "The Devil is the most beautiful creature God ever made" (45). This statement is ripe with implications. The beauty of Satan has Miltonic overtones: that Satan was the jewel of God's creation. (Mailer has stated that his image of the Devil is most influenced by Milton [*On God* 15], and he lists *Paradise Lost* in the bibliography of *The Castle in the Forest*.) The implication is that Satan was created as a higher order being suffused with goodness. His nature, then, can be understood in Augustinian terms as a "perversion of good" or "diminished good" (*City of God* 385). He was not created evil; he became evil by choice, by denying good. According to Augustine, the devils "have forsaken Him who supremely is, and have turned to themselves who have no such essence" (385). But the most telling aspect of Jesus' assessment of the Devil in the novel is that he was "made" by God. Unlike God, the Devil is a created being, and he owes his existence to God, not the other way around.

Stemming from the acknowledgment that the Devil is a creature made by God, we see that there is no creative power in the Devil's arsenal. He is a sham, a con artist, an illusionist. Just as Satan owes his existence to God, the only power he exhibits is fully dependent on the good God has made. This can be demonstrated through a brief examination of the "seven powers and demons" Mailer attributes to Satan (180–181). What Mailer's Jesus calls "the seven powers of the Devil's wrath" are attended by seven "offspring" or "demons" (180–181):

Devil's Power	Attendant Demon
Darkness	Treachery
Desire	Pride
Ignorance	Gluttony
Love of Death	Lust to eat another
Whole Domain	Defiler of the spirit
Excess of Wisdom	Urge to steal a soul
Wisdom of Wrath	Lust to lay waste a city

None of the powers and demons listed is generative or creative. Rather, each is a perversion of good. Darkness is the inverse of light and depends upon light for its existence. Light is generative, whereas darkness is merely the absence of light. Light penetrates darkness, not the other way around. Such can be said of the rest of the powers. Desire for good or for God is generative in that it takes us outside ourselves and directs our energies to others and to the Other, but desire for self-aggrandizement (i.e., pride or vainglory) perverts desire, directing our energies inward. Ignorance is a paucity of wisdom; but excess wisdom leads to the kind of desire manifested in the Devil: "the urge to steal a soul." Love of death is a perversion of the love of life. Thirst for "whole domain" results in the defiling of the soul.

In the final analysis, an incongruity exists between the stated theology of *The Gospel According to the Son* and Mailer's representation of the Devil and of evil. To say that Satan is equal to God is one thing, but to represent him as a creature of God possessing powers that are fully dependent upon God's creative powers is quite another. One answer, perhaps, is that Mailer's Dualism relies not on raising the Devil to God's height (i.e., by making him a generative, creative, all-powerful anti-God) but on bringing God down a few pegs. And this he does in the final pages of the novel, as discussed above. "Volume One" of Mailer's exploration of God and the Devil ends not with Satan's exaltation to the level of Creator-God, but God's demotion to existential being: a god of limited power, exhausted, imperiled, fighting for his life and for the lives of his creatures.

THE CASTLE IN THE FOREST—GOOD PERVERTED

> *Not all the clichés concerning the Devil are false....Evil does
> indeed seek the dark.*
>
> Deiter, Castle 457

In his review of *The Castle in the Forest* for *Commonweal*, Paul J. Griffiths claims that Mailer's depiction of good and evil in the novel is "decisively antidualist, the very reverse of Manichaean" (26). Mailer's treatment of evil is dependent upon the power of good for its existence; evil in the novel is "parasitic, pathetic, sadly strutting but internally empty...a reduction of human possibility, a loss of the good, an absence of empathy" (25). In this sense, Griffiths argues, the evil of *The Castle in the Forest* is "positively Augustinian" (25). This observation bears out in a variety of ways in the novel, beginning first and foremost with the narrator, the narrator. Dieter, who is called D.T. is a devil in service to another devil of higher rank—perhaps even the Devil himself, who is affectionately called "the Maestro." In fact there is much Dieter does not know, and what he does know will likely fade from his memory. According to Dieter, devils "develop many new qualities of mind, but soon lose them" (257). He believes he has been a devil for centuries and has been demoted after a significant rise in rank, but even of this he is unsure. As he explains it, "Few devils are permitted to retain much memory" (257). These and other passages portray devils as real beings who are in danger of dissipating to the point of extinction. What is a being without memory but a phantom, a flash in the pan? The nature of devils then seems to operate on the principle of loss (Griffiths 26). They are always in danger of becoming less, and, therefore, they are "free from moral judgment, and alert to fresh estimates" (*Castle* 282); they must ask in the case, for instance, of a sexual encounter between two people, "will this particular joining weaken our position or enhance it?" (282). Thus it is Dieter's "act of treachery" against the Evil One (72), writing a novel and thereby revealing his identity, that also simultaneously offers a kind of salvation. Through writing, memory is retained and his gradual descent toward nonbeing is arrested. Griffiths suggests that in having Dieter "become less devilish as he [writes a book], Mailer may be suggesting that those who write are performing the paradigmatically good act, the act that holds back the waters of chaos" (26). Mailer and Augustine are certainly on the same page here. According to Hannah Arendt, "Augustinian love depends on the faculty of memory, and not upon the expectation of death" (paraphrased in Bloom 275). Dieter, therefore, may owe a debt to the Bishop of Hippo: Augustine, after all, is credited with inventing "autobiographical memory" with the publication of his *Confessions* (278). So, the act of writing, especially the act of autobiographical or confessional writing like Dieter's, is "good" in an Augustinian sense because it preserves memory and produces empathy.

As Mailer depicts it, evil in the novel depends upon the presence of goodness for its existence and power. In discussing the character of Klara Hitler, Adolf's mother, Mailer said, "I think that we can't begin to understand human history until we recognize the depth and very often the ugliness of certain ironies in our life...the thought that a fine woman ended up producing a monster seemed to me in the nature of things" (Lee 208). The irony that Mailer describes here is at its essence an example of evil as perverted good. A mother's love for her child is good: a woman and man procreate (a regenerative act) and a child is born. The woman's love for her child seeks the good of the child, often at her own expense. The act of love is, therefore, expansive, relational, life-giving rather than life-taking. What characterizes Klara's love for Adi, however, is not "normal" or "healthy" behavior, but rather excess love that extends to paranoia, indulgence, and overprotectiveness. Having lost other children to death, Klara clings protectively to "Adi." She praises him, cooing, "isn't Adi an angel?" (83), and she takes unusual pleasure in keeping his anus clean. She sees breast feeding in an almost sacrificial way ("she was putting her strength into him" 83), praying earnestly while nursing, "Oh, Lord, take my life if it will help to save his" (83). As Adi grows, Klara continues to coddle and protect him, and this leads to discord between Adi and his siblings; as Alois tells her, "it breeds bad feeling if you always take Adi's side" (290). Dieter writes, "Excessive mother-love is almost as promising to us as a void of mother-love. We are keyed to look for excess of every kind, good or bad, loving or hateful, too much or too little of anything. Every exaggeration of honest sentiment is there to serve our aims" (74). In this situation, then, Dieter's power to do evil has its origin in the goodness of mother-love; he takes the "honest sentiment" and encourages exaggeration.

Besides excessive mother-love, the novel portrays other emotions and attributes such as ambition as originally good but capable of evil perversion. Dieter writes, "In our ranks, we look upon excessive ambition as a force at our disposal. We are ready to attach ourselves to any urge that mounts *out of control*. Of no passion is this more true than

out-sized ambition. Yet ambition is also related to the Lord's purposes. After all, God designed ambition for humans. (He wanted
them to strive to fulfill His vision)" (89, italics added). The paren-
thetical remark serves to remind us that ambition exists in humans
precisely because it exists in God's character. Ambition, like mother-
love, is an "honest sentiment" tied to the creative character of God
and is, therefore, innately good. We might note that "out of control"
ambition—ambition that is wrenched from its divine context and
used to build a kingdom for one's own glory—is the hallmark of
Satan (as portrayed, for instance, in Milton) and it is also the hallmark
of a fascist dictator.

In *The Castle in the Forest*, the most thoroughly explored example
of evil-power-derived-from-good is human sexuality, a good that
Mailer portrays as ripe for satanic exploitation. The act of sex, in fact,
is a divinely ordained good act because it extends life and fulfills
God's commission to "be fruitful and increase in number; fill the
earth" (Genesis 1:28). God creates, and He gives us the task of pro-
creating. For this reason, perhaps, the Devil pays close attention to
the sexual encounters of Alois and Klara. Dieter explains that "devils
are supposed to be interested in every form of bodily embrace," especially those "that fall into no established fold" (282). Incest, therefore, is of particular interest to the devils. According to Lee Siegel,
"incest represents the sick inversion of everything [Mailer] cherishes:
expansion of the self beyond one's origins; the gift of empathy with
the other; the ability to sublimate love into work and vice versa" (15).
Incest as the "sick inversion" of good makes it a powerful tool for
Mailer's devils. It is through Himmler's discourse on incest early in
the novel that Mailer introduces the satanic realm to his narrative.
Himmler's speech evokes the Augustinian notion of evil being not a
substance of itself but a perversion of what is good. Incest is at once
a perversion of good sexuality and a salient metaphor for a destructive love of self, or other-as-self. For this reason, Himmler believes
that Satan "would certainly be ready to pay great attention to
Incestuaries of advanced degree. For indeed, how could such an Evil
One not be eager to distort the exceptional possibilities that arise
from the doubling of God-given genes?" (23). While Alois suspects,
if he doesn't know for certain, that Klara is actually his daughter
(55), Klara has enough piety to understand that in having sex with
her "uncle" she is living "in the grip of the Evil One" (58). What
should be her natural joy in having sex with her husband and producing a child from their union is complicated by what she, as a pious
Christian woman, sees as several moral transgressions: incest,

fornication, and adultery. Whatever joy she feels in carnal pleasure with Alois she thus attributes to Satan. She feels that the Devil "had dug into her with the most evil enjoyment she had ever known" (59). This is not something the reader can dismiss as superstition because the devil narrator soon confirms that the Evil One was indeed present at the moment when Adolf was conceived, and this idea introduces a deeper and more profound twisting of good. Satan's presence at the conception of Adolf Hitler, Dieter suggests, becomes the inversion of the immaculate conception of Christ: "the Maestro had actually joined with the attendant devil for one instant (even as Jehovah offered His immanence to Gabriel during another exceptional event)" (79). Here the "two volumes" of Mailer's major novel on God and the Devil briefly rub shoulders.

Pedophilia is another perversion explored in the novel. Perhaps the most pernicious and hauntingly evil character in the novel, more disturbing even than the devil who narrates the story and encourages the development of Adolf Hitler, is the figure of Der Alte, "also known as Der alte Zauberer—'the Old Sorcerer'" (159). Der Alte is not a sorcerer, nor is he a Doctor of Philosophy, but he gives the impression of being both. Despite his reputation for erudition, he is the picture of depraved humanity. The contradiction between wisdom and debauchery within his character make him an emblem of Augustinian depravity. "If he had chosen in his old age to look like a confirmed drunk, an odd choice, since in fact he did not drink, he was attracted all the same to many of the slovenly habits of old sots" (167). His clothing was "filthy" and, due to incontinence, his body and dingy abode smelled of urine (167–168). However, he looked "striking" and "impressive in his person....His eyes were extraordinary, as blue as the coldest skies of the north, yet full of lights that offered a clue to many a trick he had learned" (168). Once a "satyr with the ladies" (169), he now sought to satisfy his sexual cravings with little boys. The scenes describing his sexual encounters with Alois Junior, Adolf's brother, are so degrading and disturbing that even the devil narrator admits to being "repelled" (282): "If I am free of moral judgment, I am hardly void of good taste, and Der Alte demeaned himself" (283). The combination of Der Alte's impressive qualities and lofty philosophy with his physical and moral degradation is precisely what lends the character of Der Alte a palpable air of evil. (Later in the novel, Adolf embodies the same contradiction when he wipes his ass with his school diploma [453]). Finally, the combination of pedophilia and fellatio, one an aberrant and twisted form of parental love and the other a nongenerative and unproductive form of sexual intercourse, makes Der Alte the emblem of perverted good par excellence. Siegel even connects Der Alte with the enigmatic title of Mailer's novel when he notes that "the real 'castle' is the repulsive parody of a castle: the squalid hut of...Der Alte, a sadist and child molester who is the most consequential of Adolf's twisted mentors" (15).

Unproductive, nonregenerative sexual acts abound in *The Castle in the Forest*, not the least of which is masturbation. Anyone familiar with Mailer's views on masturbation will not be surprised to learn that his Adolf is an avid wanker. Mailer argued that masturbation inspired self-pity and led ultimately to insanity (Pontifications 115, 119). "If one masturbates," Mailer once said, "the ability to contemplate one's experience is disturbed. Instead, *fantasies of power* take over and disturb all sleep" (12, italics added). This idea expressed in a 1962 interview finds its fictional realization forty-five years later in the character of Adolf. In Adolf's bizarre methods of masturbation, Mailer connects the "fantasies of power" spawned by the nonregenerative sex act with the power symbols of Hitler's dictatorship: Hilter's pencil-brush mustache and the Nazi salute, Mailer imagines, both originated with the young Fuhrer's experiments in self-pleasure. Rather than imagining nude women while he masturbates, Adolf pictures in his mind the small mustache of Empress Elizabeth's assassin in combination with the glimpse he once had of his sister's pubic hair. He also tested his masturbatory skills by performing the act while "holding one arm in the air at a forty-five-degree angle for a long time" (457).

The most powerful image of masturbatory sterility turned to a fantasy of power is illustrated in Adolf's preference for masturbating in the forest and ejaculating on leaves. Mailer believed that "if one masturbates, all that happens is, everything that's beautiful and good in one, goes up the hand, goes into the air, is *lost*" (12, italics in original). While this loss that Mailer describes is certainly applicable to Adolf's practice—masturbation is, in an Augustinian way, a negation of the regenerative potential of the sperm and thus the negation of good—the diabolic will to power manifests itself in the symbolic import of the leaves. Earlier in the novel, Dieter explained the essential goodness of the printed word over cyberspace by saying, "Even processed paper still contains an ineluctable hint of the tenderness God put into His trees" (79). By ejaculating on leaves in the forest, Adolf is thereby symbolically enacting a will to power over God. He is showing his will to dominate God by symbolically buggering Him.

MAILER'S AUGUSTINIAN DISCOVERY

The vulgarity is to...see him as an example of pure evil, unre-
strained psychopathy.

Mailer on Charles Manson, Pontifications 61

The devil's ultimate aim in this novel is to slowly and methodically turn his "client," Adolf Hitler, into a powerful tool for evil. The process of taking an innocent child and twisting him into the engineer of the Holocaust is an exercise in Augustinian theology. Griffiths writes that "Adolf is moved toward evil by being slowly emptied of love and warmth and laughter" (25). Mailer represents this draining of love most poignantly in the scene where his father uses a cake of sulphur to gas a failing bee hive. Adi's sister Angela finds the scene too disturbing and retreats to the house in tears, but Adi remains, "his eyes alive in response to his father's lecture. 'Your big sister is silly,' said Alois. 'In nature there is no mercy for the weak.' 'I'm not bothered,' said Adi" (200). But as his father opens the box to empty it, Adi is clearly bothered. He thinks of the death of Der Alte's single bee and begins to tear up. But he masters these "silly" emotions by making a comparison between Der Alte's single bee and the carnage before him. "But, of course, there was no comparison. He blinked back his tears. Der Alte had loved one little bee, but the *sick* ones here in this *bad* hive *dirtied* the place where they ate and where they slept. No comparison" (200, italics added). Adi succeeds in hardening his heart toward the bees by pronouncing them "sick," "bad," and "dirty," just as he would the Jews in years to come. The power he exhibits as the Fuhrer is, as Griffiths notes, "evil's only capacity, which is to decrease and remove" (26). Understood in this way, the extermination of a hive of bees is not so far removed from other exterminations that lie ahead in Adolf's future. The magnitude of the two acts, gassing bees and gassing humans, is clearly incongruent, but the contiguity between the two is logical. An Adolf Hitler is not born evil, but evil is what he becomes when he is drained of good. Watching the decrease and removal of good, represented by hard working creatures whose job it is to promote the growth of flowers and to produce sweet and nurturing honey, is but one step on the road to Auschwitz.

Several reviewers were disappointed in *The Castle in the Forest* because they felt the novel did not adequately portray evil. John Gross claims "there is virtually no sense of evil at all" in the book (61), and

Brad Hooper complains that the novel is "less a psychological study of evil than a fanciful one" (6). Not coincidentally, both of these reviewers saw the supernatural framework of the novel as a "gimmick" (Hooper 6) and a "whimsical contraption" (Gross 61). Perhaps Dieter was right to say that his book "can hardly be accessible to the majority of my readers." As he explains it, "Given the present authority of the scientific world, most well-educated people are ready to bridle at the notion of such an entity as the Devil. They have even less readiness to accept the cosmic drama of an ongoing conflict between Satan and the Lord" (71). But my hunch is that these reviewers were not simply thrown off by Mailer's supernatural explanation of Hitler's monstrosity, but rather by the subtlety of the evil Mailer portrays. Siegel states that in this book "Mailer has imagined himself into a raw propinquity to evil without losing either his nerve or his humanity" (15). One might expect the story of Hitler's childhood to abound in sadism, torturous episodes, abuse, and bullying. The extermination of a hive of bees can hardly count as evil by those standards. But from an Augustinian stand-point, the evil Mailer displays is right on the mark. The novel suggests that even an Adolf Hitler is not born evil. Even an Adolf Hitler is not catapulted into evil by some trauma or cataclysmic event. Rather it is the slow erosion of everything that is good. Whether it is helped along by sentient beings in the supernatural realm or not, evil is what we become when we let goodness slip away. The fact that it can happen to a little boy who is loved so deeply by his God-fearing mother makes it a frightening enough portrayal for this reader.

I can imagine two possible responses Mailer might have made to the suggestion that the world he depicted in *The Gospel According to the Son* and *The Castle in the Forest* is not at its essence Dualist. One might go something like this: "That's fine. I'm not wedded to the philosophy of Dualism." In fact, the only philosophy Mailer claimed as fully representing his views of life was existentialism. To the extent that the good and evil represented in his final two novels reveal an ongoing struggle between God and the Devil, the novel is eminently existential. It may be inconsequential to Mailer whether the evil was a power of separate origin from God or not. The second response might go something like this: "Why must we believe God is all good?" Mailer once commented in an interview, "I don't believe the Devil is the secret of all evil on earth. I believe something more complicated than that. I think God might be the source of a considerable amount of evil. Because God is embattled, He could fail to take care, much to His great woe, of people who are devoted to Him, in the same way that a general might have to surrender soldiers on a hill" *(Pontifications* 87*)*. An existential God "doing the best He can," as Mailer liked to put it, is not a God who can accomplish all the good He wishes to accomplish. We might say this is not evil so much as it is limitation, but this may be splitting hairs.

Does the existence of evil in the world necessitate a belief in God as limited in his power? To Mailer, the answer was yes. To Augustine, no. But Mailer's fictional exploration of the life of Jesus and of Hitler seems to point in Augustine's direction: evil such as Hitler's is not dependent on God's limitations but on the good that He created and what his free-will creatures choose to do with it. My analysis of evil in Mailer's final two novels—or as I would have it, in the two volumes of his final novel on God and the Devil—is not meant to be an argument with a man who, unfortunately, can no longer argue back. Rather, by showing that Mailer came to an Augustinian understanding of evil intuitively, through the creative process of writing, my analysis of evil in Mailer's last great work is meant to let the man's organic fictional world speak for itself.

Works Cited

Anshen, David. "An Enigmatic Development." *American Book Review* 28:6 (September/October 2007): 18.

Augustine. *The City of God.* New York: Modern Library, 1993.

———. *The Confessions.* Westwood, NJ: Christian Library, 1984.

Bloom, Harold. *Where Shall Wisdom Be Found?* New York: Riverhead, 2004.

Goethe, Johann Wolfgang von. *The Permanent Goethe,* ed. Thomas Mann. New York: Dial Press, 1956.

Griffiths, Paul J. "Diabolical Conception." *Commonweal* 134:9 (4 May 2007): 24–26.

Gross, John. "Young Adolf." *Commentary* 123:3 (March 2007): 59–63.

Hooper, Brad. Rev. of *Castle in the Forest. Booklist* 103:6 (15 November 2006): 6.

Lee, Michael. "The Devil in Norman Mailer." *Literary Review* 50:4 (Summer 2007): 202–216.

Lewis, C.S. *The Screwtape Letters.* New York: Collier, 1982.

Mailer, Norman. *The Castle in the Forest.* New York: Random House, 2007.

———. *On God: An Uncommon Conversation.* New York: Random House, 2008.

———. *The Gospel According to the Son.* New York: Ballantine, 1997.

———. *Pieces and Pontifications.* Boston: Little Brown, 1982.

Milton, John. *Complete Poems and Major Prose,* ed. Merritt Y. Hughes. Indianapolis: Bobbs-Merrill, 1984.

The NIV Study Bible: New International Version. Grand Rapids, MI: Zondervan, 1985.

Siegel, Lee. "Maestro of the Human Ego." *New York Times Book Review* 21 January 2007: 1, 12–15.

Tolkien, J.R.R. *The Fellowship of the Ring.* London: Collins, 2001.

PART III

Politics

CHAPTER 7

Imperial Mailer: *Ancient Evenings*

Ashton Howley

[E]go is awareness of one's will.

Norman Mailer, Conversations 226

Is it not true that defending the One involves, ipso facto, rejecting the unconscious; since the latter implies that part of the psyche exists which is acting in its own interests, thwarting the empire of the ego?

André Green, Life Narcissism, Death Narcissism 9

When heroic consciousness dominates, one thinks one knows better than the unconscious who one is and feels one should therefore be in control of one's life.

John Beebe, Introduction to Jung's Aspects of the Masculine *xii.*

As we know from ancient Egyptian history, [events which are in accord with an end of an era] are manifestations of psychic changes which always appear at the end of one Platonic month and at the beginning on another. Apparently they are changes in the constellation of psychic dominants, of the archetypes, of 'gods' as they used to be called, which bring about, or accompany, long-lasting transformations of the collective psyche. This transformation started in the historical era and left its traces first in the passing of the aeon of Taurus into that of Aries, and then of Aries into Pisces, whose

beginning coincides with the rise of Christianity. We are now
nearing that great change which may be expected when the spring-
point enters Aquarius.

Carl Jung, Flying Saucers: A Modern Myth of Things Seen in
the Skies, 5

This essay offers a Jungian reading of *Ancient Evenings*. Inspiring it is
the fact that the novel's central character, Menenhetet, corresponds to
Jung's description of the aimlessly peripatetic heroes of Egyptian
mythology, who figuratively resemble "the wandering sun" (*Aspects*
22), a symbol of the ego, moving in repetitive cycles toward and away
from the dark, primordial waters of the unconscious. Specifically, the
tendencies and traits definitive of the ego inhabiting the second of
three stages of the Hero archetype are similar to the features of
Ancient Evenings that have resulted in its main critiques. Literalism,
egotism, projection, narcissism, and sadomasochistic violence—interestingly, these terms itemize both the "unfortunate results" (Beebe,
Aspects 14) of the ego's "rejection of the unconscious" in the second
stage of heroic-archetypal development, and the reasons that *Ancient
Evenings* is commonly disparaged. For instance, the result of Mailer's
intention "to treat mythology as if it were real" (Whalen-Bridge,
"Karma" 4) is its "outrageous literalism" (Bloom 33). Another criticism centers on the fact that the novel is set in ancient Egypt and
based on the Egyptian *Book of the Dead,* but patently reflects the
author's fascination with his own ego (De Mott 3). A third involves
the ways in which *Ancient Evenings* blurs distinctions between
Egypt's ancient culture and concepts about the United States that can
be found throughout Mailer's *oeuvre* (Olster 63). A fourth is that
Ancient Evenings, containing elements of "orientalist fantasy"
(Whalen-Bridge, "Karma" 3), might impel some readers to regard it
as "pro-imperialist." Finally, the novel's critics objected to its sadomasochistic brutality occurring (mostly) between men (Cf. Bloom
33; DeMott 3). For those who complain about Mailer's obsession
with aggressive masculinity, *Ancient Evenings* is a sort of *locus
classicus.*

Necessarily psychobiographical, "the most largely practiced
method of research in psychoanalysis of art since Freud's *Leonardo da
Vinci and a Memory of his Childhood*" (Gaillard, qtd. in Papadopoulos
331), this essay assesses the reasons that *Ancient Evenings* is so out of
favor and asserts that the reasons for its unpopularity make it important as a psychological allegory about men's collective difficulty in

accessing their unconscious, an allegory that epitomizes the fact that most stereotypical heroes fail to glimpse, let alone enter, their archetype's final frontier. In what follows, after discussing the links between Egyptian mythology and Jungian psychology, I briefly elaborate on the latter before turning to a discussion of the literal manner in which Mailer employs a number of concepts that Yeats explores in *Ideas of Good and Evil* and *A Vision*, which derive, in part, from Egypt's *Book of the Dead*. Mailer's exoteric treatment of Yeatsian motifs makes it inevitable that the sadistic voices of the gods and of the Pharaohs, flowing continuously in Menenhetet's thoughts, impede his heroic-archetypal progress. I then examine another instance of the novel's "horrible literalism" (Bloom 33), Mailer's treatment of palingenesis as his hero's conduit of regression. Forced to play a subordinate/masochistic role in the military and political hierarchies of Egypt's government, Menenhetet, stuck, for much of the novel, in stage two of the hero archetype wherein the achievements of superordinate male figures serve as mirroring ego-ideals, repeatedly retreats to stage one, that of "containment/nurturance" (Papadopoulos 199) wherein ego-consciousness becomes bound up with maternal figures in what Jung called *participation mystique*. "In my second life" (787), Menenhetet tenderly recalls, "I grew up in the Gardens of the Secluded as the son of Honeyball, and slept in her bed every night."[1] Striving for power, becoming humiliated (raped, demoted, exiled) and retreating to the womb—this pattern is the result of Mailer's obsession with "power relationships among males" (*Conversations* 331), an obsession that Jungian psychology can help to contextualize. Finally, while drawing on Edward Said's *Orientalism*, I argue that *Ancient Evenings*, in its depictions of imperial warfare and violent brutality, in its sheer bulk and its relentless exotericism, reflects the era in which it is set, the period in which Egypt's rulers sought to extend the boundaries of their empire and in doing so destroyed it. Mailer's achievement is to delineate, consciously or otherwise, an earlier imperial culture as a mirroring image of our present global one.

Egyptian mythology provides the common ground between Jungian psychology and *Ancient Evenings*. For Jung, the story of Osiris allegorizes the ways in which the disintegration of ego-consciousness brings the ego into psychology's underworld, the unconscious. Showing how the unconscious lures into herself "the forward-striving libido which rules the conscious mind" (*Aspects* 17), Isis is the archetype of the " 'sister-wife-mother,' the woman in man," who appears "during the second half of life" and "effects a forcible change of personality" (20). She connects the ego's split-off parts, symbolized by Osiris's fragmented body, after which it returns to the light of consciousness equipped with the knowledge of the contents of the unconscious. Her poisoning of Ra signifies how "the demands of the unconscious act at first like a paralyzing poison on a man's energy and resourcefulness" (18). The battle between Set and Horus represents the destructiveness of ego-consciousness and the ardors of male competitiveness, inviting sabotage by the feminine unconscious. In betraying Horus, Isis upsets his hard-won victory over Set, but her cruelty is of saving benefit to him. Here she represents the return to awareness of buried memories, hiding from the light of consciousness (denial, repression), but arising unbidden to effect the proverbial mid-life crisis, often instigated by "an unwelcome accident or a positive catastrophe" (20), also of saving benefit. Even as Horus becomes morose and isolated, the ego enters a "state of introversion," as it "sinks 'into its own depth'" (12), becomes dominated by the mother and reexperiences "the world of the child" (12). A final element of Egyptian mythology yielding significance as psychological allegory is the incest occurring among Egypt's theogonic figures. "In so far as the mother represents the unconscious" (14), Jung explains, "the incest tendency, particularly when it appears as the amorous desire of the mother ... is really only the desire of the unconscious to be taken notice of." Development "in the first part of life" (14) requires "over-coming the actual mother," but "in the second half of life," it neces-sitates reconciling with "the mother-symbolic," feminizing men by getting them in touch with their unconscious, a process that makes the heroic ego feel "like one buried in the earth, a dead man who has crawled back into the mother" (22).

These characters and scenarios in Egyptian mythology, which Mailer draws on extensively in *Ancient Evenings*, constitute the foun-dational elements in Jungian psychology. A brief summary of these elements can help to elucidate the psychodynamics that Mailer's gran-diose hero dramatizes so exuberantly. Actualized during the first transitional period in which the ego moves out of stage one of the hero archetypes, the maternal symbolic realm, the ego's "archetypal energy ... kills the dragon (i.e., the incest wish)" (Papadopolous 207). Once advanced into the second stage, that of "adapting / adjusting" (199), it requires the assistance of paternal figures to help it conform to the standards of society. As Herbert Read argues, "[f]or the boy, the father is an anticipation of his own masculinity, conflicting with his wish to remain infantile" (319). Crucial to its development, the heroic ego must cease its idealizing of father figures so as to ensure that the dragon of *participation mystique* not rear its ugly head again in the second stage. Threatened by its regressive desire for affection and affirmation, its forging "the confidence, call it bravado, to face up to the father and meet the challenges of the patriarchal world" (Papadopoulos 211) entails detaching from its ego-ideals.[2] During this second identity-crisis, ego-consciousness, detached from maternal/paternal support, becomes aware of the unconscious as it experiences the proverbial "death of the ego," the dualistic phase in which the "dominant position formerly held by external authority, by the voice...the 'father'" (212) gives way to the "new structure that emerges from the inner world of the psyche," that of the transformed, Phoenix-like "Self (capitalized to denote its transcendence and essential difference from the ego)" (212). Unlike the ego's "persona" in the first and second stages, which consists mostly of prevailing cultural stereotypes, individuated identity in the third stage becomes "grounded in the archetype of the Self rather than in the unconscious mother or father images" (212).

Such are the stages of archetypal development, as Jung described them. In practice, however, various pathologies arise when the ego is compelled to "procrastinate and delay" in the first and second stages, "by trickery and subterfuge and self-deception" (Papadopoulos 207). Among the neurotic characterological traits that hinder the ego's transition to the third life-stage is the literalism caused by its alienation from the unconscious, troubling its efforts to access, intuitively, the resonant depths of symbolic language. Fascination with its own personality and heroic achievements, another indicator of its inhabiting the second stage, develops into its narcissistic inability to acknowledge the autonomy of others and into aggressive attitudes toward father figures. The narcissism, megalomania, "acrobatics of the will" (Storr 198), and "unconscious automatism" to which it succumbs drives it to "go on re-staging the drama of separation, using endless women and men as stand-ins" (Papadopoulos 208). These neurotic traits "are joined by necrophilia" (Fromm 108): Eros joins Thanatos as "the craving for death and destruction" becomes synonymous with the "craving to return to the womb and to the past." The heroic ego, then, while journeying through these three life-stages, "can choose only between two possibilities: to regress or to move forward" (Fromm 119).

Readers of *Ancient Evenings* will recognize the relevance of at least some of these citations from psychology. For Menenhetet is literally a dead man recounting the times he enters the womb of a woman and, dying while ejaculating, rebirthing himself so as to experience another blissful childhood and another agonized adulthood, characterized by his competitive compulsion for political power, monetary gain, violence, and sex, all of which serve as his means to attaining his desire to replace the Pharaoh(s) as Lord of the Double Crown, or, at least, to become Vizier. Throughout his four lives and his long afterlife, Menenhetet's quasisurgical dissections of his every memory, thought and mood, his ingestion of body organs and fluids, and bat dung and scorpions, reveal how maniacally anxious he is to probe the depths of himself. But he searches for answers to the important questions both about himself and his fate in all the wrong places. In his filth there is no wisdom.[3]

The first section of *Ancient Evenings*, "The Book of the Gods," shows Menenhetet narrating the dramas of Egypt's ur-figures to Meni while regarding them as historical events much like a fundamentalist discussing cosmogony in Genesis. Foreshadowing the rest of *Ancient Evenings*, the straight-forward manner in which he relates the events of his four lives, seminally transmitting them to Meni, is Mailer's *modus operandi,* his blending of elements in Egyptian myth and in Yeats's "Magic" and *A Vision.* Capitalizing on the fact that the "Egyptian religion was pre-eminently a manly religion, and therefore calculated to develop manhood" (Massey 242), Mailer literalizes a passage from *The Book of the Dead* attributed to Ra—"I poured seed into my mouth, I sent forth issue" (Bishop 127; cf. Budge 282–292)—just as he does the Yeatsian doctrine, cited in the novel's epigraph, that the shifting "borders of our mind" enable "many minds" to "flow into one another...and [to] create or reveal a single mind, a single energy." The second Yeatsian doctrine that Mailer includes in his epigraph and renders literally throughout *Ancient Evenings* states that "the borders of our memories are as shifting"; while the third, "[t]hat this great mind and great memory can be evoked by symbols" (Finneran 351) is omitted in Mailer's epigraph—a surprising omission, given that the chapter subtitles in *Ancient Evenings* bear hieroglyphs that symbolically evoke their content. A fourth Yeatsian motif is structural. The novel "moves in a spiral" (*Conversations* 328), Mailer remarked, invoking Yeats's apocalyptic image of the widening gyres in "The Second Coming." As Meni, in his opening moments, passes out of one state of existence and into another—"I have a thirst like the heat of earth on fire. Mountains writhe. I see waves of flame. Washes, flashes, waves of flame (3)—he dramatizes another image that Yeats borrowed from *The Book of the Dead*, of world-departed souls having to "mount to heaven by means of a ladder" (Budge lxx), a fiery one, after which they arrive at "the point...where...[they] may escape the constraints of [their] nature and that of external things, entering upon a state where fuel becomes flame" (Ellmann 50). For Jung, such imagery denotes the heroic ego's plunging into and returning from its encounters with the contents of the unconscious. But Meni's confusion constitutes his narrative. Before entering the mode of consciousness in which he recounts his awakening in the Pyramid of Khufu (3), he envisages "[a] burning number": "[t]he flame showed me an edge as unflickering as a knife, and I passed into that fiery sign.... [i]n fire I began to stream through the clear and blazing existence of the number 2." He is far from entering what Jung referred to as the dualistic phase that the transformed ego enters as it passes into the third life-stage. Here the number prefigures his becoming one with his great-grandfather, in the first of many examples in *Ancient Evenings* of the blurring of distinctions between male identities, a defining tendency of the ego in the second life-stage. As Meni listens to Menenhetet narrate stories about his four existences, his memories become intertwined with those of his great-grandfather, so that, ultimately, distinctions of identity vanish, as together they embark as one person in the Boat of Ra, voyaging to the stars.

Yeats operates in the decorous world of the novel's semiabstract concepts, some of which Mailer translates into precisely those graphic details that have offended so many readers. Meni, having returned to the Pyramid of Khufu, now in company with Menenhetet, wonders: "Was that a cave in the sky by which I had been ready to enter the Duad? .... [b]ut I had no taste for such questions" (105). He discerns that he "was looking into a large bowl of water, and the star was a reflection" (111). Moments later, Menenhetet, after placing his penis in Meni's mouth, begins his long narration. Eight-hundred pages later, Meni again sees the "light of a star reflected in a bowl of water" (819). But then: "I could no longer see the star .... [o]nly a navel before my eyes.... and I was back in all the stink and fury of the old man's phallus in my mouth.... [t]hen all of him came forth, and in great bitterness.... I had to take into me the misery he felt" (819–820). This exploitative dynamic between men, enabled by the lack of borders—physical, emotional, mental—subtends the dramatic apices of *Ancient Evenings'* seven books. In the first, Meni ends up, surprised and disgusted, with Menenhetet's member in his mouth. In the second, Horus and Set battle for supremacy, with the elder attempting to rape, inseminate, and kill the younger. The third book conveys infant Meni's observations of his childhood, as he remains enfolded in his mother's security, full of admiration for his father/great-grandfather, but forced to observe them having intercourse with her, enraging him. The fourth book stages Ramses II's rape of

Menenhetet, after which the ashamed charioteer fights bravely along-side the Pharaoh in the Battle of Kadesh, is then scorned, demoted, and exiled. In the fifth, Ramses II sodomizes him again before making him governor in the House of the Secluded, where Menenhetet takes his revenge by forming a sexual relationship with Usermare's most rebellious mistress. Habitually angry and jealous, Menenhetet spends his time voyeuristically observing his master's sexual performances, mightier than his own, his anxiety toward his father-figure counterbalancing his admiration of him. He then becomes the "companion to Rama-Nefru," Pharaoh's second wife, again playing the voyeur and turning the available mistresses into stand-ins for her, as he acts out Usermare's role. Menenhetet endures these prolonged periods of agitated stasis by contemplating such unheroic topics as the lifestyles of the eunuchs (611) and women's "moonblasts" (662), all the while suffering a "stampede of restlessness" (677). Sensing this, Pharaoh orders him to become Rama-Nefru's governness.

With Mailer persisting in his dramatizing of this sadomasochistic dynamic and of its emotional and political consequences for Menenhetet, *Ancient Evenings* threatens to become insufferably tedious. Most of the sixth book portrays the neglected charioteer overshadowed by Usermere's ithyphallic coronation, as Menenhetet frantically searches for Nefertiri, has sex with her, then mentally replays every last nuance of their encounter (oral, anal, vaginal), obsessively recalling them again later that evening because he feels "like a madman without her" (743)—goes looking for prostitutes and, after spending all night in a local brothel, devotes the next day to cherishing his obsessively sexual thoughts about her (731–776). That evening, during Usermare's ceremonial feast, Menenhetet has sex with her again, this time autogenetically, but her son (at her behest) kills him in the act (777). He dies, is reborn, and, nine months later, becomes what he has all along unconsciously wanted to be, her son, raised in Honeyball's care. He then relives another boyhood (758–842), gregariously enjoying his surrogate mother's affections. World-weary, he dies, rebirths and recycles himself again in stages one and two of the hero archetype. Toward the end of *Ancient Evenings*, Meni, misinformed about Menenhetet's death, learns that he goes looking for Hathfertiti, his daughter and Meni's mother, in order to have sex with her. Menenhetet survives the ordeal; she gets pregnant but aborts their child. After failing to engender himself in her, Menenhetet, succumbing to indigence and despair, dies offstage. Even in death, however, he is driven by his dynamic of failure and neediness: literalizing the links between the seminal and the semantic a final time, he vanishes into his last resort for a surrogate mother, Meni. Before they enter the bottomless river of feces, Meni, knowing neither his origin nor his end, neither who he is nor whose memories are his own, becomes a prominent candidate for the most abused/confused character in all of literature. However, it is little wonder that Meni is still enraptured in a vertigo of questions about his identity since Mailer distinctly set his novel in the two dynasties in which "the hated pharoahs regarded [incest] almost as a royal requirement" (Tannahill 77).

What becomes clear is that palingenesis is Menenhetet's way of regressing into the womb. The "art of palingenesis" (15), in Léon Surette's words, "the topoi of metamorphosis and descent" (16) is a "'backward birth' for the male partner." Despite Menenhetet's repeated "[e]ntry into the mother" (Jung, *Aspects* 21), his many deaths and rebirths, merely physical in nature, do not constitute the proverbial rite of passage from the second to the third stage of the hero archetype. His recycled consciousness, inscribed in almost 900 pages, undergoes no psychological transformation whatsoever. Hence Bloom's remark that "this is a book in which every conceivable outrage happens, and yet nothing happens, because at the end everything remains exactly the same" (35). Applicable to young boys, Jung's comment about the fact that "fear of the father may drive the boy out of his identification with the mother" (Read 321), but that "it is possible that his fear will make him cling still more closely to her," is apposite to Menenhetet. Indeed *Ancient Evenings* "moves in a spiral" (*Conversations* 328), but its circularity is that of the "vicious circle" (Jung, *Aspects* 17) describing the ego's "fear of life and people" that "causes more shrinking back" and that "leads to infantilism and finally 'into the mother.'" Full of "regressive longing to return to the blissful state of infancy in a world dominated by his mother" (von Franz, qtd. in Jung, *Man* 111), Menenhetet is Mailer's entirely exoteric adaptation of the story of Osiris, the oldest extant paradigm of the born-again self that lies at the heart of tribal and religious rituals the world over. As M.-L. von Franz explains, "the hero figure is the symbolic means by which the emerging ego overcomes the inertia of the unconscious mind" (qtd. in Jung, *Man* 111). What makes the Osirian hero heroic is his/her confrontation with the contents of the unconscious, which become his/her source of the primordial energy needed to journey through to stage three of the hero's archetypal narrative. Originating in the story of Osiris, primal initiation rites "take the novice back to the deepest level of the original mother-child identity or ego-Self identity, thus forcing him to experience a symbolic death" (von Franz, qtd. in Jung, *Man* 123) in which "his identity is temporarily dismembered," before becoming "ceremonially rescued by the rite of the new birth." The archetype of striving heroes has a crucial double valence, the exoteric narrative of their victorious struggles and the esoteric story of their self-renewal, but Mailer's treatment of it does not.

The lack of dynamism in Menenhetet's character accounts for the lassitude of *Ancient Evenings*, the dearth of kinetic energy in its plot. His four lives do not effect any significant changes in him because Mailer, in fulfilling his desire to explore the dynamics of power between men, expunges the feminine symbolic from his treatment of Egyptian mythology. His male characters, devoid of an unconscious, undergo no life-transforming experiences in their ardor to accrue more power over one another, militarily, politically, and sexually. In terms of the dialogues that the novel's female characters are given, Hathfertiti, Nefertiri, Honeyball, Rama-Nefru, and the Whore of Tyre, among others, often sound similar to the men, for they are just as hungry for power and prestige and mainly serve as receptacles of the men's compulsive lust. Contrastively, the men who are made to "become a woman" are raped, so Pepti mockingly puts it to the embarrassed Menenhetet, as Mailer bowdlerizes one of his own ideas, that, for a man, becoming "more masculine" entails "first satisfy[ing] something feminine" (*Presidential Papers* 298). Pepti, speaking "in a stern voice, imitating an officer" (761) and prompting "wild laughter" from the soldiers present, tells Menenhetet to "[t]ake heart...the way to become a man is by way first of learning how to be a woman." It was not until Mailer wrote *Tough Guys Don't Dance* that he fully explored in fiction his ideas about the psyche as a composite of male and female principles. The novels that come after *Ancient Evenings*, featuring embattled sons probing the underlying causes of their fathers' masculinist credos and their compulsions toward power and violence, represent Mailer's efforts to overcome his commitment to these same attitudes, credos, and compulsions. The perspectival distance that they gain is the result of their sons' incipient awareness of the contents of their unconscious and nurturance of their "feminine component" (*Tough Guys* 195), as narrator Tim Madden puts it.[4]

Ancient Evenings lavishly demonstrates why Mailer's detractors often regard his male characters as representative examples of an "imperialist" and "pathological masculinity" (Savran 163, 63), of "rogue traits" (Faludi 37) such as "toughness, struggle and conquest" (Segal 104), of "frontier psychology" (Olster 44) and of fascism (Millett 314–355). Had *Ancient Evenings* been published a decade earlier, the feminists would surely have had a great deal more grist for their ideological mill. Anyone reading *Ancient Evenings* while bearing in mind Susan Sontag's definition of the fascist aesthetic in "Fascinating Fascism," for example, could find ample grounds for comparison. Sontag's analysis provides some of the indicators: men's finding in mountains and supersized phallic statues "a visually irresistible metaphor for unlimited aspiration toward the high mystic goal" (76), both "beautiful and terrifying, a fetishizing of the monumental" (76); their fascination with "victory of the stronger man over the weaker" (89) and with "success in fighting" serving as the "main aspiration of a man's life"; the "rendering of movement in grandiose and rigid patterns" (91) such that the feminine "masses are made to take form, be design"; the "blunt massing of material" (94); "fantasies about armor and uniforms" and about the "righteousness of violence" (99); "verbal fetishism" (100). Such elements constitute lengthy tableau in *Ancient Evenings*. "The Book of Queens" is, in toto, "sexual theatre, a staging of sexuality" (Sontag 102). And throughout Mailer's novel, sadomasochism, which "is to sex what war is to civil life: the magnificent experience" (Sontag 103). *Ancient Evenings* is one long "ritual of domination and enslavement" (104) in which "masters and slaves" become "consciously aestheticized" (105).

Yet the author of *Ancient Evenings* was no more an imperialist than Melville was a "blubber capitalist"[5] or Hawthorne a Puritan or Nabokov a pedophile. What the novel's critics overlooked is that the features of the novel that they found regrettable were definitive of the ancient warrior-culture in which it is set. The similarities between Mailer's contemporary context and Egypt's nineteenth and twentieth dynasties have gone unnoticed in commentaries on *Ancient Evenings,* a novel that validates Jung's comment about the recurrence of "psychic dominants" at the end of Platonic months.[6] Aesthetically, as the Age of Aries came to a close, the esoteric substance of Egypt's artistic productions diminished as the "New Kingdom tendency toward the massive in art and architecture reached its apex" (Wilkinson 39). The "symbolic statement made by the massive was especially important from a political standpoint" (40), for the "representational program from the Egyptian temple reliefs" depict "scenes of warfare, the delivery of captives to the deity [and the] smiting of captives." The aesthetically massive was a reflection not only of the "pharaohs' excessive pride inflated by imperialism" (39), but also of the nation's "loss of traditional behavior" and of "the disintegration of [its] recognized culture." These and other "changes brought in by empire" (204) accelerated the demise of Egypt's ancient civilization, a civilization that existed "for some four hundred generations with but slight changes in their basic structure" (Mills 21)—"six and a half times as long as the entire Christian era, which has only prevailed some sixty generations," and "about eighty times as long as the five generations of the United States' existence." With its government shifting from being "a 'logistical' to a 'predatory' empire" (Joxe 183), with violence increasingly "dominat[ing] the economy" and with its "love of sports" (199) serving the ruling elites' ideological agendas, it was the era in which the Pharaohs' enthusiasm as both sportsmen and warriors "inspired a new literary genre." This genre consisted of state-commissioned narratives "glorifying the successful sportsm[e]n and athletes" (Wilson 195) and celebrating the Pharaohs' "galloping [their] horses across the desert." The perennial means of mobilizing sociopolitical support for imperial war that today's archons and solons of empire implement differ little from their counterparts' in the ancient world: propagandistic icons of warrior-heroes.[7]

"The Book of the Charioteer" can serve to show that the novel's critics were too quick to criticize Mailer for delineating the warrior-culture he chose as his novel's setting. Egyptologists have shown that Ramses II did not overcome their enemies, although Mailer, true to the spirit of the imperial age in which he wrote, renders it a victory. The Kadesh section reads like Mailer's literary tribute to both Hemingway and de Sade. However, ego-consciousness and warrior-mentality, as *Ancient Evenings* massively dramatizes, are causally linked, and the consequence of both is entirely the same—the tendency to invalidate the autonomy of others. Like Egypt's imperial rulers, Mailer aesthetically invaded ancient Egypt's literary culture without worrying that he showed indifference to another nation's right of autonomous identity. Later in the novel, when Menenhetet makes the surprising claim that he has "imparted" Egyptian history to Meni "in the way that these Romans and Greeks tell it to each other.... [f]or out Land of the Dead now belongs to them" (839), at least two implications of Mailer's having gleaned his narrative material through the lenses, as it were, of Occidental eyes, become clear. The first is that the esoteric substance of Egypt's mythology was, when writing *Ancient Evenings,* entirely lost to him. As Schwaller de Lubicz writes, "[o]ur exoteric evolution, through the Greek metaphysical phases" (55), fostered rationalistic attitudes about the ancient Egyptians" that make interpreting their esotericism difficult. The Greek's conception, based mainly on Herodotus's descriptions, "presents a view of Egypt's past which shows no genuine understanding of Egyptian history" (qtd. in Shaw 13), as British Egyptologist Alan

Lloyd observes, "[e]verything has been uncompromisingly custom-ized for Greek consumption and cast unequivocally into a Greek mold." Whereas the first implication of Menenhetet's claim that he has been relating the Greek's version of Egyptian history is that Mailer aligns himself with the tradition of rationalist exotericism, another is that his character's statement makes it difficult for him to defend himself against the charge of "orientalizing" his subject matter, a point first raised by John Whalen-Bridge in his interview with Mailer.

During this interview, Mailer, musing about how the novel might have turned out, claimed that he "could have restricted it to the cam-paign of the battle of Kadesh" ("Karma" 3), making it "a very good 200-page novel." Originally *Ancient Evenings* was to be part one of a trilogy whose third narrative he envisaged as a work of science fiction, as he described it: "the world would have to be destroyed in order to save a few people.... the only thing they have a lot of information on was a writer of the period in the second half of the twentieth century named Norman Mailer.... the biography of Norman Mailer as seen by those people on the spaceship" (9). His sci-fi ambitions reveal them-selves as a wry attempt to imagine imperializing the future, with himself as the messiah-figure whose works and days create the quilt-work of fact and fiction out of which later peoples of the book, the book of Norman, will have woven their cultural mythologies. If Whalen-Bridge and Mailer's verbal sparring can be likened to arm-wrestling, it is as if Mailer unconsciously lends the support of his left hand to his opponent.

Recalling the process of composing *Ancient Evenings*, Mailer remarked: "I'd write directly out of the unconscious.... [which] is so much deeper than one's own self" and "is connected as a taproot into something else.... [s]o, if something's going on when I write it, I'll just obey it.... I'll follow it" ("Karma" 6, 7). The problem with his statement is that it seems to be suggesting that the contents of his unconscious are no different from that of his consciousness. Again, Jung can help sort this out. It "is in the nature of the conscious mind" (*Psyche* 139), he says, "to concentrate on relatively few contents and to raise them to the highest pitch of clarity." And "when a part of the psyche is split off from consciousness," he continues, "it is only *appar-ently* inactivated...in actual fact it brings about a possession of the personality, with the result that the individual's aims are falsified in the interests of the split-off part" (139). In *The Aesthetics of Excess*, Allen Weiss describes this total possession of the psyche by the ego's obsessions as its "[i]mpossible [s]overeignty" (26) over itself, the con-sequence of which is its need to dominate everyone else.

Mailer's *obiter dicta* on *Ancient Evenings* reveal what they do, that "part of the psyche exists which is acting in its own interests, thwarting the empire of the ego" (Green 9). The ancient adage, that one hand doesn't know what the other is doing, makes a psychological point. Consider Mailer's statements about his composing of *Ancient Evenings*. On one hand, he says that "unless we are truly able to comprehend cultures that are initially alien to us, I don't know if we are going to make it" (Busa 31); on the other, that "this ability to reinvent cultures, to make imaginative works of them that are more real than any pieces of journalism, is crucial to our continuation" (Busa 31); that, when writing it, he "was interested in finding what was going on possibly in the people who were in that society" ("Karma" 3), and that, while doing so, " I was making it up," himself the source of his knowledge about "what was going on" for them. The "real excitement" he felt as a novelist, he claimed, occurs "when I do it myself, when I'm not dealing with a legend, what I make up the story, as I did in *Ancient Evenings*" (Busa 31). Obviously the tension created by these contradictory stimuli helped to make the novel such an important one in his career.

When Mailer, speaking of *Ancient Evenings*, insisted that he had "a right to imagine a work...of the imagination" (*Conversations* 324, 325, 327), and when he anxiously defended himself—"[i]n the case of the writer the risk is to his ego.... [b]ut I will say once again, that I've taken a field—I'm a bully—where there's no competition"—he may not have realized that his comments put him in good company. Writers' attempts to "raise Egypt from the dead" are motivated by its "extraordinary remoteness" (Hare, qtd. in Shaw 9) and by "its 'timelessness'": all the "potency of nostalgia" fuels their tendency to treat mythological material as sites of their own unconscious projections. Providing support for Edward Said's claim, that "[e]very interpretation, every structure created for the Orient...is reinterpretation, a rebuilding of it" (158), contemporary Egyptology accepts the premise that nothing written by Western writers about ancient Egypt can be taken as authentically Egyptian. The pioneering Occidental revisitings of Egypt that Said explores—Napoleon's *Description de l'Egypte*, Chateaubriand's *Itineraire*, Lamartine's *Voyage en Orient*, Flaubert's *Salammbo*, Edward Lane's *Manners and Customs of the Modern Egyptians*, and Richard Burton's *Narrative of a Pilgramage to al-Madinah* (Cf. 86, 158)—show that "[w]hat mattered to them was the structure of their world as an independent, aesthetic, and personal fact." Surely Mailer's egocentric literalizing of himself as a heroic writer of mythic proportions is responsible for the fact that *Ancient*

Evenings has been "consigned to the purgatory of neglect" (Glenday 118). "The idea of the heroic author is *ridiculous* in this 'death of the author' age, but Mailer was our last quixotic/heroic writer." (Mailer's Later Fiction 185).

In *The Sense of an Ending* (167), Frank Kermode has thoughtful things to say about an author's "emotional attachment to the paradigms" of a former epoch, which cause books ultimately to fail to move their readers because they "represent the world of potency as a world of act." Old paradigms were persistently attractive for Mailer, whom Quentin Anderson invokes in *The Imperial Self* as a representative example of American writers whose works illustrate how "shifts from communal modes of self-validation to a psychic self-reliance have always been a part of magic and religion, and perhaps action itself" (237). Napoleon-like, Anderson writes, such authors—Emerson, Whitman, Henry James, for example—"incorporate" (237) into themselves prevailing "cultural forms" (18) only in fulfillment of their own "emotional demand[s]" (19). These demands are tantamount to the "inner imperialism" (Anderson 244) driving them to seek self-definition, not in "the self reciprocally known" (243), but in their "exhibition of the power of the self to image the world [they have] incorporated" (14). However "absolutist" (ix), "hypertrophied" (xi), and "trans-historical" (10) the components of their "imperial self-hood" (238) might seem, their "projections out of the self" (57) *are* their contributions to the American literary canon, Mailer's no less.

NOTES

1. All citations in this essay are taken from the Warner Books paperback edition.
2. Here is Menenhetet, speaking of the Pharaoh: "as Horus with His weak legs is a fool among Gods...so I wept because I did not love my King well enough...wept because I hated His heart for stirring my old love for Him" (756). Mailer claimed that this codependent dynamic is common to us all: "[w]e're always in competition with God the same way we're in competition with one's parents.... [y]ou revere that initial source and you wish to pre-empt it" (Whalen-Bridge, "Karma of Words" 5).
3. Selected arbitrarily, according to J. Michael Lennon, the message in hieroglyph on some hardcover editions of *Ancient Evenings*, transliterated, reads: "Wicked devils write about filth as a favorite way of entering darkness," and on others, "In filth is wisdom." The latter renders Menenhetet's ideas about filthy wisdom ironic while validating Jung's about synchronicity.

4. For a detailed examination of Mailer's treatment of gender dualism in *Tough Guys* see "Heterophobia in *Tough Guys Don't Dance.*" *JML* 30:1 (2006): 31–46.
5. This term is Laura Saunders'.
6. As R. A. Schwaller de Lubicz writes, in *Symbol and the Symbolic: Egypt, Science and the Evolution of Consciousness* (39), Platonic months "correspond...to the [earth's] precessional cycles," each "last[ing] approximately 2,160 years": "Taurus (Montu), Aries (Amun), the end of Pisces (the Christian era), today.
7. The particular similarities between these dynasties and Mailer's America are salient. "Our social, economic, and political institutions (308), Wilson argues, are "generally the same as those of Egypt." Its most important administrative structure was called "the White House" (de Beler and Cardinaud 2005, 98), where finances were managed and where the pharaoh, "the chief of the army and of diplomacy," resided. Ideologically, similarities appear in the fact that the ruling elites of these Egyptian dynasties "effectively ended any advocacy of the rights of the individual and forced every citizen into a disciplined and submissive acceptance of the transcendent rights of the state" (Wilson 314), a state of affairs emergent in the United State since Bush's signing of the Patriot Act. As a manifestation of their attitudes toward foreign policy, Egyptian rulers coined the political maxim, "let them hate so long as they fear," that the Romans perpetuated—*oderint dum metuant*—and that members of the Bush administration employed—for example, James Woolsey, when he commented on "the silence of the Arab public in the wake of America's victories in Afghanistan," a silence that, for him, "proves that 'only fear will re-establish respect for the U.S.'" (Cited in Blum 392).

WORKS CITED

Anderson, Quentin. *The Imperial Self: An Essay in American Literary and Cultural History.* New York: Alfred A. Knopf, 1971, ix, xi, 10, 14, 18, 19, 57, 237, 244, 243.
Bishop, Clifford. *Sex and Spirit: Ecstasy and Transcendence, Ritual and Taboo, the Undivided Self.* New York: Little, Brown, 1996, 127.
Bloom, Harold, ed. *Norman Mailer: Modern Critical Views.* New York: Chelsea House, 1986, 33, 35.
Blum, William. *Killing Hope: U.S. Military and CIA Interventions Since World War II.* Monroe, Maine: Common Courage Press, 1995, 392.
Budge, E.A. Wallis. "Introduction: the Doctrine of Eternal Life," in *The Egyptian Book of the Dead (The Papyrus of Ani): Egyptian Text Transliteration and Translation,* ed. and trans. E. A. Wallis Budge. New York: Dover, 1967 (1895), lv–lxxxi.

Busa, Christopher, ed. "Interview with Norman Mailer." *Provincetown Arts* 14 (1999): 24–32.

DeMott, Benjamin. "Norman Mailer's Egyptian Novel." *New York Times Book Review* 10 April (1983): 1–4.

Ellmann, Richard and Robert O'Clair, eds. 1973. *Modern Poems: An Introduction to Poetry.* New York: W.W. Norton, 1976, 50.

Faludi, Susan. *Stiffed: The Betrayal of the American Man.* New York: William Morrow and Company, 1999, 37.

Finneran, Richard J., ed. *The Yeats Reader: A Portable Compendium of Poetry, Drama, and Prose.* New York: Scribner, 1997, 351.

Fromm, Eric. *The Heart of Man: Its Genius for Good and Evil.* New York: Harper Colophon Books, 1980 (1964, 1968.), 108, 119.

Glenday, Michael K. *Norman Mailer.* New York: St. Martin's Press, 1995, 118.

Gos de Beler and Marina Cardinaud. *Egypt.* China: Molière, 2005, 98.

Green, André. *Life Narcissim, Death Narcissism,* trans. A. Weller. London and New York: Free Association Books, 2001, 9.

Joxe, Alain. *Empire of Disorder,* trans. Ames Hodges, ed. Sylvère Lotringer. Los Angeles and New York: Semiotext(e), 2002, 183, 199.

Jung, Carl. *Aspects of the Masculine.* Selected and introduced by Violet S. de Laszlo, trans. R.F.C. Hull. New Jersey: Princeton University Press, 1991, xii, 17, 20–22.

———. *Flying Saucers: A Modern Myth of Things Seen in the Skies,* trans. R.F.C. Hull. New York: MJF Books, 1978, 5.

———. *Psyche and Symbol.* Selected and introduced by Violet S. de Laszlo, trans. R.F.C. Hull. New Jersey: Princeton University Press, 1991, 139.

Kermode, Frank. *The Sense of an Ending: Studies in the Theory of Fiction.* New York: Oxford University Press, 1967, 167.

Lennon, J. Michael, "Norman Mailer: Novelist, Journalist, or Historian?" *Journal of Modern Literature* 30:1 (2006): 91–103.

Mailer, Norman. *Ancient Evenings.* Boston, MA: Warner Books, 1983.

———. *Conversations with Norman Mailer,* ed J. Michael Lennon. Jackson: University Press of Mississippi, 1988, 226, 324, 325, 327, 328.

———. *The Presidential Papers.* London: Corgi Books, 1965 (1963), 298.

———. *Tough Guys Don't Dance.* New York: Random House, 1984, 195.

Massey, Gerald. *Ancient Egypt: The Light of the World,* vol. 1. New York: Samuel Weisner, 1970 (1907), 242.

Millet, Kate. *Sexual Politics.* New York: Doubleday, 1970, 314–355.

Mills, C. Wright. *The Power Elite.* 1956. New York: Oxford University Press, 1967, 21.

Olster, Stacey. *Reminiscence and Re-Creation in American Fiction.* New York: Cambridge University Press, 1989, 44, 63.

Papadopoulos, Renos K. *The Handbook of Jungian Psychology: Theory, Practice and Applications.* London and New York: Routledge Taylor and Francis Group, 2006, 199, 207, 208, 211, 212.

Read, Herbert, ed. *The Collected Works of Carl Jung: Bollingen Series XX*, vol. 4, trans. R.F.C. Hill. New York: Pantheon Books, 1961, 319, 321.

Said, Edward. *Orientalism: Western Conceptions of the Orient.* New York: Penguin Books, 1995 (1978, 1985, 1991), 86, 158.

Saunders, Laura. "Blubber Capitalism." 11 October 2004 http://www.forbes.com/ forbes /2004/1011 /096.html.

Savran, David. *Taking It Like A Man: White Masculinity, Masochism, and Contemporary American Culture.* Princeton, NJ: Princeton University Press, 1998, 63, 163.

Schwaller de Lubicz., R.A. *Symbol and the Symbolic: Egypt, Science and the Evolution of Consciousness,* trans. Robert and Deborah Lawlor. Massachusetts: Autumn Press, 1974, 39, 55.

Segal, Lynne. *Slow Motion: Changing Masculinities, Changing Men.* Great Britain: Virago Press, 1990, 104.

Shaw, Ian. *Ancient Egypt: A Very Short Introduction.* Oxford and New York: Oxford University Press, 2004, 9, 13.

Siegel, Lee. "Maestro of the Human Ego." *New York Times Book Review* 21 January (2007): 1, 12.

Sontag, Susan. *Under the Sign of Saturn.* New York : Doubleday, 1991 (1974), 76, 89, 91, 4, 99, 100, 102, 103, 105.

Storr, Anthony. *The Essential Jung.* Princeton, NJ: Princeton University Press, 1983, 198.

Surette, Léon. *The Birth of Modernism.* Montreal, Québec, and Kingston, Ontario: McGill-Queen's University Press, 1993, 15, 16.

Tannahill, Reay. *Sex in History.* Great Britain: Hollen Street Press, 1984 (1980), 77.

Von Franz, Marie-Louise. "The Process of Individuation," in *Man and His Symbols,* eds. Carl Jung and Marie-Louise von Franz. New York: Bantam Doubleday, 1968 (1964), 111–123.

Weiss, Allen S. *The Aesthetics of Excess.* New York: State University of New York Press, 1989, 26.

Whalen-Bridge, John. "The Karma of Words: Mailer Since *Executioner's Song.*" *Journal of Modern Literature* 30:1 (2006): 1–16.

Wilkinson, Richard H. *Symbol and Magic in Egyptian Art.* London: Thames and Hudson, 1994, 39, 40, 204.

Wilson, John A. *The Culture of Ancient Egypt.* Chicago and London: University of Chicago Press, 1956 (1951), 195, 308, 314.

CHAPTER 8

Spooks and Agencies: *Harlot's Ghost* and the Culture of Secrecy

Brian J. McDonald

Intelligence agencies are supposed to resolve national obsessions, not cause them, but this is what gives a novelist something to do after breakfast.

DeLillo to Mailer 2 September 1991

In an interview with Scott Spenser, which appeared in the *Guardian* following the publication of *Harlot's Ghost*, Norman Mailer provides this insight into his shift in attitude toward the CIA precipitated by his research for the novel:

> By the time I started *Harlot's Ghost* my attitude towards the CIA was no longer hostile. At one point, I believed that the CIA was the most sinister organization we have, but I came to think it was the most sinister bureaucracy—and my novel became a comedy of manners. (Spenser 21)

In fact, it is Mailer's rather comic representation of the CIA, as "an overgrown bureaucracy, forever tripping over its own feet," that Louis Menand, reviewing *Harlot's Ghost* in *The New Yorker*, finds most disagreeable about the novel (118). Menand objects to Mailer's characterization of the Cold War CIA on the grounds that it fails to adequately or seriously address the political, intellectual, economic, and human consequences of forty years of dubious CIA activities undertaken in the name of national security and justified in the cause of anticommunism. Menand's conclusion, that *Harlot's Ghost* is essentially an apology for the CIA and Mailer an example of a prominent former critic of American Cold War policy "jumping on the bandwagon" of "winner's history," is damning indeed.

However, a more sympathetic reader, perhaps one not looking for a blanket condemnation of "the Cold War mentality," might plausibly regard *Harlot's Ghost* as Mailer's imaginative attempt to account, not for the contribution of the CIA and its methods to the West's victory in the Cold War, but rather for the curious failure of the CIA to provide accurate intelligence, its inability "to see clearly the nature of the Soviet threat" that was, as Daniel Patrick Moynihan reminds us in his 1998 book *Secrecy*, "the very purpose it [the CIA] was designed to serve" (181). Rather than expressing outright condemnation or disdain, Mailer, in *Harlot's Ghost*, encourages a better understanding of the nature of the CIA, in part as a means of coming to grips with the many historical, political, and ethical controversies that cluster around the apparent failure on the part of the American government, despite the immense expense and expansion of American intelligence agencies, to foresee the collapse of the Soviet Union.[1] Both Moynihan and Mailer point the finger directly at what Moynihan calls "the culture of secrecy" that developed around issues of national security during the anxiety-ridden days and years of the Cold War (16).

While the two writers pursue a similar historical theme—the nature and impact of the burgeoning of state secrecy in America—Mailer, having recourse to the tools of a novelist rather than those of a senate committee member or a social scientist, argues he is afforded "a unique opportunity" to fashion a "superior" history of the CIA "out of an enhancement of the real, the unverified, and the wholly fictional" (*Harlot's Ghost* 1173). In *Harlot's Ghost*, Mailer attempts to "offer an imaginary CIA that will move in parallel orbit to the real one," an approach he contends grants him the necessary latitude to delve more deeply into the broader meaning of the CIA's secretive actions during the Cold War than would be offered by a more empirical effort to outline and assess "the spectrum of facts and often calculated misinformation that still surrounds them" (1173–1174). Claiming that following the evidential rules of traditional historical enquiry—providing the reader "every instant with a scorecard of what actually happened and what was made up"—would fail to adequately engage the imagination of his audience, Mailer mingles "the factual with the fictional" in order to better "nourish [. . .] our sense of reality" (1173). For his fictional CIA to be convincing, however, Mailer would also, to some degree, have to demystify the image of the agency as the masterly, all-knowing, shadowy presence in national life that haunts conspiracy theories and often finds reinforcement in popular culture. Rather than present a historically accurate, an ideologically correct, or a clichéd conspiracy-minded portrait of the CIA, *Harlot's Ghost*, according to its author, endeavors to "understand the tone of its inner workings" (1169). It is an approach Mailer shares with his fellow member of the so-called paranoid school of American fiction, Don DeLillo. In *Libra*, his fictional account of the assassination of President John F. Kennedy, DeLillo is forthright in discussing his fictional methodology, assuring his readers in an "Author's Note" that what he offers is "a work of imagination" that makes "no attempt to furnish factual answers to any questions raised by the assassination." In fact, it is DeLillo's intention that *Libra* offer its readers "refuge" from the "gloom [...]" of unknowing" that perpetually surrounds the Kennedy shooting—"a way of thinking about the assassination without being constrained by half-facts or overwhelmed by possibilities, by the tide of speculation that widens with the years" (*Libra* "Author's Note"). Also, like Mailer, DeLillo asserts the novelist's entitlement to assume the proportion of truth without claiming factuality, and seeks to "nourish our sense of reality" while simultaneously altering and embellishing it (*Harlot's Ghost* 1173). This speaks to what DeLillo has referred to as the novelist's pursuit of a "kind of redemptive truth," the capacity of fiction to "leap across the barrier of fact" in order to release our imaginations from a too confining desire for certainty or a too bewildering confrontation with ambiguity (DeCurtis 48).

In *Harlot's Ghost*, Mailer traces the development of the CIA, from its origins in the OSS after World War II through the heady days of the early Cold War period, the remarkable episodes of the Cuban missile crisis and the Bay of Pigs invasion, the turbulent era of the Vietnam War, the murky events of Watergate, and into the early Reagan era, depicting the decline of the CIA into a breeding ground, not just for conspiracy and covert activity, but also for elitism, adventurism, and egotism. In effect, Mailer offers an account, partly fiction and partly fact, of the downward path of the CIA, from an agency designed to help defend American democracy by providing its duly elected representatives with vital intelligence, into a vast and seemingly unmanageable bureaucracy capable, in the name of national security, of indulging its most absurd fantasies of power and control—how else should one characterize a plot to kill Fidel Castro with an exploding seashell?

It is not difficult to see why many critics characterize Mailer's narrative approach in *Harlot's Ghost* as an expression of a paranoid style of fiction, or an example of the fascination of contemporary American culture with conspiracy theories. Peter Knight, in particular, points to Mailer's "deep attraction to the generic conventions of the thriller and the clandestine romance of the intelligence agencies" as an example of the "dialectic of fear and fantasy" about "the world of secret power" that permeates post–Word War II American fiction and films (29–30). Indeed, there is little doubt that as a tale rife with conspiracies, cover-ups, official secrets, and clandestine operations, *Harlot's Ghost* contains all the conventions of a spy thriller—the fact that the novel's protagonist and narrator, Harrick "Harry" Hubbard, works as a ghost-writer of pro-CIA novels as part of his duties as an agent does suggest that Mailer is quite aware of the appeal and power of these conventions. However, as a rather detailed immersion into the technocratic inner structure of a vast bureaucracy whose primary function seems to be the systemic creation and retention of secrets, Mailer's novel spends at least as much time and effort relating the intricacies and rituals of a rationalized organization as it does romanticizing about some murky and sinister "clandestine other world" (30).

Still, there is little doubt that *Harlot's Ghost* taps into postwar America's fascination with conspiracy. Mailer calls on the suspicion and mistrust of government that colors the image of the CIA in the popular American political consciousness to lend plausibility to the host of speculations he offers concerning CIA activities, ranging from the well-worn suggestions of possible agency involvement in the assassination of President Kennedy and the death of Marilyn Monroe, to a rather complicated plot involving CIA finances, the Watergate break-in, and the death of agency operative, and author of spy novels, E. Howard Hunt's wife in a plane crash. Public disclosure of the covert, unauthorized, and illegal nature of many CIA operations and activities—particularly those brought to light by the 1975 Senate Select Committee on Government Operations with Respect to Intelligence Activities (whose investigation Harry Hubbard refers to in the novel as "the exposure of the Family Jewels"[2])—together with the revelations about Watergate, the Iran-Contra affair, the existence of FBI files on 1960s dissidents and protest groups, and the ever-lingering doubts regarding the official explanation for the Kennedy assassination, have cultivated a general atmosphere of scepticism and suspicion. It is this widespread culture of secrecy, Mailer argues, that bestows on the events as he describes them in *Harlot's Ghost*, if not the authenticity of a historical account, at least the sense that they respect the "proportions of the factual events" (1174).

Mailer seems to have embraced the logic of what Richard Hofstadter, in his seminal 1952 essay, refers to as "The Paranoid Style in American Politics." Hofstadter argues that what "distinguishes the paranoid style" is not "the absence of verifiable facts [. . .] but rather the curious leap in imagination" that is always employed "at some critical point in the recital of events" (37). Mailer's "paranoid style" in *Harlot's Ghost*, his manner of bringing together an accumulation of factual personages and circumstances that he then extrapolates into a fictional narrative that moves toward conspiracy as an explanation for real historical events, is exemplified in the following passage in which the formidable figure of Harlot, Harry Hubbard's godfather and mentor, sets Harry straight regarding the real priorities of the CIA in the Cold War world:

> [Harry asks Harlot] "But isn't it our priority in Europe to know when the Soviets might attack?"
> [Harlot responds] "That was a pressing question five or six years ago. The Red onslaught, however, is no longer all that military. Nonetheless, we keep pushing for an enormous defense buildup. Because, Harry, once we decide that the Soviet is militarily incapable of large military attacks, the American people will go soft on Communism. There's a puppy dog in the average American. Lick your boots, lick your face. Left to themselves, they'd just as soon be friends with the Russians. So we don't encourage news about all-out slovenliness in the Russian military machine."
> [. . .] "I'm confused," I [Harry] said. "Didn't you once say that our real duty is to become the mind of America?"
> "Well, Harry, not a mind that merely verifies what is true and not true. The aim is to develop teleological mind. Mind that dwells above the facts; mind that leads us to larger purposes. Harry, the world is going through exceptional convulsions. [. . .] Communism is the entropy of Christ, the degeneration of higher spiritual forms into lower ones. To oppose it, we must, therefore create a fiction—that the Soviets are a mighty military machine who will overpower us unless we are more powerful." (355)

By accounting for the apparent failure of the CIA to predict the collapse of the Soviet Union by hypothesizing about a conspiracy amongst high ranking agency figures to hide CIA intelligence of Soviet military and economic weakness from the government and the American people in the name of a messianic anticommunism, Mailer's novel, if we accept Hofstadter's terms, is following in a long-standing American tradition, perpetuated by voices coming from both the

Right and the Left, of hunting for secret conspiracies to explain historical events. This tradition, according to Hofstadter, is the product of a mentality unable to grasp that "mistakes, failures, or ambiguities" must always be taken into consideration when attempting to explain historical events, and that any attempt to understand history in terms of a "motive force," or "one overreaching, consistent theory," is a fundamental misunderstanding and distortion of how things happen (36–37, 29).

It is, however, exactly the ambiguities and failures in the American democratic system that have been highlighted by repeated revelations in recent decades of conspiracies, cover-ups, and abuses of power that Mailer does take into consideration with his narrative method in *Harlot's Ghost*. As Mailer himself tells us, *Harlot's Ghost* is a product of his long-standing preoccupation with the "ambiguous and fascinating moral presence of the agency in national life" (1169). It calls attention to the conflict between the American liberal democratic ideal of openness and transparency in public affairs, and the many instances of secret interventions and illegal subversions perpetrated by a state intelligence apparatus that acts under the auspices of a democratic government. The critique of America's culture of secrecy in *Harlot's Ghost*, however, goes beyond just reinforcing this fundamental observation concerning democratic values. Mailer seems to suggest, in *Harlot's Ghost*, that the CIA, and the significant place it has come to occupy in the American psyche, reflects a distinctive development in the character of postwar American society.

Why are Americans so fascinated with secrecy and conspiracy? For Mailer, as his interview with Scott Spenser indicates, the answer seems to lie in the growing bureaucratization and corporatization of postwar America. To borrow a common idiom of Mailer, not for nothing is the CIA nicknamed "the Corporation." There is a sense in which *Harlot's Ghost* represents a persevering populist political sensibility for Mailer, a determination to continue to assert a kind of democratic subjectivity in the face of the organizational and corporatist forces that, as Mailer never tired of arguing, have come to increasingly dominate the lives of American individuals. What Mailer offers his readers is a possible, perhaps even plausible, narrative of events, but one that is self-consciously fictional, that responds to the skepticism and suspicion engendered by the seemingly habitual and systemic overuse and abuse of secrecy at the highest levels of the American government with a novelist's imagination rather than a paranoid sensibility. In this sense Mailer is working in the same mode as Don DeLillo, not as conspiracy theorists anxiously laboring to wring the ambiguity and contingency out of history, but rather as novelists who enliven their narratives with the interplay between fictional and historical ambiguities as a means of dramatizing the haunting of the American political and cultural imaginary by what DeLillo calls in an article in *Rolling Stone*, a "clandestine mentality," referring to the individual and collective fascination with secrecy as one of the keys to the exercise of power in contemporary America.

For his part, DeLillo has resisted the characterization of his work as paranoid, arguing that his fiction is in fact "clear sighted" and "reasonable," that he is "a completely rational person who is simply taking what he senses all around him and using it as material" (DeCurtis 66). DeLillo recognizes that in many ways the exaggerated levels of anxiety and suspiciousness in contemporary America represent a quite reasonable reaction to the democratic illegitimacy of the intensification and expansion of state and corporate power during the Cold War (and continued more recently under the "war on terror"), but one whose tendency to Gothicize, in Mark Edmondson's sense of the term, to portray that power as preternatural, ubiquitous, and proof of the existence of a "vast world that serves as a dark double to the visible everyday world," serves only to encourage cynicism and fatalism rather than a sense of popular political engagement (Edmondson 22).[3]

And while this often melodramatic reaction to the mundane exercise and expansion of bureaucratic and systemic power yields some crucial insights regarding the routinization of antidemocratic practices within state, cultural, and economic structures, it ultimately offers no purchase or leverage on those systems since, as Patrick O'Donnell tells us, paranoia functions largely as a mode of perceiving the monolithic networking of power rather than as an effective mode of resistance to it. Resistance requires the capacity to identify vulnerabilities or ambiguities in the system to which one is opposed, thus preserving some sense of agency, intention, or subjectivity capable of directing, restraining, or influencing it.[4] Conspiracy theories often posit a world where contingency plays no part, where events are determined by forces whose power is ubiquitous, total, and invisible, and thus beyond the moral, ethical, or political reach of democratic action or constraint. DeLillo reflects, in *Libra*, on the political and social context in which conspiracy as a mode of popular politics is no longer easily dismissible as unreasonable, but also insists on the inescapable role that chance plays in events as a vital element in affirming that a "clear sighted" response to the challenge to democratic legitimacy and agency posed by the expansion of state secrecy, corporate power, and globalization remains viable.

In *Libra*, David Ferrie, an eccentric and shadowy figure with ties to the CIA, the mob, and various clandestine political organizations—as well as a penchant for astrology and mysticism—gives voice to the novel's "aspir[ation] to fill some of the blank spaces in the known record" ("Author's Note") without resorting to the causal logic of either conspiracy or contingency by invoking a quasimetaphysical force with the capacity to impose some sense of narrative cohesion on events:

> "Think of two parallel lines," he [Ferrie] said. "One is the life of Lee H. Oswald. One is the conspiracy to kill the President. What bridges the space between them? What makes a connection inevitable? There is a third line. It comes of our dreams, visions, intuitions, prayers, out of the deepest levels of the self. It's not generated by cause and effect like the other two lines. It's a line that cuts across causality, cuts across time. It has no history that we can recognize or understand. But it forces a connection. It puts a man on the path of his destiny." (339)

Peter Knight suggests that Ferrie's "third line" is that level at which "the conspiratorial has become inseparable from the coincidental, or more accurately," as he qualifies, the point at which "we need to read coincidences *as if* they were signs of a conspiracy, without necessarily equating the two" (108). DeLillo's novel certainly insists on blurring the line between accident and intention in history, but it is unclear how Knight's interpretation addresses the notion raised by Ferrie that what connects conspiracy and contingency, Oswald to the plot of renegade CIA agents, the lone gunman of the Warren Commission to the paranoid sensibility of conspiracy theories, "comes of our dreams, visions, intuitions, prayers, out of the deepest levels of the self." Knight is correct to insist on DeLillo's willingness to question historical explanations based on either causal or contingent metanarratives of history, however, as Paul Maltby points out, "*Libra* is neither consistently nor unequivocally postmodern," and it is important to keep in mind DeLillo's appeal to "the truth and sovereignty of 'the deepest levels of the self,' " to the transhistorical forces whose invocations Maltby calls DeLillo's Romantic metaphysics, when considering the terms of the social and political critique DeLillo offers in *Libra* (Maltby 510).

Neither a theory of conspiracy nor a theory of contingency, the "third line" is a metaphor for an impression of truth rooted deep in the psyche of "the idiosyncratic self" that DeLillo poses against "the forces of history, so powerful, visible and real" (DeLillo, "Power" 5). DeLillo, like Mailer, champions the veracity and creative power of the novelist's imagination, and its respect for the influence of the deeper ambiguities of human desire and belief on the unfolding of historical events, as a release from the kind of paralyzing uncertainty that plagues Nicholas Branch, the former CIA researcher in *Libra* who is working on a secret history of the assassination. Branch finds himself in a dilemma. He is reluctant to risk interpreting the evidence he has spent three decades collecting regarding the assassination for fear he might be guilty of distorting, misrepresenting, or even fabricating the real meaning of the event. Branch is also overwhelmed by the sheer quantity of related material and evidence he has collected and his choice seems to lie between giving up his search for the truth or giving in to paranoia, either "despair of ever getting to the end" or accept "the powerful and lasting light, exposing patterns and links" which the assassination appears to emit (*Libra* 57–58).

As Knight and other critics have pointed out, Branch's situation is representative of a particular condition of consciousness that "is very much in tune with a postmodern distrust of final narrative solutions" (Knight 116). Branch's anxiety and paralyzing uncertainty are, for Knight, a result of his never-ending search for closure, his perpetual pursuit of a narrative able to encompass the "endless suggestiveness" of the facts (*Libra* 300–301). Timothy Melley agrees that Branch "finds himself in an epistemological crisis," but suggests that his crisis is also, in part, historiographical (Melley 139). Stuck between his obsession with accumulating evidence and his lingering desire to determinately solve the historical case, Branch, according to Melley, abandons his effort to produce a coherent historical narrative of the assassination and adopts an approach Melley describes as "archeological," replacing the work of historical interpretation with the collection and organization of artifacts, the amassing of materials and documents that generate their own series of links and connections.

What often gets overlooked or discounted in such discussions, however, is the valuable nature of what Branch is able to glean from his stubborn efforts to interpret the evidence. Despite Branch's (and perhaps DeLillo's) recognition that any final narrative of intention or coherence he might construct from the historical evidence would be incomplete and distorting—as much a product of his own ordering consciousness and imagination as an objective reflection of the facts— the insights Branch gains for his troubles affirm the worth and significance of his project and the interpretive desires that continue to haunt it.

One such insight regards the essential flaw of conspiracy theories, their inability to account for the role contingent elements of chance and coincidence play in the outcome of events. Those on the outside, as Branch comes to understand, tend to assume a conspiracy is "the perfect working of a scheme"; that all conspiracies are "the same taut story of men who find coherence in some criminal act" and that conspirators possess a "logic and a daring beyond our reach" (*Libra* 441).

> But maybe not. Nicholas Branch thinks he knows better. He has learned enough about the days and months preceding November 22, and enough about the twenty-second itself, to reach a determination that the conspiracy against the President was a rambling affair that succeeded in the short term due mainly to chance. Deft men and fools, ambivalence and fixed will and what the weather was like. (441)

Such a provisional conclusion, while not venturing another "gleaming theory, supportable, assured," does have the effect of undermining the notion of the assassination as the result of a monolithic and masterful conspiracy. It suggests a way of thinking about the assassination that allows for the popular skepticism surrounding the version of events offered by the Warren Commission without accepting the totalizing logic of the paranoid style.

It also, as Skip Willman points out, undermines the conception of the CIA as "the 'invisible Master' of the geopolitical sphere"—a fantasy embraced by the conspiratorial imagination and often encouraged by elements of the CIA itself—while also calling attention to the corrosive effect of the Cold War culture of secrecy on the democratic legitimacy of the state (414). Rather than reflect its mastery of events, in *Libra* the CIA's obsession with secrecy appears to have the more mundane and bureaucratic function of providing the CIA with an effective means of shielding its activities from democratic accountability, public scrutiny, congressional oversight, and administrative rivalry,[5] as the following passage from the novel describing the CIA's plans for the Bay of Pigs invasion suggests:

> Knowledge was a danger, ignorance a cherished asset. In many cases the DCI, the Director of Central Intelligence, was not to know important things. The less he knew, the more decisively he could function. It would impair his ability to tell the truth at an inquiry or a hearing, or in the Oval office chat with the President, if he knew what they were doing [...]. The Joint Chiefs were not to know. [...]. The Secretaries were to be insulated from knowing [...]. The Deputy Secretaries were

interested in drifts and tendencies. They expected to be misled. The
Attorney General wasn't to know the queasy details [...]. The White
House was to be the summit of unknowing [...] the system operated
as an insulating muse. (21–22)

The routinization of secrecy by the CIA is, for DeLillo, more an indication of a lack of absolute power, or an illusion of absolute control,
than a confirmation of its status as a shadowy plenipotentiary of a
ruthless secret state. Like Mailer's depiction of the CIA in *Harlot's
Ghost*, DeLillo's CIA in *Libra* is ultimately revealed as more "sinister
bureaucracy" than "invisible government."

The bureaucratic routinization of secrecy in America during the
Cold War, epitomized by Mailer's depiction of the CIA, in *Harlot's
Ghost*, as the fusion of rationalized administration and the generalized fantasy world of spies and clandestine plots, has not only lent
paranoid political sensibilities and conspiracy theories a semblance of
plausibility and even reasonability, but has also led to an overdevel-
oped fascination with state secrecy, and with the idea of secrecy in
general, that works to undermine the American individual's faith in
the value of democratic politics. Rather than as a sinister means for
the CIA to manipulate and control political and historical events,
secrecy, as Mailer's novel punctuates, was often utilized by the CIA as
a tool in the internal battle for influence and resources between gov-
ernmental bureaucracies. It is a case that Senator Moynihan also
makes when he points out how "within the confines of the intelligence community, too great attention was paid to hoarding information, defending boundaries, securing budgets, and other matters of
corporate survival" (79). As one character in *Harlot's Ghost* puts it,
when it comes to the CIA, "We're dealing with bureaucracy, and
that's a whole other kingdom" (218).

This antidemocratic and disproportionate emphasis on secrecy
magnified its significance and prominence in the American political
imagination. Confronted with a series of very public scandals detailing how arms of the American government sought to circumvent
democratic processes and procedures to cover up illegal and unethical
activities, generally justified in the name of national security,
Americans' faith in the democratic legitimacy of their government
was significantly eroded.[6] Richard Gid Powers is quick to point out
that while, during the Cold War, most Americans were more skeptical
regarding the presence of a secret and pervasively powerful "invisible
government" than the proliferation of conspiracy theories and paranoid culture might indicate, the notion that important information

was being collected, manipulated, and kept secret by the state, and that significant power was being wielded by institutions whose practices flouted democratic openness and accountability, did have a profound effect on the mainstream American political consciousness. Encouraged by revelations concerning the state abuse of secrecy, a growing chorus of voices amongst journalists, academics, and political commentators for whom, as Powers puts it, "secrecy became the explanation for almost everything that ailed America," and a government that continued to utilize official secrecy to an absurd extent,[7] secrecy was increasingly presumed to be a measure of the inherent value of knowledge and an indication of the influence and power of an organization (41). In other words, the situation seems to have developed within American politics and culture that anything kept secret accrues a greater aura of importance and power, whatever its actual significance, than that which is not.

Mailer's style of narrative speculation certainly engages and reflects the suspicious and conspiracy-minded mood of contemporary American political sensibilities; however, his fictional effort in *Harlot's Ghost* to "understand the tone of [the CIA's] inner workings" reveals a CIA more Weberian than Machiavellian. We are told that in order to concentrate on writing the "detailed memoir of [his] life in the CIA," referring to the fictional "Alpha" manuscript that constitutes the bulk of *Harlot's Ghost*, Harry had to abandon his agency-sanctioned literary project, "a monumental work on the KGB whose in-progress title was *The Imagination of the State*" (30). The notion, implicit in the title of Harry's abandoned work, that the purpose of official secrecy is to serve and enhance the mythological or fabulous elements of state power, is the constant subtext of Mailer's narrative. As the state becomes more rationalized and bureaucratic, secrecy as a means of controlling information has less to do with the sensitivity of the content of this or that particular fact to the interests of the state, and more to do with the exercise of structural or administrative power by those with political interests at heart. In a society becoming increasingly technocratic, the measurement of any bureaucracy's, and by extension any bureaucrat's, power, is largely based on the amount of knowledge and information it/he/she controls. As John Ralston Saul points out, "One of the truly curious characteristics of this society is that the individual can most easily exercise power by retaining the knowledge which is in his hands" (287). This fundamentally undemocratic tendency creates a general atmosphere in which individuals "must treat the secret as a cult," and encourages the rise of a political and cultural logic based around "a generalized fantasy life" in which "the fictional spy [...] [becomes] a glorified reflection of the citizen" (288). The act of keeping something secret, of retaining the most banal piece of information is transformed by the technocratic imagination into proof of its importance. Of course, the fact that something is not kept secret, that information is public, is, by the same shaky logic, proof of its unimportance.

Saul recognizes that much of the damage wrought by the heightening mood of suspicion and skepticism in American politics and culture can be measured by the influence that this "worship of the idea of secrecy" has on the individual's conception of his/her democratic agency (287). He argues that if the perception that the real power determining the historical and political fate of the country is always wielded in secret continues to gain strength in the American imagination, and if, as Saul puts it, government bureaucracies continue to function as if "everything is secret unless there is a conscious decision to the contrary," the view that participation in democratic politics is an important and worthwhile exercise will continue to lose credibility (287). As Saul observes,

> [t]he generalized secret has introduced such a terrible uncertainty into our society that citizens' confidence in their own ability to judge public matters has been damaged. They constantly complain that they don't know enough to make up their minds. They have a feeling that the mass of information available would not be available if it were truly worth having. The result is a despondent mental anarchy which prevents them from actively using the considerable powers democratic society has won. They are convinced that essential information is being held back. (288)

For Saul, as for Moynihan and Mailer, one of the residual effects of the "culture of secrecy" that flourished during the Cold War is the cultivation, in America, of a widespread belief that all the important decisions are taken by secretive government agencies and corporations, a perception that leads to a general cynicism and fatalism regarding the value of political engagement. The overwhelming image of the CIA that one takes away from *Harlot's Ghost* is not that of a powerful invisible government or shadowy puppet-master of history—though Mailer's portrayal of agency elitists whose desperation to believe just that conception of the CIA greatly enhances the novel's "comedy of manners" sensibility—but rather that of a massive, convoluted, poorly scrutinized bureaucracy whose obsession with collecting, retaining, and controlling information, mostly of the most mundane and banal nature, achieved fetishistic, and often paranoid, proportions.

Rather than simply confirm the notion of an irredeemably corrupt invisible government that has taken over the reigns of the Republic, what Mailer attempts in his fictionalization of the Cold War history of the CIA is to dramatize the tensions that always exist between the exercise of state power and the values of transparency and public accountability that legitimize American democracy. At the core of Mailer's imaginative depiction of the CIA—and particularly evident in his theory of the "High Holies"—is a bureaucracy with an inherent tendency to seek to hide, or even free itself altogether, from the limitations and scrutiny of democratic processes and procedures. The critique of secrecy that Mailer offers in *Harlot's Ghost* is consistent with the liberal tradition in which state secrecy and democracy represent conflicting political values. Mailer's perspective, however, is not reducible to the promotion of the universal maxim that "openness is good and secrecy is bad," which K.G. Robertson ascribes to the more "normative" elements of that tradition (9). Nowhere in *Harlot's Ghost* does Mailer insist that state secrecy is, in every case, an illegitimate and insidious enemy of the interests of liberal democracy. What is insistent, however, is the determined effort Mailer makes in the novel to represent the banal bureaucratic details underlying the clandestine fantasy world of intelligence agencies in order to provide his readers with a vantage point—somewhere between "those separate playhouses of paranoia and cynicism" that Harlot mentions in his High Thursday lectures—from which to consider the dilemma that the need for "sinister bureaucracies" like the CIA continues to pose for American democracy.

NOTES

1. The contention that the CIA overestimated the strength of the Soviet military and failed to predict the collapse of the Soviet Union is a matter of ongoing debate amongst historians of American intelligence. For perspectives that reject Moynihan's charges see MacEachin and Haines and Leggett. Haines and Leggett, in particular, respond to Moynihan's arguments in *Secrecy*. Tim Weiner's 2007 history of the CIA, *Legacy of Ashes*, comes down largely on the Moynihan/Mailer side of the issue.
2. In June 2007, the CIA declassified and released nearly 700 pages of documents detailing CIA activities considered illegal or inappropriate from the 1950s to the mid-1970s. This set of internal reports has come to be known as "the family jewels."
3. The discussion of the connection between populism and conspiracy theory that follows is greatly indebted to Fenster.

4. This is the democratic "problem of the political" as Sheldon Wolin identifies it: "The problem of the political is not to deny the ubiquity of power but to deny power uses that destroy common ends" (198).

5. See Millard, who argues that in the national security state as it is depicted by DeLillo, the "deliberately fragmented bureaucracy" that is "the form of rationality peculiar to such organizations [CIA] depends precisely on minimizing the possibility that anyone might know enough to comprehend the full narrative" (218).

6. For a discussion of this "massive erosion of trust the American people have in their government," see Cliff (57).

7. Moynihan argues that "The Cold War has bequeathed to us a vast secrecy system that shows no sign of receding," pointing, as partial evidence, to the fact that by 1996 the United States was still producing over 6 million classified documents per year (214). A recent study by Freedom House, "Today's American: How Free?" pegs the number of documents classified as secret in 2005 at 14.2 million (cited in "Land of the Free?").

Works Cited

Cliff, Lionel. "Explanations: Deceptions in the US Political System," in *The Politics of Lying: Implications for Democracy*, by Lionel Cliff, Maureen Ramsay, and Dave Bartlett. Houndmills: Macmillan Press, 2000. 56–79.

DeCurtis, Anthony. " 'An Outsider in This Society': An Interview with Don DeLillo," in *Introducing Don DeLillo*, ed. Frank Lentricchia. Durham: Duke University Press, 1991. 43–66.

DeLillo, Don. "American Blood: A Journey through the Labyrinth of Dollars and JFK." *Rolling Stone* 8 December 1983, 24+.

———. *Libra*. New York: Viking, 1988.

———. "To Norman Mailer" 20 September 1991, Ransom Center Mailer Archives. *The Mailer Review* 1 (2007): 169.

———. "The Power of History." *New York Times Book Review* 7 September 1997. www.nytimes.com/library/books/090797article3.html.

Edmundson, Mark. *Nightmare on Main Street: Angels, Sadomasochism, and the Culture of Gothic*. Cambridge, MA: Harvard University Press, 1997.

Fenster, Mark. *Conspiracy Theories: Secrecy and Power in American Culture*. Minneapolis: University of Minnesota Press, 1999.

Haines, Gerald K. and Robert E. Legget. *CIA's Analysis of the Soviet Union 1947–1991*. Washington, DC: Center for the Study of Intelligence, 2001.

Hofstadter, Richard. *The Paranoid Style in American Politics and Other Essays*. London: Jonathan Cape, 1966.

Knight, Peter. *Conspiracy Culture: From Kennedy to the X-Files*. London: Routledge, 2000.

"Land of the Free?" *The Economist* 10 May 2008, 44.

MacEachin, Douglas J. *CIA Assessments of the Soviet Union: The Record Versus the Charges*. Washington, DC: Center for the Study of Intelligence, 1996.

Mailer, Norman. *Harlot's Ghost*. New York: Ballantine, 1992.

Maltby, Paul. "The Romantic Metaphysics of Don DeLillo," in *White Noise: Text and Criticism*, ed. Mark Osteen. New York: Penguin, 1998. 498–516.

Melley, Timothy. *Empire of Conspiracy: The Culture of Paranoia in Postwar America*. Ithaca: Cornell University Press, 2000.

Menand, Louis. "From Here to Eternity." *New Yorker* 4 November 1991, 113+.

Millard, Bill. "The Fable of the Ants: Myopic Interactions in DeLillo's *Libra*," in *Critical Essays on Don DeLillo*, ed. Hugh Ruppersburg and Tim Engles. New York: G.K. Hall, 2000. 213–228.

Moynihan, Daniel Patrick. *Secrecy: The American Experience*. New Haven: Yale University Press, 1998.

Powers, Richard Gid. "Introduction," in *Secrecy*, by Daniel Patrick Moynihan. New Haven: Yale University Press, 1998. 1–58.

Robertson, K.G. *Secrecy and Open Government: Why Governments Want You to Know*. Houndmills: Macmillan Press, 1999.

Saul, John Ralston. *Voltaire's Bastards*. Toronto: Penguin, 1992.

Spenser, Scott. "The Old Man and the Novel." *Guardian* 5 October 1991, 20+.

Weiner, Tim. *Legacy of Ashes: The History of the CIA*. New York: Doubleday, 2007.

Willman, Skip. "Traversing the Fantasies of the JFK Assassination: Conspiracy and Contingency in Don DeLillo's *Libra*." *Contemporary Literature* 39 (1998): 405–433.

Wolin, Sheldon S. "On the Theory and Practice of Power," in *After Foucault*, ed. Jonathan Arc. New Brunswick: Rutgers University Press, 1988. 179–201.

CHAPTER 9

The Nazi Occult and *The Castle in the Forest*: Raw History and Fictional Transformation

Heather Wolffram

MAILER AND THE OCCULT

In an interview with National Public Radio (27 January 2007) about his final novel *The Castle in the Forest*, Norman Mailer spoke of his attitude to the occult and his use of diabolism in his imagining of Hitler's conception and childhood. The book, narrated by the putative SS man Dieter (D.T.)—in fact a demon assigned to monitor the spiritual and psychic development of young Adolf—presents a Hitler who is literally the progeny of the devil; his conception occurring in a primal scene at which the Maestro (Satan) is present. D.T. guides the reader not only through Hitler's formative years, encouraging the child's peccadilloes and fostering petty hatreds; he infiltrates Himmler's inner circle, in which race, incest, and mysticism are researched in pursuit of the *Übermensch* (8). According to Mailer, the genesis of this extraordinary novel, in which he invites the reader to follow him into both serious and cryptohistorical thinking, was his reading of the journalist Ron Rosenbaum's book *Explaining Hitler*. Rosenbaum considers the many and varied hypotheses surrounding the Fuehrer, ranging from Hugh Trevor-Roper's mesmeric messiah to Christopher Browning's dithering, hesitant Hitler, and what these hypotheses tell us about Hitler and the "Hitler explainers" (xii). Unconvinced by any of the theories he found here, or perhaps intrigued by the sense of inexplicability that pervades Rosenbaum's book, Mailer says he sought an exceptional explanation for Hitler, one that he found in the occult (National Public Radio). The cosmology Mailer develops in *The Castle in the Forest*—a Miltonian struggle between the Maestro and the Dummkopf (God) in which human thought and action is manipulated by armies of devils and cudgels (angels)—allows him to envision a Hitler whose power derives from occult sources. Although Mailer declares that he does not have a fixed opinion on the paranormal, unable to decide whether it is nonsense or real, he nonetheless contends that the historical Hitler dabbled at the edges of the occult, reluctant to fully engage with it because like others who believe they possess extra or magical powers, he was aware that any such involvement would draw unwanted attention to him (National Public Radio).

Mailer's interest in the occult and in particular the connection between occultism and Nazism predates *The Castle in the Forest*, manifesting explicitly in his foreword to Peter Levenda's book *Unholy Alliance* (also reprinted as part of a chapter on the occult in *The Spooky Art*). Here Mailer points to the presence of occultists on both sides during World War II, but most particularly among the Nazis. He also outlines the cosmology that he later develops in *The Castle in the Forest*, stating that "[i]f a Creator exists in company with an opposite Presence (to be called Satan for short), there is also the most lively possibility of a variety of major and minor angels, devils and demons, good spirits and evil, working away more or less invisibly in our lives" (*The Spooky Art* 230–231). While Mailer does not go as far as Levenda in claiming that Hitler believed in magic, he does attribute the Fuehrer with an uncanny political sense for the separate uses of magic and magicians (232). Hitler's persecution of occultists, particularly following Rudolf Hess' flight to Britain in 1941, can be understood, Mailer argues, as an attempt to deflect attention away from his own reliance on an occultist of no small dimension, Heinrich Himmler (232).

Of course, Mailer is far from alone in connecting occultism with National Socialism's policies, personnel, and symbolism. There is a veritable industry in books and documentaries that do the same, as well as a significant number of popular cultural texts—films, video games and comics—that market the *frisson* derived from the marriage of Nazism and the occult. Unlike many of these other texts, however, there is reflectivity in the way that Mailer utilizes the occult. Just as he "workshops" and evaluates other elements of Hitler historiography (incest, Jewish heritage, sexual pathology, homosexuality) in *The*

Castle in the Forest, making use of a substantial bibliography, so does he engage, often playfully, with the scholarship and speculation that surrounds Hitler's relationship to the occult. This essay seeks to contextualize Mailer's book, looking not only at the historical realities of Hitler's connection to the occult, but also the historiographical trends in scholarship on National Socialism and occultism and the ways in which the "Hitler-occult-question" has been transformed into both fictional accounts and cryptohistorical works. My hope is that this approach will highlight the way Mailer has woven historical fact, speculation, and fantasy into *The Castle in the Forest* and the manner in which his novel contributes to the ever-expanding popular and scholarly discourse on Hitler.

RAW MATERIAL: THE NAZIS AND THE OCCULT

Mailer's contention that Hitler came into contact, if only peripherally, with the modern occult movement is based in historical fact. Indeed, given the ubiquity of occultism in Central Europe during Hitler's childhood and youth, it would have been difficult for him to avoid acquaintance with the occult milieu in some form or the other. The modern occult movement, apparent in Central Europe, as elsewhere, between the late 1840s and the late 1930s, centered on the practice of mediumship, that is, the ability to communicate with the spirits or access other states of being (Webb 1974, 2). Performed by mediums in a state of either self-induced or hypnotic somnambulism, this practice generated phenomena such as clairvoyance, telepathy, and spirit communication, providing the basis for a wide range of occult sciences, including spiritualism, Theosophy, and Christian Science. Eminently versatile, occultism attracted proponents from across the social and political spectrum, their interest in the occult piqued by grief, scientific curiosity, reformist ambitions, or the artistic possibilities offered by trance states. The venues in which the occult sciences manifested also varied widely, ranging from the parlors of the middle classes to socialist clubrooms, theaters, university laboratories, popular newspapers, and scientific periodicals. Occultism was an extraordinarily flexible set of beliefs that changed its outer forms in order to better suit both individual requirements and sociopolitical exigencies. It enabled its proponents to naturalize their worldview and to convey their ideological beliefs in the guise of either scientific laws or religious revelations, in order to convince others of the need for social and spiritual renewal and political reform.

Hitler's initiation into this occult milieu came in two forms: through his reading of a Viennese mystical-racist periodical and his infiltration of the German Workers' Party. During his time in the cosmopolitan multiracial capital of the Habsburg Empire (1906–1913), Hitler familiarized himself with contemporary race and racist theory through his consumption of cheap pamphlets and periodicals (Goodrick-Clarke 194). Among these publications was an occult journal, titled *Ostara,* that promoted the idea of a Manichean struggle between blond blue-eyed Aryans and dark non-Aryans. This periodical was launched by Jörg Lanz von Liebenfels (1874–1954), a follower of the clairvoyant völkisch thinker Gudio von List (1884–1919), who combined spurious Teutonic beliefs and customs with occult thought (Treitel 25). Ariosophy, as Lanz von Liebenfels labeled this brand of race mysticism, bore some resemblance to Theosophy; an occult science that enjoyed considerable popularity in central Europe during the late nineteenth and early twentieth centuries. Both of these occult sciences sought secret knowledge possessed by mysterious grand masters and both incorporated ideas about racial hierarchy, but that was where the similarity ended (103–105). While Theosophy promoted universal brotherhood and rejected discrimination on the basis of race or gender, the supremacy of the Aryan race was central to the Ariosophists' ideology. The small group of nationalist anti-Semitic Germans and Austrians who were attracted to Ariosophy used it not only to channel their disgust with modernity and political liberalism, but also to support their racial prejudices and advocate German world rule (Goodrick-Clarke, 1–6).

Hitler appears to have encountered Lanz von Liebenfels in 1909 when he attempted to acquire some back issues of *Ostara.* According to Lanz von Liebenfels, Hitler said he was interested in his racial theories and wanted to complete his collection of the journal (Daim, 14–17, 20–27; Goodrick-Clarke 195). Although some authors have made much of Hitler's interest in *Ostara* and the apparent congruence between some of Lanz von Liebenfels ideas and those of Hitler, evidence suggests that Hitler was more interested in the racial doctrine espoused in this journal than its occult or mystical elements (Goodrick-Clarke 198). Hitler was, however, to come into contact with the Ariosophists again this time in Munich after World War I when he was sent by the army to spy on the newly formed German Workers' Party (DAP). This small nationalist political party, which changed its name to the National Socialist German Workers' Party (NSDAP) in February 1920, had emerged from the political wing of the Thule Society, a völkisch-occult group ideologically indebted to

Guido von List (Treitel 25). In spite of this heritage the DAP and its successor were not concerned with Aryan-racist-occultism, but with extreme nationalism (Goodrick-Clarke 150).The two groups were linked, however, by their use of symbols, the NSDAP adopting the swastika, which had also been the emblem of the Thule Society and a number of other contemporary Ariosophical and Theosophical groups, in May 1920. While their mutual use of occult iconography may have suggested an affinity, Hitler's attitude to the Thule Society, as expressed in *Mein Kampf,* was clear: he had nothing but contempt for the woolly and impractical völkisch mysticism of this group of Ariosophists (151).

Hitler's links to the modern occult movement as outlined here were obviously tenuous, highlighting his disinterest in and contempt for occultism, rather than his engagement with occult groups or themes. A small number of his party colleagues, however, were deeply interested in occult matters, most particularly Rudolf Hess and Heinrich Himmler. Like many Germans who participated in the occult milieu, these high ranking National Socialists had become receptive to occultism through their adherence to alternative and natural medicine. In early twentieth-century Germany, natural thera-pies, temperance, and vegetarianism were seen by some as a way of reversing the negative effects of rapid urbanization and industrializa-tion on social cohesion and health (Hau 10; Meyer-Renschhausen and Wirz 325–28). This reform movement, known as *Lebensreform* (life-reform), intersected with modern occultism, facilitating the exchange of ideas, beliefs, and personnel between the two move-ments. Many practitioners of alternative medicine also offered occult services—mesmerism, graphology, and dowsing—and their clientele often sought to mesh the principles of life-reform with occult thera-pies and ideas. Hess, for example, combined his commitment to homeopathy and organic food with astrology, magnetic healing, and clairvoyant consultations (Treitel 213). Similarly, Himmler began his acquaintance with occultism via natural medicine, dabbling in both astrology and Ariosophy as an extension of his interest in alternative therapies (Kersten 39–51; Treitel 214). While these esoteric interests clearly situate Hess and Himmler within the occult and *Lebensreform* milieu, it was an occult seer named Karl Maria Wiligut (1866–1946) who forged the strongest link between National Socialist institutions and modern occultism.

Karl Maria Wiligut, under the pseudonym Karl Maria Weisthor, was appointed the head of the Department for Pre- and Early History, part of the SS Race and Settlement Main Office, in 1933 (Treitel 215).

Wiligut, a clairvoyant whose blood link to a group of German sages called the Uiligotis of the Asa-Uana-Sippe ostensibly allowed him knowledge of ancient Germanic history, helped design a number of ceremonies and symbols that were intended to lend authenticity to SS ideology (Goodrick-Clarke 177–179). In consultation with Himmler, Wiligut helped design the death's head ring worn by the SS and conceived of an SS order-castle, which was established at Wewelsburg. Himmler's patronage of Wiligut occurred in the context of his desire to ground the ideological and moral purpose of the SS in Germanic prehistory. In this way the *Reichsführer's* use of Wiligut is contiguous with his establishment of the Ahnenerbe, which pursued archaeological research into the Germanic past (178).Wiligut, whose association with the SS ended in 1939 as information about an earlier confinement in a mental institution became common knowledge, imbued SS ritual with an occult aura and provided the most tangible connection between Nazism and the occult milieu (Treitel 215).

Although there was clearly some sympathy for occult belief among high ranking party members, such as Hess and Himmler, there is little proof that their fascination with the occult affected their decisions or that it provided the motivation for their racist policies; it may have provided, as the case of Wiligut demonstrates, a sense of authenticity and tradition for some of their ideologies. The occult pursuits of Hess and Himmler certainly did not affect the belief of a number of their colleagues', most prominently Joseph Goebbels and Martin Bormann, that the ideological dangers posed by occultism were too great to allow it to flourish unmolested. Goebbels was able to vent some of his long-held vitriol against the medieval superstitions that made up the modern occult movement when Hess made his ill-fated flight to England. Whether or not he truly believed that Hess had been motivated by the advice of his astrologers, Goebbels used the event to crack down on occultism (Treitel 216–217). Similarly, Bormann believed that occultism and its practitioners were sources of discontent and dissent that required eradication (217). Both of these men and many of their colleagues ultimately envisioned occultism as a kind of insidious disease that threatened the Nazi social body (217).

The Nazis tended to view occultism as an ideological menace that promoted a corrosive individualism and dangerous internationalism antithetical to the Nazi worldview (Treitel 211). Indeed, if we look at Theosophy or the occult thought of the vitalist-biologist Hans Driesch, we can see an emphasis on international brotherhood and racial harmony that was radically different from the racial "survival of the fittest" dogma ascribed to by the National Socialist state (Wolffram 158–159). This ideological chasm between most forms of modern occultism and Nazism ensured hostility toward occult practitioners when Hitler took power in 1933, but also extended to those occult groups like the Ariosophists who shared the regime's racial aspirations. This treatment of Ariosophy may have been a result of Hitler's well-known disgust for so-called wandering völkisch scholars, but may have also resulted from a desire to sever the putative links between Hitler's thought and that of occultists like Lanz von Liebenfels (Goodrick-Clarke 202). In the course of 1937 the National Socialists' negative stance on occult practice became official when they issued a decree for the protection of the people and the state, which dissolved occult, Theosophical, and psychical research groups effectively outlawing occultism (Treitel 224). Ironically, this decree was issued by the head of the German police and SS, Heinrich Himmler. With this new law the Nazis' long-held hostility toward occult practice, as a medical, psychological, and ideological danger to the German *Volk*, now became manifest not only in official and legal discourse, but also in physical intimidation and arrest (Linse 1996, 164–174). Large numbers of occultists were imprisoned by the Gestapo during the early 1940s, for example, as part of a campaign known as Action Hess, a campaign launched against Germany's occultists after Hess' dramatic flight to England. A number of astrologers who had had contact with Hess were shipped off to concentration camps and other occultists found themselves interrogated by the Gestapo.

While there are certainly some historical connections between Nazism and occultism and high ranking Nazis such as Hess and Himmler and esoteric practice, these links seem to be the result of the pervasiveness of modern occultism in Central Europe during the late nineteenth and early twentieth centuries, rather than a direct confluence or synergy between the two movements. Occultists cannot in any serious way be seen as an important source for or sinister force behind Hitler's genocidal dream. So, why do so many books (both fictional and cryptohistorical), films, games, and comics continue to rehearse this theme? In part it may be, as Treitel argues, that "locating Nazism's roots in the "lunatic fringe" and the occult "flight from reason" makes it easier to evade the hard question of what connects the proud heights of German (or even European) culture to the ignoble depths of Nazi barbarism"(26). But, this persistent fascination with linking occultism and Nazism may also be the result of a historiographical tradition that emerged following World War II and is only now beginning to be revised and refuted.

HISTORIOGRAPHICAL TRENDS: FROM RIGHT-WING IRRATIONALISM TO LIBERALISM BY OTHER MEANS

There is a significant body of serious historical work on occultism in Germany and other parts of Central Europe, which deals not only with the relationship between National Socialism and the occult but also the broader occult movement. Historiography in this field has developed from an initial interest in the link between irrationalism— epitomized by occultism—and right-wing politics to attempts to see modern occultism as a movement that resonated across the political and social spectrum and intersected with modernism. The bibliography that Mailer provides at the end of *The Castle in the Forest* indicates his familiarity with at least some of the scholarship in this field, most particularly Nicholas Goodrick-Clarke's *The Occult Roots of Nazism*. This section will put the arguments of Goodrick-Clarke and others into historiographical context.

In an effort to comprehend the horrors of the Nazi era a significant number of German historians in the period following World War II adopted a historiographical approach, known as the *Sonderweg* (special path), which stressed the peculiarity of modernization in the German context (Blackbourn and Eley 2–4; Kocka 40–50). Locating the roots of the German disaster in the failure of a bourgeois revolution, these historians examined Prussian militarism and contemporary intellectual currents in order to establish the eccentricity not only of Germany's institutional and political development, but also of the German mind (see Bossenbrook, Fraenkel, Krieger, and Stern, for example). The focus on irrationalism, which marked examinations of a German mentality during the 1950s and 1960s, saw occultism, like other forms of "unreason" native to the late nineteenth and early twentieth centuries, linked to both antimodernism and reactionary politics. In this context historians were particularly concerned to ascertain the links between Nazism and Ariosophy, ideologies that had become connected in the historical consciousness by the fact that a group of Ariosophists in Munich had hosted the meeting at which the German Worker's Party was founded in 1919. Ariosophy, an ideology that derived from the thought of the Austrians Jörg Lanz von Liebensfels and Guido von List, combined occultism, racism, anti-Semitism, and nationalism.

In an article published in 1950, Joachim Besser made much of the supposed connection between Hitler and the Ariosophists of Austria and Bavaria, arguing that the mixture of anti-Semitism and occultism prevalent in this milieu provided the ideological basis for National Socialism (763–784). Building on Besser's work, Wilfried Daim conducted a study of Jörg Lanz von Liebenfels in 1957, which maintained that Hitler's racial theories had their basis in Lanz's writings. George Mosse's 1961 article "The Mystical Origins of National Socialism" expanded on both these arguments. Mosse maintained that the reaction against positivism in Germany during the *fin de siècle* became intimately entwined with a mystical view of nature and with a romantic vision of the Aryan past, a combination that influenced a number of Nazism's intellectual architects (81–96). He concentrated in particular on the occult and Theosophical connections of men including Ludwig Klages (1872–1956), Stefan George (1868–1933), and Franz von Hartmann (1838–1912) whose approach to the problems of modernity in many instances overlapped with those of the Ariosophists.

During the 1970s the notion that occultism and National Socialism were intimately linked found support in the work of James Webb, who while cognizant of occultism's significance beyond the German context, found sufficient evidence to support the argument for a connection between Nazism and the German occult movement (1976, 275–344). Webb's two-volume work began with a survey of occultism in Europe and the United States during the nineteenth century. The occult, he argued, was an underground of knowledge existing in opposition to the establishment to which Europeans turned in their disgust with those scientific and philosophical developments that threatened to denude life of both moral and spiritual meaning (*Occult Underground* 2). In the second part of his study Webb maintained that World War I, viewed by many as the culmination of rationalism and materialism, exacerbated the crisis of consciousness that had caused the occult revival of the nineteenth century. In the interwar period the "flight from reason" inspired by this crisis became apparent not only in forms of religious occultism but also in the entanglement of occultism and mysticism with questions of ethics and social order (*Occult Establishment* 12–13). This combination of occultism and politics was most apparent in the Nazis' adoption of occult philosophies. For Webb this signified occultism's emergence from an intellectual underground to join the establishment. While Webb's work reiterated the link between Nazism and occultism, it also hinted that the significance of occultism, which manifested itself across Europe and America during the nineteenth and twentieth centuries, might be far broader than as a foundation for anti-Semitic and nationalist beliefs.

In 1985 Nicholas Goodrick-Clarke conducted a reassessment of the link between occultism and National Socialism in a book titled *The Occult Roots of Nazism*. Goodrick-Clarke argued that while a connection did exist between the Thule Society, the Germanenorden, and the early Nazi Party, Hitler's interest in Ariosophy was confined to the racial and Pan-German aspects of this doctrine, leading him to conclude that Ariosophy was a symptom rather than an influence in its anticipation of Nazism (192–204). Hitler's interest in the occult, as Goodrick-Clarke demonstrated, was minimal. The strongest link that he could establish between Hitler and the Ariosophists, for example, was the Führer's visit to Jörg Lanz von Liebenfels during 1909 in an effort to obtain back copies of the mystical-racist periodical *Ostara*. Hitler in fact tended to be highly critical of mystical and *völkisch* thought arguing that they were ineffective weapons in the fight for Germany's salvation because of their antiquarianism and emphasis on ceremony (Goodrick-Clarke 202).

A number of recent studies of German occultism reflect the departure from the *Sonderweg* that occurred within German historiography during the mid-1980s as a result of a questioning of normative assumptions about the development of Western democracies (Kocka 43–45; Repp 1–18). This new approach has allowed historians to demonstrate occultism's significance in the German arena. Moving beyond those analyses of the occult movement, which have viewed it solely in terms of its links to National Socialism, these studies have considered German occultism as a mode of cultural critique utilized by Germans from across the social and political spectrum. Replacing our conception of a straightforward process of secularization with the more complex and uneven processes of disenchantment and reenchantment, these studies have also added immeasurably to our understanding of what constitutes modernity. Ulrich Linse, for example, has rejected James Webb's designation of the occult movement as a "flight from reason" by those unable to come to terms with the frantic pace of modernization. He has argued instead that far from rejecting reason, spiritualists, Theosophists, and parapsychologists embraced both rationality and empiricism by extending them to the study of supernatural phenomena (*Geisterseher und Wunderwirker* 10–11). His studies of spiritualism in Germany and of the spiritualist publishing company Ostwald Mutze in Leipzig have also helped sever the historiographical ties between occultism and Nazism in the German context (*Der Spiritismus in Deutschland* 95–113; "Das Buch der Wunder" 219–244). Demonstrating the manner in which plebeian spiritualists in Saxony combined, or at least were perceived by the authorities to combine, spiritualism and socialism, Linse's work proves that occultism was not the exclusive purview of the nationalist right ("Das Buch der Wunder" 232–238).

Treitel's 2004 book *A Science for the Soul* not only considers occultism across the social and political spectrum in Germany but also argues that occultism can be understood both as a form of cultural critique and as a continuance of the liberal project by other means. Germans' engagement with the occult, she argues, was an attempt to reconcile their faith in science with their longing for meaning. Occultism also offered pragmatic solutions to modern problems. Treitel's analyses of both the occult movement's commercialization and its engagement with the new sciences of self and detection during the Weimar Republic have added depth and color to our understanding of occultism in this period (254–288). Her research into the relationship between occultism and Nazism has revealed the ambivalence of the National Socialists toward the occult movement. While there were undoubtedly a number of high ranking Nazis with an interest in astrology and race mysticism, the message of universal brotherhood promoted by occult philosophies such as Theosophy clashed with the *völkisch* and nationalist ideologies of the Party. Such scholarship in its rehabilitation of the occult provides a richer and more nuanced view of modernity in the German context and allows concentration upon the epistemological, social, and cultural issues that were central to those who participated in Germany's occult movement.

Fictional Transformations: Cryptohistory, Fiction, and *The Castle in the Forest*

Though the putative link between National Socialism and occultism has been all but severed by recent historical work, this bond continues to persist in the popular imagination. In part this is a result of the existence of a flourishing cryptohistoriography in this field. There appear to be three main strands within this cryptohistorical tradition. The first, inspired by Theosophy, links Nazism and the shadowy occult groups supposedly behind it to the mystical wisdom of the east, usually Tibet. Such books, including Louis Paulwels and Jacques Bergier's *Le matin des magiciens* (1960), and Dietrich Bronder's *Bevor Hitler kam* (1964), claim that the Nazi leadership tried to harness the occult knowledge and power of a group of mysterious Himalayan Grand Masters in order to ensure Germany's domination of the world (Goodrick-Clarke 219). The second strand within this historiography utilizes Anthroposophical sources, connecting Grail legends and the so-called spear of destiny to Hitler. In Trevor Ravenscroft's *Spear of Destiny* (1972), Hitler is convinced that he is a reincarnation of the sorcerer-king who appears in the *Parzival* legend. His aim is thus to regain the spear, held by the Habsburg's, and use its power (221–224). According to Ravenscroft, the retrieval of the spear was Hitler's first priority following the *Anschluss*. The final strand within Nazi occult cryptohistory is Ariosophy. In this tradition, apparent in Michel-Jean Angebert's *Les Mystiques du Soleil* (1971), Lanz von Liebenfels and List are seen as Nazism's occult architects, Lanz von Liebenfels supposedly meeting Hitler as a child at the choir school in Lambach (224). All of these works, which claim to reveal the secret history of the Third Reich, are based on myth and speculation rather than true history, catering for what is seemingly an insatiable appetite for the mystification of Nazism and its causes.

Some of the ideas posited in the cryptohistory of Nazism and occultism have been reiterated in popular fiction and film. James Herbert's thriller *The Spear* (1978), for example, revolves around the idea of the survival of the Thule Society, which having reestablished itself in England is obsessed with reenacting the Parzival legend, resurrecting Himmler and creating global terror. Katherine Kurtz's *Lammas Night* pits Nazi magicians and English witches against each other in a story set during World War II and Daniel Easterman's *The Seventh Sanctuary* (1985) features the Ahnenerbe, which having survived the collapse of the Third Reich searches for the Ark of the Covenant deep in the Saudi desert. Umberto Eco's *Foucault's Pendulum* (1989), a conglomeration of occult conspiracy theories, mentions the Thule Society on several occasions as the protagonists fabricate an occult philosophy using a computer program. Similar themes have been explored in film. For example, a group of occult-obsessed Nazi archaeologists, inspired by the Ahnenerbe, feature in the Indiana Jones movies *Raiders of the Lost Ark* (1981) and *Indiana Jones and the Last Crusade* (1989). The Thule Society also appears in the 2005 film *Unholy*. Like Herbert's book, this film imagines the survival of the Thule Society and its infiltration of powerful positions within modern liberal democracies.

The emphasis in these texts, both cryptohistorical and popular, on an occult conspiracy behind National Socialism's meteoric rise and the possibility of the survival of Nazi leaders and the occult forces behind them is a crystallization of our deepest fears about Nazism (Goodrick-Clarke 217–218; Rosenbaum xi). The occult element here appears to represent both the inexplicable nature of National Socialism and its crimes and the sense of inevitability that pervades even serious historical work on Hitler and the Holocaust; that is, the rise of the Nazi Party could not have been prevented because supernatural forces were in play. The survivalist concept that features in many of these texts similarly plays on our fear that Nazism could happen again. Mailer's use of occultism in his imagining of Hitler's conception and childhood is considerably more subtle than that which features in either the cryptohistoriography or other popular incarnations of the Nazism-occultism myth, but his novel clearly engages with this tradition.

There are several parts of *The Castle in the Forest* in which this engagement is put in the foreground, Mailer playfully weaving historical fact, myth, and speculation into his narrative. In the section titled "Der Alte and the Bees," for example, Mailer introduces the idea that Adolf may be or may come to believe that he is clairvoyant. In preparation for Adi's first meeting with the beekeeper, Der Alte, D.T has provided a dream-etching intended to deeply impress upon the child's mind. D.T. exclaims:

> We now knew that when Adi met Der Alte on this Sunday, he would feel a sense of personal importance, for he would believe he had the power to peer into the future.... No surprise, then, that Adi, etched by the dream, was marked by his visit. His expectation that he would often be able to picture in advance people he had not met would become an asset for us. We would exercise this device often during Adolf Hitler's service as an Army courier over the two years and more when he had to carry messages up to the trenches, then work his way back to regimental Headquarters. Since his duties incurred real danger, his belief that he could anticipate the future proved of no small assistance to his courage. (160–161)

Here Mailer utilizes Ken Anderson's work on Hitler and the occult, which analyzes a number of the occult myths surrounding the Fuehrer, including his putative obsession with the spear of destiny and his supposed clairvoyant powers. Hitler claimed that he had survived the shelling of a dugout during World War I because a mysterious voice had warned him to move to another position. Only minutes after evacuating the trench, the dugout was hit by a shell killing everyone inside. While Anderson argues that this story of precognition was part of the process of self-mythologization undertaken by Hitler, Mailer uses it as part of his narrative of diabolical patronage.

Similarly, in the same section, while the narrator D.T. laments a lost opportunity, Mailer intimates young Hitler's growing belief in his ability to channel occult power. D.T. states:

> Adi was certain. This was one night when you could feel free to breathe the night air, no matter how cold. For the Son of God was present.

Would He grant the power Adi needed to kill the mouse by force of his thoughts? To kill the mouse by force of his thoughts? I knew the limitations of my agents. They could not have conceived of such a notion. This had come from Adi. It was his. His alone. If I had been present, I would have raised the stakes. I might have gotten the boy ready to believe that he could save certain lives by exercising the special power he possessed to destroy others. That is one of the most useful suppositions we can implant in clients, but it does call for a sequence of dream-etchings. (191)

It is not, however, just the use of the myths concerning Hitler's occult powers of mind that links Mailer's work to the historiography and cryptohistoriography on Nazism and occultism. Mailer also integrates material on both the early relationship between Hitler and the swastika and Hitler and Lanz von Liebenfels into his story.

Making use of Goodrick-Clarke's book on the occult roots of Nazism, Mailer points to the presence of a swastika at the choir school attended by Hitler at Lambach. Here he uses elements of both cryptohistory and legitimate historiography by including the narrator's warning not to put too much emphasis on the swastika, a warning that is reminiscent of Goodrick-Clarke (224). D.T. says:

Over the entrance to the monastery was a large swastika carved into the stone of the arched gate. It was the coat of arms of the previous Abbot named von Hagen, who had been Abbot Superior in 1850, and von Hagen must have enjoyed the propinquity to his own name—a hooked cross was also called a *Hakenkreuz*. Not too much, I hasten to add, should be made of this. Hagen's swastika was subtly carved, and so offered no striking suggestion of the phalanxes yet to march beneath that symbol. Nonetheless, there it was, a hooked cross. (341–342)

Goodrick-Clarke relates the manner in which the cryptohistoriography casts von Hagen as a widely traveled scholar of astrology and the occult. While he argues that there is no evidence for either von Hagen's travels or his occult interests and thus the occult significance of his family's emblem, he points out that the story of Hitler's supposed veneration of the swastika at Lambach circulated even during the Third Reich. This notion was reinforced by the sale of an icon, which showed the child Hitler kneeling before the Lambach swastika (Goodrick-Clarke 224).

The choir school at Lambach also features in stories about an early meeting between Hitler and Lanz von Liebenfels. The Ariosophist is, according to cryptohistorical accounts, supposed to have resided at the Lambach monastery during 1898 as he studied von Hagen's occult library. While Mailer does not explicitly identify the mean-spirited cleric who discovers Hitler smoking under the swastika his words intimate—just as the crypto-history does—that this is Lanz von Liebenfels. D.T. states:

> Given the many clients I was overseeing in that part of Austria, I can-not claim to have been always in the right place at the best moment, but on this occasion I was. Our mean-spirited cleric—small surprise!—happened to be one of my finest clients in Lambach and had of course been alerted to take a quick stroll over to the gate where von Hagen's hooked stone cross was emblazoned. (343)

In creating this episode Mailer has closely followed Goodrick-Clarke who has outlined the most persistent strands of the Nazi occult cryptohistoriography (224).

While there are several more instances within *The Castle in the Forest* in which Mailer has D.T. attempt to instill in young Adolf the notion that he is in communication with supernatural powers and that his life has a special purpose (394–395), those mentioned above most clearly illustrate Mailer's attempt to weave historical fact and crypto-historical myth into his narrative. The question remains: to what pur-pose has Mailer used the Hitler/Nazi occult theme in this novel?

CONCLUSION

In the introduction to *Explaining Hitler*, Ron Rosenbaum explores the schism that divides the Hitler explainers, that is, the question of evolution or metamorphosis, or whether there was a defining moment, event, or person that made Hitler *Hitler*, he writes:

> It's a search impelled by the absence of a coherent and convincing evolutionary account of Hitler's psychological development, one that would explain his transformation from a shy, artistically minded youth, the dispirited denizen of a Viennese homeless shelter, from the dutiful but determinedly obscure army corporal, to the figure who, not long after his return to Munich from the war, suddenly leapt onto the stage of history as a terrifying incendiary, spellbinding street orator. (xiv)

It is arguable that what Mailer has tried to achieve in *The Castle in the Forest*, with its exploration of incest on the one hand and its intima-tions of the occult on the other, is just such an evolutionary account of Hitler's psychological development. He clearly engages not only the occult historiography concerning Hitler, but almost all of the major theories about the sources of Hitler's evil as well. In combining different hypotheses, the novel produces a Hitler theory that is more than the sum of its parts.

Hitler historiography, as Rosenbaum has shown, has moved since the late 1940s from seeing Hitler as directly responsible for the Holocaust at one extreme to all but dismissing him as an agent at the other, looking instead to irresistible historical forces to explain the murder of the Jews (389). Mailer's novel, with its conglomeration of theories, combines the two apparently antithetical historiographical trends. While the cosmology D.T. develops in *The Castle in the Forest* suggests that human history, society, and politics are manipulated by two invisible opposing forces, he also stresses the difficulty of grooming clients and expresses delight, surprise, and dismay at various times over Hitler's independent actions, thoughts, and fantasies. Mailer's young Adolf, thus, seems a product of both grand historical forces (diabolic and occult) and free will. Mailer's historical research into the relationship between occult texts and Nazism, including his playful nods to the cryptohistoriography in this field, can thus be seen as part of this larger project of creating a grand theory.

In spite of his attempt to create an all-encompassing account of what made Hitler *Hitler*, Mailer leaves the reader with a sense of the inexplicable. His story ends as the teenaged Adolf completes his studies at the *Realschule*, but Mailer goes on to provide an epilogue in which D.T. describes the liberation of a concentration camp, ironically called "the castle in the forest" by its inmates. This leap from the representation of an unlikeable, but sensitive youth to the aftermath of genocide is similar to Rosenbaum's philosophizing on Hitler's baby photos and the Holocaust—the gap between the two defies explanation. As Rosenbaum writes,

> [n]o explanation or concatenation of explanations can bridge the gap, explain the transformation from baby picture to baby killer, to murderer of a million babies. It's not just a gap...it is an *abyss*. (xviii)

Finally, then, despite his use of what could have been the ultimate explanatory device, that is, the devil made him do it, Mailer (deliberately I think) leaves the reader staring into the abyss.

WORKS CITED

Anderson, Ken. *Hitler and the Occult*. Amherst, NY: Prometheus Books, 1995.

Angebert, Michel-Jean. *Les mystiques du soleil*. Paris: Lafont, 1971.

Besser, Joachim. "Die Vorgeschichte des Nationalsozialismus in neuem Licht." *Die Pforte*. *Monatsschrift für Kultur* 2:21/22 (1950): 763–784.

Blackbourn, David, and Geoff Eley. *The Peculiarities of German History: Bourgeois Society and Politics in Nineteenth-Century Germany*. Oxford and New York: Oxford University Press, 1984.

Bossenbrook, William. *The German mind*. Detroit: Wayne University Press, 1961.

Bronder, Dietrich. *Bevor Hitler kam: Eine historische Studie*. Hannover: H. Pfeiffer, 1964.

Daim, Wilfried. *Der Mann, der Hitler die Ideen gab. Jörg Lanz von Liebenfels*, 3rd ed. Vienna: Ueberreuter, 1994.

Easterman, Daniel. *The Seventh Sanctuary*. London: Grafton Books, 1987.

Eco, Umberto. *Foucault's Pendulum*. London: Pan Books, 1990.

Fraenkel, Ernst. *Deutschland und die westlichen Demokratien*. Stuttgart: Kohlhammer, 1964.

Goodrick-Clarke, Nicholas. *The Occult Roots of Nazism. Secret Aryan Cults and Their Influence on Nazi Ideology. The Ariosophists of Austria and Germany, 1890–1935*. New York: New York University Press, 1985.

Hau, Michael. *The Cult of Health and Beauty in Germany: A Social History, 1890–1930*. Chicago: University of Chicago Press, 2003.

Herbert, James. *The Spear*. London: New English Library, 1978.

Howe, Ellic. *Urania's Children: The Strange World of the Astrologers*. London: William Kimber, 1967.

Kocka, Jürgen. "Asymmetrical Historical Comparison: The Case of the German *Sonderweg*." *History and Theory* 38:1 (1999): 40–50.

Krieger, Leonard. *The German Idea of Freedom*. Boston: Beacon Press, 1957.

Kurtz, Katherine. *Lammas Night*. London: Severn House, 1986.

Levenda, Peter. *Unholy Alliance: A History of Nazi Involvement with the Occult*, 2nd ed. New York: Continuum, 2002.

Linse, Ulrich. *Geisterseher und Wunderwirker. Heilsuche im Industriezeitalter*. Frankfurt am Main: Fischer, 1996.

———. "Der Spiritismus in Deutschland um 1900," in *Mystizismus und Moderne in Deutschland um 1900*, ed. Moritz Bassler and Hildegard Châtellier. Strasbourg: Presses Universitaires de Strasbourg, 1998.

Mailer, Norman. *The Castle in the Forest*. New York: Random House, 2007.

———. *The Spooky Art: Some Thoughts on Writing*. New York: Random House, 2003.

Meyer-Renschhausen, Elisabeth and Albert Wirz. "Dietetics, Health Reform and Social Order: Vegetarianism as a Moral Physiology. The Example of Maximilian Bircher-Benner (1867–1939)." *Medical History* 43 (1999): 323–341.

Mosse, G.L. "The Mystical Origins of National Socialism." *Journal of the History of Ideas* 22 (1961): 81–96.

National Public Radio. *Norman Mailer Digs into Hitler's Childhood.* Interview with Jacki Lyden. 27 January 2007.

Pauwels, Louis, and Jacques Bergier. *The Dawn of Magic,* trans. Rollo Myers. London: Panther, 1964.

Ravenscroft, Trevor. *The Spear of Destiny: The Occult Power behind the Spear that Pierced the Side of Christ.* London: Sphere Books, 1973.

Repp, Kevin. *Reformers, Critics, and the Paths of German Modernity. Anti-Politics and the Search for Alternatives, 1890–1914.* Cambridge, MA, and London: Harvard University Press, 2000.

Rosenbaum, Ron. *Explaining Hitler: The Search for the Origins of his Evil.* New York: Harper Perennial, 1999.

Stern, Fritz. *The Politics of Cultural Despair: A Study in the Rise of the German Ideology* Berkeley: University of California Press, 1961.

Treitel, Corinna. *A Science for the Soul: Occultism and the Genesis of the German Modern.* Baltimore and London: Johns Hopkins University Press, 2004.

Webb, James. *The Occult Establishment.* La Salle, IL: Open Court, 1976.

———. *The Occult Underground.* La Salle, IL: Open Court, 1974.

Wolffram, Heather. "Supernormal Biology: Vitalism, Parapsychology and the German Crisis of Modernity, c. 1890–1933." *European Legacy* 8 (2003): 149–163.

PART IV

Fame

CHAPTER 10

History Looks at Itself: On the Road with the Mailers and George Plimpton

Lawrence Shainberg

Vienna, 2002. On a warm wet evening in late October, Norman Mailer is greeted by a full-house rousing ovation as he parts the rear curtain and moves onto the stage at the Funkhaus Theatre. It is fifty-five years since his first book, *The Naked and the Dead*, propelled him into a celebrity that has so proliferated through the years that it seems to him now "an anchor I'm dragging through the sand." Next year, on his eightieth birthday, he will publish his thirty-second book, a collection of essays about writing called *The Spooky Art*, which includes this sentence: "If a writer is really good enough and bold enough he will, by the logic of society, write himself out onto a limb that the world will saw off." He likes to say that all novelists are actors at heart. Over the years, it's been a useful metaphor, completely subjective, of course, a reference to the voices and identities he explores at his desk, but tonight it is no metaphor. The writer is an actor and the role he plays is of another writer who may have been, on the public stage at least, as much engaged with acting as any writer who ever lived, including Norman Mailer. As Ernest Hemingway, Mailer is about to assume the voice he sought to emulate when he discovered it more than sixty years ago and, when it vanished with Hemingway's suicide some forty years ago, made him realize, as if for the first time, the immeasurable risk of the profession he had chosen.

In pursuit of his role, Mailer wears khaki pants and a matching jacket with epaulettes, an ensemble designed to make him look like a man embarking on safari—to hunt elephants, maybe, or no less an adventure, revisit a voice he had to jettison in order to find his own. Fatigue—a result of jet lag, a round of press interviews this afternoon and several official ceremonies in his honor the past two days—weighs on his posture, but his face is animated by the pleasure he derives from being on stage. Squeezed beneath his arm because his hands are occupied by the pair of canes his arthritic knees demand of him these days, he carries the script from which he'll read this evening. He is followed onto the stage by his wife, Norris Church Mailer, and George Plimpton, his longtime friend, once a good friend of Hemingway's, who happens to be the coauthor of the script from which they'll read. Left and center, schoolhouse desks are set up for Mailer and Plimpton and, to their right, a lectern and a higher stool for Church. When they're settled into their chairs, Mailer's canes neatly arranged in parallel on the desk beside his script, Plimpton addresses the audience,

What you're about to hear is a collection of letters and prose that describes the arc of friendship between Ernest Hemingway, F. Scott, and Zelda Fitzgerald. You'll hear snippets from letters that Zelda wrote Scott and parts from twenty-nine letters between Fitzgerald and Hemingway. For reasons you'll see as we go along, Zelda and Hemingway did not exchange letters. They did not, it seems, like each other very much. The adaptation also includes short sections from Zelda Fitzgerald's novel, *Save Me the Waltz,* and a mention, toward the end, of a second novel she never finished. You'll hear a section from Hemingway's book on his days in Paris, *A Moveable Feast,* and one from *The Great Gatsby* and also a transcript of a painful conversation between Zelda and Scott that took place in the presence of a psychiatrist. You'll hear a shocking letter from Scott to Scottie Fitzgerald, his daughter with Zelda, which, in effect, condemns her mother for her effect on his writing. You'll also hear, from both Scott and Ernest, letters to someone called "Max." This is Maxwell Perkins, the legendary editor, who worked with both of them as well as Zelda. In case you're confused, Norman Mailer is Papa Hemingway. As you see, he's suitably attired. Norris Mailer is Zelda Fitzgerald, and I'll play Scott. That's why I'm wearing my orange Princeton tie which is alas somewhat shorter than it should be. Forgive me—it's the best I could do under the circumstances. OK, here we go. "Zelda, Scott, and Ernest."

*   *   *

Plimpton had once been my editor on a novel I published with Paris Review Editions. It was during lunch with him a couple of years ago, May 1999, that I first heard about this play. I knew that Mailer and he had long been friends, so I mentioned to him that Norman and I, who lived near each other on Cape Cod, had developed a happy ritual of quiet dinners now and then on bleak winter nights in Provincetown. As it happened, George said, he had plans to visit the Mailers in Provincetown that summer. "We'll be doing our play up there in August." He described the script as he'd describe it later, from the stage, in Vienna. They'd already performed it, he said, in Washington and New York and, after Provincetown, they were scheduled for Amsterdam and Paris. This trip to Vienna, which began two days ago in Fitzgerald's birthplace, St. Paul, Minnesota, and, after this stop, will take us to Berlin, Moscow, and London, was not yet planned, but in its wake the cast will be deluged with publicity and interest, invitations from Cuba, India, San Francisco, the United Nations, and other venues, a host of performances that will never happen because of Norris' cancer, which strikes just a few months after our return to the States, and Plimpton's sudden death, in his sleep, one year later. Three more times, after tonight, these six American archetypes will meet on stage, and then the play will succumb to the mortality and impermanence that are the unspoken heart of its matter.

Like those that preceded it, tonight's performance, in Vienna, is strictly noncommercial. Since the Hemingway and Fitzgerald estates own most of the material from which the play derives, all performances are philanthropic. Paris benefited the James Jones Society, Provincetown the Provincetown Repertory Theatre. The proceeds from tonight's performance will go to victims of recent floods in Europe. As always, the cast will not be compensated beyond its expenses. They do it for love of each other and the people they play, of performance itself no doubt and the mind-boggling contradictions—wisdom and ignorance, success and failure, love and hatred, joy and sorrow—they envelop as they perform. Then too, none of them is oblivious to the mythic realm they are exploring. "When it comes to culture," Mailer says, "the U.S. is like an empty rich man who doesn't know what to do with his money. Mythos is culture, a nutrient. I would love to be able to do this play all over America. I'd take it to five towns in seven days, do it maybe twenty or thirty times a year. I think it could bring back the equivalent of Chautauqua."

Over that lunch two years ago, George explained that not a single word of the script had been invented. It was all an edit, searched out, composed, and organized with his coauthor, Terry Quinn, and fine-tuned by Norman, Norris, and himself. The play was a kind of Appropriation Art, suitable, perhaps even inevitable, at a time when the onslaughts of media and information had made the creation of new material a somewhat different proposition than it had been in the past—the days, for example, when Hemingway and Fitzgerald were publishing their masterpieces; when there was no such thing as a quality paperback; when 24,000 books were published in a given year, as opposed to the 120,000 that compete for shelf-space today; and Plimpton's *Paris Review* received less than 2,000 submissions annually rather than the 20,000 it received last year. Given that Plimpton had written or edited twenty-six books and appeared in thirty films, while Mailer, in addition to his thirty-two books, had directed four films and written ten screenplays and countless magazine articles, it struck me as both ironic and appropriate that they were involved, this time around, in what was essentially an act of recycling.

Since Plimpton had made a career of leaving his own for other identities, it was no surprise that the play had begun with him. As endless articles and newscasts reported after his death, his own myth no less celebrated than Hemingway's, Fitzgerald's, and Mailer's, his unique brand of participatory journalism had taken him into bull-fighting, professional golf, basketball, football, baseball, and boxing. He'd explored the trapeze with the Ringling Brothers Circus and, by his own account, suffered one of the greatest traumas of his life when he missed Leonard Bernstein's cue while playing the gong in Mahler's Fourth with the New York Philharmonic. As a soccer goalie, he'd been scored on by Pele, as a hockey goalie, by Bobby Hull. As an amateur pianist, playing his own composition, he'd placed second at Amateur Night at the Apollo. Finally, however, it was his excursion into Edmund Wilson, during Wilson's epistolary argument with Vladimir Nabokov, that led to this night in Vienna. In *Dear Bunny, Dear Volodya,* an adaptation by Quinn of the Wilson-Nabokov letters, Plimpton was Wilson in colloquy with Nabokov's son, Dmitri, as his father. The form of that work had so captivated him that he'd turned his attention to the Hemingway-Fitzgerald letters and sought out Quinn to collaborate with him.

Over lunch, George described the happy coincidence that had set the play in motion. "Actually, we came together as a cast because of John Irving. Just at the time when Terry and I were working on our final draft, John asked the Mailers to do him a favor." Irving's children were attending a school in Manchester, Vermont, which was about to hold a benefit, and he asked the Mailers if they would do a reading from A.R. Gurney's Lanford Wilson's *Love Letters.* Sympathetic to the cause but not the role, Norman suggested that Plimpton might do it with Norris. "I told him I had a better idea—something the three of us could do together. I sent it to him in Provincetown, and he liked it a lot. Next thing I knew, we were working on it together in John's kitchen the day of the performance in Manchester. The audience response astonished us. I remember one guy crying out during the Q and A after the performance, "This should be done in every high school in America!" Norman told John that the play ought to be done by professional actors, but John saw it differently. "It's you three make it work—listening to you and thinking back to the originals. This is about history looking at itself."

Unlike the audience in Moscow, tonight's, in Vienna, does not require simultaneous translation. The laughs are less frequent than in St. Paul but, thanks no doubt to various collisions and intersections of English and Russian syntax, more abundant than they will be in Moscow three days later. Even so, the most striking discovery of this trip will be the stamina of American Literature as it travels the world. All performances—with minimal advertising—are sold out, and there is as much appreciation for the actors as those they portray. "It's nice to know," Mailer says, "that in Europe I'm probably read more seriously than in America. But that's an old story, of course. I'm sure many American writers could say the same. I get the same feeling in small American cities, like St. Paul. It's as if a sort of city patriotism takes over. People take a sort of pride that an author visits them." The owner of a restaurant in Potsdam, where the entourage will be taken for lunch the day after tomorrow (and treated, of course, to a tour of the rooms in which Stalin, Truman, and Churchill negotiated at the end of World War II), will confide that she named her son after Mailer. Asked what brings them here, more than one member of the audience will talk about reading *The Naked and the Dead* in high school. A young writer in Moscow talks about permission to read Hemingway ("the essence of America to us") as one of the happier results of Glasnost, and a secondary schoolteacher in Berlin says of Mailer that he "represents the American Left to us. And now, of course, because we are so afraid of the American Right, we're all the more anxious to hear what he's got to say." Most impressive of all was a talk given yesterday, the day after our arrival in Vienna, by Guenther Nenning, former publisher of the German magazine FORUM and founder of Austria's Green Party, on the occasion of Mailer's receipt of the Cross of Honor, which happens to be the highest distinction Austria can bestow upon an artist. Nenning addressed Mailer as a way to address America:

> Dear Norman Mailer, we small Austrians have a very clear position towards your great America. We are always for America and always

against America. Always for America because we want to be protected and because, in the global clash of civilizations, we belong after all to the West. Always against America because in our Central-European souls, there is a lot of arrogance coupled with anger and envy. It is therefore a great relief when Mailer shoulders our anti-American burden, because you can't be more anti-American than this great American. Norman Mailer has a European concept of patriotism: he loves his country not how it is but how it should be.

*　*　*

Four days after we leave Vienna, Plimpton, his wife Sara and I, sharing a taxi from Moscow's airport to our hotel near Red Square, pass a soccer stadium that sports a banner advertising a local team called the Dynamite. "Hey," says George, "I played goalie against those guys! They scored on me!" He tells us how he was introduced to the Dynamite players as a veteran of renown, how impressed with themselves they were that they scored on him so easily. He talks about Bobby Hull and Pele and goal-tending in general, and then—another kind of goal-tending?—the night he introduced Hemingway—over dinner at the Colony Restaurant in New York—to thumb-wrestling.

"As it happened, the whole thing came about because of Norman." Earlier that day, I'd had an idea that Norman might come to dinner with us. He'd been wanting to meet Ernest for years of course. As it happened, Ernest was interested. Not because of *The Naked and the Dead* but because of *The Deer Park*, which he'd just read, and liked. I set it up with Norman but for various reasons the meeting did not come off. As a matter of fact, they never met. But like I said, Ernest was interested in him, and at dinner he started plying me with questions. "What's he like? What's he interested in?" I told him that one of the things Norman was into was thumb-wrestling. "Thumb-wrestling?" Hemingway said. "What the hell is that?" I took his hand and set about demonstrating for him. I'd been warned that he was intense about any sort of physical confrontation, but before I knew it, we were into it for real. He was very bad at it. Very bad. He couldn't stand when I beat him. The table was shaking, dishes rattling. The mark of his fingernails stayed on my palm for a week.

I asked George what he was up to these days. He told me about three books—a biography of Ernest Shackleton (published in April 2003), a boxing anthology, and an account of a fifteen-year birdwatching project that had grown out of articles he'd written for *Audubon Magazine*. It had taken him to India, Antarctica, and thirty other countries. In addition, this seventy-four-year-old man who'd interrupted work at his desk, which was dominated, as it had been for nearly fifty years, by his editorial duties at *Paris Review*, who was traveling the world with a play he'd distilled from other writers' letters, was writing two *New Yorker* profiles and working on a children's opera, "Animal Tales," with Lucas Foss. Participatory journalism? "Nothing planned just now, but I've got an idea. I want to manage a wrestler. Get this big guy—350, 400 pounds—call him 'The Grecian Urn.' He's got tattoos all over his body. 'Beauty is truth and truth beauty.' That sort of thing. I've got it all worked out. He comes into the ring strumming a little harp or lyre. When he's angry, he swears in Shakespearean odes. 'Devil damn thee black thou green-faced moon!' I took the idea to ABC. Thought maybe we'd do a sort of retrospective of all the things I've done, many of which are on film, you know. I wanted to intersperse it with story of the Urn. Seemed to me they were interested at first, but their pencils stopped when I started talking about the tattoos and the harp. They looked at me like I was crazy."

* * *

ZELDA, SCOTT, AND ERNEST begins with a typically hyperbolic exchange between Zelda and Scott—tender expressions from the early days of the famous, high-octane romance that, if you know their biography, makes you wince with fear for them. Drawn from her own youth, in Arkansas, Norris's accent is a drawly suggestion of Zelda's Alabama roots; and if one had ever had the opportunity to hear Fitzgerald read aloud, one imagines he'd sound a lot like George, whose patrician accent is delivered so off-handedly that he might be addressing a small group of friends over dinner or, as was the case, with sad excess, throughout most of Fitzgerald's adult life, drinks.

The play is set in motion by a 1919 telegram from Scott to Zelda: "Darling heart: ambition, enthusiasm and confidence. I declare everything glorious! This world is a game, and while I feel sure of your love, everything is possible." Scott finds himself in a "land of ambition and success" and declares that his "only hope and faith is that my darling heart will be with me soon." Zelda, matching Scott's mood, tells him that "[t]oday seems like Easter." "Everything smells so good and warm, and your ring shines so white in the sun—like one of the church lilies with a little yellow dust on it. Everyone thinks it's lovely, and I am so proud to be your girl."

Like no small number of women these days, Norris is captivated by Zelda's story, but there are parallels between the two women that push her interest toward an identification that's almost uncanny. Born just two months after Zelda died, she sometimes wonders if she's not a reincarnation of the woman she plays. "Maybe she came back to see if she could do it better this time." Both women were born in the South and married writers of renown, and both were themselves accomplished writers who abandoned their work for years. Both were talented painters and had aspirations—Zelda as a dancer and Norris as an actress and playwright—toward the stage.

Mailer's notorious battles with feminists had once made him a virtual archetype of male chauvinism, and, at first glance, it would seem that Norman/Norris will echo the destructive relationship evolving in the play between Scott and Zelda. The differences between the relationships are as significant as the similarities. While Scott raided Zelda's letters and diaries for his own work and was often mean-spirited in his attitude toward her writing—"You're a second-rate writer! Compared to me, you are—well, there is just not any comparison!"— Mailer has been unqualified in his support of Norris, who published her first novel *Windchill Summer* in 2000 and her second, *Cheap Diamonds*, in 2007. "Some of the dialogue between Scott and Zelda," Norris told me, "makes you want to cry. Part of it, of course, is the era she grew up in. Women didn't have the vote. They were totally subjugated to men." Norris reminds me that Zelda's problems were personal, not just institutional: "She was in and out of mental hospitals for the last twenty years of her life. But she once told Scott that she'd rather be in an asylum than living with him. 'At least they allowed me to write there.' It was if she had no right to her own life. Their life together was Scott's material. 'I'm the writer,' he said. 'How dare you use the name Fitzgerald?'" In the end Zelda capitulated; she had no life of her own.

With Norman it was quite different. "Norman has been totally supportive. He's never held me back at all. He's not that kind of person." Norris acknowledges that Norman has made a number of inflammatory statements in the heat of the moment but feels that feminists have used him as a punching back. "He's no enemy of women."

* * *

Mailer is eighty years old. Talk to his friends these days and you'll hear—with amazement that mounts in proportion to the length of time they've known him—how age has mellowed him. About the man who used to be called "Stormin Norman," who ran an eccentric, often bizarre, and distinctly unsuccessful campaign for mayor of New York City in 1969 and spent two weeks in Bellevue after a much-publicized stabbing of his wife in 1960, adjectives of the moment run from "kind" and "sweet" to "serene" and "avuncular." He's not always pleased to hear himself described like this but he can't deny the complexities to which time is introducing him. "One of the few benefits of old age is that I don't get nearly as exercised about questions I can't answer." Or: "It's hard to keep up the old vendettas because for the most part I've forgotten them." To my astonishment, I heard him, at one point on this trip, celebrate the benefits of short-term memory loss: "It makes you a better editor of yourself. You're much more objective when you come back to something you did the day before because you can't remember writing it."

My own experience confirms the endearing adjectives. I trace our friendship to a book I sent in search of a blurb. I barely knew him, but I'd heard about his generosity toward Cape Cod writers. Inundated though he is with such requests, he read the book and responded three days later. I know at least half-a-dozen other writers who've had similar experiences with him.

One thing that hasn't changed, however, is his passion for argument. The old vendettas may be forgotten but he is hardly reticent toward new ones. When *The New Republic* published a defamatory cover five years ago (a picture of Mailer in a loin cloth over a caption reading "He is Finished!") in response to his just-published *Gospel According to the Son,* he punched out its publisher, Martin Peretz, outside a Provincetown restaurant. He doesn't get to the gym these days, as he did for years when he was boxing or, in his mid-fifties, rock-climbing, but you only have to watch his eyes to see how sparring feeds his energy. Though at this time he'd been with Norris—his sixth wife, mother of the ninth of a brood of children that ranges in age from fifty-one to twenty-four—for twenty-eight years and, for the most part, seems content with their current life in Provincetown, their arguments are frequent and public, sometimes nasty, sometimes playful, often both, as if they're testing each others' tolerance and patience and, together, how near they can get to the edge of the cliff without going over. Norris describes such confrontations with a metaphor that seems to me appropriately mixed. "Kind of like dancing. He wins a few, I win a few." Norman? "Marriage is an excrementious relationship. One can take all that's bad in oneself and throw it at one's mate. She throws it back at you and you both shake hands and go on with your business—you can't do that when you're out in the world."

But even when he's angry, it's not clear how much he means to be taken seriously. Testing theories, risking offense, edging away from moderation and sometimes, as in the early days, even rationality, he seems at times to enjoy nothing so much as controversy. I suspect he'd not like to hear this, but I can't disabuse myself of the notion that his arguments are play, his interviews play, that an impulse toward play is always present in his work. Play—and gambling. As he says, "I'd classify myself and half the people I know as wicked. Gamblers. People just upping the ante." Needless to say, a writer's gambling is often solitary and not entirely confined to his work. For years, he's begun his work day with a long bout of solitaire, and ever since Norris got mad at him for losing money on football (she once remodeled their Provincetown kitchen to get even with him for his losses), he's pursued a sort of solitaire-football of his own invention, tracking the NFL and its weekly betting line but making "mind bets" against himself. Show me a better metaphor for a man who defines a novelist as a compendium of opposites. What Mailer once wrote of Hemingway,—"His contradictions are his unity. His dirty fighting and his love of craft come out of the same blood"—is remodelled in *The Spooky Art*, where Mailer writes, "To know what you want to say is not the best condition for writing a novel." While we were in Europe, he was hell-bent on the Monday *Herald Tribune* for the results of Sunday's NFL games, so as to see how he'd fared, against himself, the day before. Bad days bothered him not inconsiderably. Real bets or "mind-bets," sparring and argument were at once matters of import and games to be played with full intensity. What's more serious to a player than his game? At times, as in the fight with Peretz or some of his battles with femininists, he'd had real money on the line, but with Norris, the bets were always paradoxical. Not exactly safe but less about hostility than one's capacity to enjoy it. One played to win but the chips on the table were not the sort one expected to cash. He sometimes imagines Hemingway's suicide as an accidental loss of another sort of bet. "I think it was his need to be a man that killed him. He had all the male fears that were strong in those days—of being a coward, of ending up gay, of basic dread, etcetera. His solution was to dare death…become a prizefighter, seek out the risks that frightened him. I can imagine him going into his study and putting a gun in his mouth, pulling the trigger in a sort of Russian roulette, just to test himself against his dread." On the other hand, mind bets have an ante like any other and, as he says, antes have to be upped if you want to keep the risk alive. He was particularly hard on Norris' Baptist background, perhaps because, as Norris suggested, he knew that nothing bothered her more. "Petty honesty" was what he accused her of. "It's worse than petty thievery. Where you come from, it's a big thing to find a way to pass the time without offending God." Anything but apologetic, he talked about their battles with no less abandon than he pursued them. A few hours before this evening's performance, for example, in a limo hired by our hosts in Vienna (heading out on a sightseeing tour that included, among other sites, the house in which Beethoven spent his formative years), he'd explained their game, apropos of nothing, like a first-time realization. "Norris and I are like two old gym rats. Fighting is our hobby." And then, a moment later, as if displeased by such benevolence, turned the screw in the other direction. "When you're my age and you've been married as long as we have, your wife can have half your IQ and twice your rage and you still argue like equals." Gazing out the window, Norris had not been paying much attention, but this last found her ear:

> "Did you say half?"
> "Well, maybe 55%."
> "Fuck you, Norman."
> "Fuck you too, baby. You act like my older sister. Christ, I've got to be the only eighty-year-old in the world who's treated like a six-year-old. When I leave you, I'll say it's 'cause you frustrated my late adolescence."
> "If you leave me, who'll arrange for your wheelchair at the airport?"

Unsure how angry they were, I worried for a moment, but I was quickly reassured by the grin on Norman's face. I don't know that it had ever occurred to me that one can laugh and scowl simultaneously, but that's what he was doing, and I doubt he'll ever come closer to defining his love of play, and gambling and, come to think of it, his relation to his work, than he did with that expression.

*　*　*

Fitzgerald had already published *The Beautiful and the Damned* and was close to finishing *The Great Gatsby* when he and Zelda made their way to Europe for the first time. It was a few months after that that he and Hemingway met for the first time. Drawing from *A Moveable Feast* in its description of this first meeting, Hemingway/Mailer says: "He had come into the Dingo Bar in the rue Delambre, where I was sitting with some completely worthless characters." He thought him, he (as Mailer) offers, "a man who looked like a boy, with a face between handsome and pretty. He had very fair, wavy hair, a high forehead, excited and friendly eyes—and a delicate, long-lipped Irish mouth that, on a girl, would have been the mouth of a beauty." Fitzgerald's features, he goes on, "should have added up to a pretty face, but that came from the coloring, the very fair hair and the mouth. The mouth worried you until you knew him—and then it worried you more. 'Ernest,' he said. 'You don't mind if I call you Ernest, do you? Tell me, did you and your wife sleep together before you were married?' "

"'I don't know,' I said.
"What do you mean you don't know?"
"I don't remember."
"But how can you not remember something of such importance?"
"'I don't know,' I said. 'It's odd, isn't it?' "

A few minutes later, Mailer/Hemingway confides in the audience at Fitzgerald's expense. The latter has loaned out his last and only copy of his new book but wants Hemingway to read *The Great Gatsby* as soon as he can get it back. As we know from their history, this reading changed everything for them. "He had many good, good friends—more than anyone I knew. But I enlisted as one more, whether I could be of any use to him or not. If he could write a book as fine as *The Great Gatsby*, I was sure he could write an even better one. I did not know Zelda yet, and so I did not know the terrible odds that were against him."

* * *

Thus began a friendship that has generated as much interpretation and scholarship as any in American literature. Fitzgerald was already successful at this time, Hemingway just starting out. Supporting and advising him, Scott would introduce him to Maxwell Perkins, offer editorial help, and convince him to delete, from a preliminary draft of *The Sun Also Rises,* seventeen pages that would have badly weakened the book. Profoundly important to both, the friendship was passionate, perhaps homoerotic, increasingly colored, as the years wore on, by resentment, mistrust, and competition, not to mention the mutual antipathy between Ernest and Zelda. The mistrust increased as Hemingway's career outstripped Fitzgerald's. Here is Fitzgerald/Plimpton, summing it up in 1937, when he was forty-one: "I really loved Ernest, but of course it wore out like a love affair. We began trying to walk over each other with cleats...I talked with the authority of failure, Ernest with the authority of success. We could never sit across the table again."

Mailer says he's never, himself, known a literary friendship like Hemingway's with Fitzgerald: "I'm not certain two writers of the same stature can really afford a profound friendship with each other. Imagine a marriage between a beautiful actor and a beautiful actress. How long's it gonna last? There's more imbalance than balance in the relationship." Even so, he and Plimpton have known each other for almost fifty years, differ though they do in vision and stature; the benefits of the friendship are apparent to both and anyone who knows them. If they don't completely mirror Fitzgerald and Hemingway, they surely offer, in their lives, an echo of the echo they're offering on stage. Norman counts the opportunity to work with George as one of the play's principal attractions, and on the same subject George can sound almost reverential. "Norman says 'Vienna' and I start packing. Even if I'm busy and tired of the play, I can't say no to him." Physically, they differ as much from each other as they do from Hemingway and Fitzgerald or, for that matter, as the latter two did from each other. At 5-7, Mailer is six inches shorter than the man he plays, and Plimpton, 6-3, nine inches taller. They're both Harvard graduates, but their backgrounds are as disparate as their bodies. Mailer was born in Brooklyn, his parents Jewish, his father an accountant who was a fairly chronic gambler. He went to public school before he went to Harvard. Plimpton, whose father, Francis Plimpton, was a Wall Street lawyer and a Deputy Representative to the United Nations, went to Exeter and, after Harvard, Cambridge.

No less different, the roads they took to their collaboration on stage tonight are a celebration of the endless tributaries that feed and branch off the river of their profession. Each was clearly influenced by the man he is portraying, and like any writer in the grip of major influence, including, of course, Hemingway and Fitzgerald, each has struggled to wean himself from it. Plimpton first tapped his literary voice in a class at Harvard with Archibald MacLeish. "I'd started a novel about murder—patricide, I think, or maybe fratricide—but suddenly I realized I had to do something different. I wrote a light piece, coming out of my work on the *Lampoon*. MacLeish praised it. My greatest influence, for sure, was Mark Twain, but in retrospect, I think that first piece was influenced by Fitzgerald. I'd just read 'Diamonds Big as the Ritz.' In any event, I understood that I had to avoid the solemn at any cost."

Mailer was writing what he calls "crude imitations of Hemingway" eight or nine years before *The Naked and the Dead* was published. "I was sixteen or seventeen when I read that first collection of Hemingway stories, *The Fifth Column*. I read them over and over like a Bible. It was his style that moved me, of course, its manliness. I loved him the way some actors love John Wayne. I wanted to be like him as much as I wanted to write like him." After college, Plimpton turned to editing, founding (with Peter Matthiessen, Harold Humes, Thomas Guinzburg, and Donald Hall) the *Paris Review* in 1953 and interviewing other writers—E.M. Forster, William Styron, Irwin Shaw, and Hemingway, to name a few—for its famous "Writers at Work" series. Opting for journalism, he wrote occasional pieces and played small parts in film and on television until 1961, when he published *Out of My League,* a collection of his participatory journalism pieces for which Hemingway wrote this blurb: "Beautifully observed and incredibly conceived, this account of a self-imposed ordeal has the chilling quality of a true nightmare. It is the dark side of the moon of Walter Mitty." Though journalism remained his métier, he tried his hand at fiction in 1987 with a wonderful comedy called *The Curious Case of Syd Finch.* The story of a mystical baseball player whose spiritual realization leads to phenomenal success in the Major Leagues, it was critically and commercially successful. Many filmmakers have shown interest in it but, optioned by Warner Brothers and still their property, it has never been produced.

Mailer started with fiction, but of course, even more than Plimpton, he's worked in nonfiction too. Of his thirty-two books, twenty-six—including *Armies of the Night* and *Executioner's Song,* which won him Pulitzer Prizes—have been nonfiction. He differs from Plimpton in literary ego as much as he does in his work. In 1958, with a grandiosity that might embarrass him today, Mailer said: "I am imprisoned with a perception that will settle for nothing less than making a revolution in the consciousness of our time." Plimpton's ambitions, to say the least, are of a different magnitude. His nonfiction is subjective, his language and narrative skills sure-footed and original, but his self-image as a writer is almost diffident. If Mailer, in the view of almost any American writer, is the ultimate professional, Plimpton might be one of the few writers for whom "amateur" is a complimentary label. Say that he seems to risk himself at the typewriter the way he risked himself on the trapeze. As critic Gerald Clarke once noted, "It is Plimpton's triumph that he has restored the word *amateur*—which today is so often a synonym for bungler—to its original and true connotation: someone who takes up an art or craft not for gain but for love."

What Plimpton and Mailer share, and both of them share with Hemingway and Fitzgerald (at least the Fitzgerald who wrote *The Crackup*), is defiance of the life-work boundary and courage in the face of what Mailer calls the "perils" of their profession. Say that all four have struggled to reject Yeats' famous dictum that one must choose between perfection of the life and perfection of the work. Mailer could have been speaking for them all, no less than for Zelda and Norris, when he said of Hemingway, over dinner one evening in Provincetown, "Writing was a species of religion for him. He had a detestation of the abuse of English. I think he gave that to me as he did thousands of young writers. I can't think of a writer who was more aware of the danger implicit in language. He had plumbed its nature enough to know that it was not to be taken for granted." Mailer's "species of religion" claim is not mere exaggeration, but rather an open display of devotional understanding: "He was the ultimate master of 'show, don't tell.' It was implicit in the way he approached things. Everything was manifest for him. In that sense, he was an existential writer. More, he was a writer who was full of immanence, which is to say he was no less interested in the silence behind language than language itself." Mailer's performance at the dinner table is celebratory, but the dramatic description of "Zelda, Scott, and Ernest" opens up a different sort of communion, that of shared pain. On stage in Vienna, Mailer/Hemingway reads a letter written to Scott: "That terrible mood of depression, of whether it's any good or not, is known as Artist's Reward. Summer's a discouraging time to work—you don't feel death coming on the way it does in the fall, when the boys really put pen to paper. Everybody loses all the bloom—we're not peaches." This is the ultimate in writerly shop-talk, but the audience knows that Fitzgerald will die too young and that Hemingway, in a "terrible mood of depression," will end his life. The letter continues: "That doesn't mean you get rotten...you lose everything that is easy, and it always seems as though you could never write. You just have to go on when it is worst and most hopeless. You damned fool, go on and write the novel."

*   *   *

Thirty-five requests for interviews greet Mailer at the airport in Vienna. Pressed for opinions on George W. Bush ("the president we deserve—a man who can't stand a question that takes longer than ten seconds to answer"), Iraq, the 9/11 terrorist attacks, and, of course,

the present state of American Literature, his presence here, as in
Berlin, Moscow, and London, is close to Head-of-State news. Of
course, the cameras and the questions bring out the gambler in him.
Check this out for one of the mind-bets that, via this article in Berlin's
Zeitung Am Sonntag, he wins:

> WHEN I FIRST CAME TO BERLIN, I HAD AN ENORMOUS ERECTION
> Muhammad Ali once called him "the writing champion." And at
> 79, deaf and walking on crutches, the legendary American writer with
> the whiskey-colored voice has still got a crystal clear mind and enjoys
> provocation and dirty talk. "When I arrived here first in 1959, I had
> an erection when I got off the plane."

As he sees it, his enthusiasm for interviews is a by-product of marriage. "When you've been married as long as I have, you'll do most
anything to get yourself a situation where you don't get interrupted."
Whatever the reason, it's clear that nothing caffeinates him like an
interview or the random questions from the audience that follow
these performances. Even after the Q and A—at the end of a day that
began with a 10:00 AM press conference—he's witty and thorough
and endlessly patient with the reporters who surround him before he
leaves the stage. As it happens, our sightseeing tour this afternoon
was an introduction to the main event. As it draws to an end, our
guide directs our driver toward the outskirts of Vienna. We ascend
till we reach the famous Vienna Woods that are said to have been a
source of inspiration for Beethoven, Mozart, and Schubert. Rain
came on a while ago and seems just now to be getting heavier. We
park outside a restaurant in a lot already packed with cars and vans,
equipment trucks, and media vehicles. Huddled beneath umbrellas, a
crowd surrounds our car. As the Mailers emerge (Plimpton is back at
the hotel where, facing a deadline, he works on the galleys of his
Shackleton book), cameras appear, and books—*The Naked and the
Dead, Executioner's Song, The Gospel According to the Son,* and, to
Norris's delight, several copies of *Windchill Summer*—are offered for
autographs. We are joined by Norman's longtime friend, the Austrian
journalist, Hans Janitschek, and a number of other luminaries:
Austria's secretary of state, Franz Morak; Hans Dichand, publisher of
the most widely read paper in Austria, *Der Krona*; and finally by
Ernst Strasser, Austria's minister of police. A procession forms, and
we set out along a hilly, graveled path. The rain continues. Snaking
through the gloom, interrupted here and there by cameras, lights and
sound booms, the reds and yellows and blues and greens of umbrellas

are like a streak of color in a black and white film. Adapting its pace to Mailer's, even slower now because the terrain is hard on the knees, we shuffle along for fifteen or twenty minutes to reach a small, white, stucco building deep in the woods. It's fronted by a brick patio on which a pack of Paparazzi are already encamped. Walking beside me, Janitchek, a buoyant fellow with an unwavering enthusiasm for history, politics, and, most of all, Norman Mailer, offers narration. He's been a close friend of Mailer since they met, more than twenty years ago, when Janitchek was president of the Second Socialist International. Presently the New York correspondent of *Der Krona*, he was Kurt Waldheim's chief deputy when he was secretary general of the United Nations, and he ran for president of Austria in 1992. He explains that the building we face is the famous Sissi Chapel, one of the great legends of Austrian history, built by Emperor Franz Joseph in the late nineteenth century in an attempt to win back the affections of his beautiful young wife, Elizabeth, or Sissi. She rejected him when she discovered he had syphilis. Assassinated by an anarchist in 1898, she was radically independent, so indifferent to the conservative principles of her day that she is often called "the first European feminist." Later I'll learn that Norman has no idea at this moment of the ceremony at which he's about to preside, but he conducts himself as if carefully rehearsed and perfectly cast. While most of us watch from the edge of the patio, he and Norris are seated at a picnic table facing the chapel's door. Janitschek explains that this tiny building was maintained by the Catholic Church until World War II, when it was plundered by the occupying Russians. Since then, its windows and doors have been sealed with brick to protect it from decay. Today's ceremony celebrates the bricks' removal and the beginning of its renovation, and the entire ceremony, as it happens, is built around Mailer. Dichand and Morak sit across from him. While cameras flash and search for angles, and aides hover with umbrellas, the speeches begin. Janitschek attempts a rough translation from the German but for the most part leaves the content to my imagination. Twenty minutes later, an elegant elderly woman in a yellow slicker approaches Mailer with a wooden panel containing an array of dials and lights and gauges. It looks something like a children's game but would not be out of place in the cockpit of a 747. At the top right-hand corner is a large, illuminated red button that Norman is directed to press. Immediately, as he does so, the doors of the chapel, illuminated by stage-lights, swing open dramatically. A great spray of smoke rises from the threshold and, amidst the applause, we hear the yearning chords of a Beethoven Sonata played by a cellist within the chapel. Mailer handles it all with calm and what seems to me a kind of amusement, but it's not a little moving to think of him, an American writer, here to portray one of his forebears opening doors on a new chapter in Austrian history.

* * *

Onstage, the shop-talk continues, and the relationship gets rockier. Scott/Plimpton reads from a letter to Ernest, one in which Fitzgerald urges Hemingway to make cuts in *Farewell to Arms* because the story is, well, dull? Targeting pages 114–121 of the novel, Fitzgerald writes: "It's slow and it needs cutting—it hasn't the incisiveness of the other short portraits in this book or in your other books: the characters are too numerous and too much nailed down by gags. Please cut!" Fitzgerald complains that there's no psychological justification in introducing the singers—"it's not even bizarre." If the characters were consequential for the plot—if they got drunk with the protagonist and caused him to get tossed out of the hospital, say, "it would be OK. At least reduce it to a sharper and self-sufficient vignette. It's just rather gassy as it is." Fitzgerald goes on to say that pages 133–138 could also stand improvement. In general, says Plimpton for him on stage, "these conversations sometimes take on a naive quality that wouldn't please you in anyone else's work. Have you read Noel Coward?"

To which Mailer, as Hemingway, replies, "Kiss my ass!"

* * *

Mailer was seventeen years old and Plimpton thirteen when F. Scott Fitzgerald, a serious alcoholic down on his luck, writing screenplays in Hollywood three years after publishing *Tender Is the Night*, died of a heart attack at the age of forty-four. This was 1940. Hemingway did not go to the funeral. He and Scott had met twice, briefly, in 1937, but it was years since they'd pretended to be friends. Mailer reads a 1939 letter to Maxwell Perkins that sums it up for Ernest: "I always had a very stupid little boy feeling of superiority about Scott, like a tough, durable little boy sneering at a delicate but talented one." Hemingway was also, by this time, a serious alcoholic. For years, he'd taken pride in his drinking, bragging about his capacity and unequivocal about its value in his work. "We always called it the Giant Killer," he said of alcohol. "Nobody who has not had to deal with the Giant many, many times has any right to speak against the Giant Killer." Other Giants for sure were the depression he'd been dealing with all his life and, as Mailer suspected, the fear of suicide that his father had bequeathed Hemingway by ending his own life. Whatever it was, the alcohol Giant was proving harder and harder to kill. By the time Lillian Ross wrote her *New Yorker* profile of him in 1949, he was less often sober than drunk. *The Old Man and the Sea,* published in 1952, was the last of his major work. He was after all a man who, as his son Gregory wrote, "could never develop a philosophy that would allow him to grow old gracefully." Physical problems—eyesight, liver, high blood pressure, much of it related to injuries he'd suffered in a 1954 plane crash, in Africa—cut into his writing, his sex life and eventually, the drinking itself. His marriage was so embattled that his Cuban doctor removed all the guns from his house because he and his wife were threatening to shoot each other. In addition to his father, his uncle was a suicide. Now he was on his way to his own. By 1959, extreme paranoia had him imagining phones tapped, government agents tracking him, and most of his friends allied against him. He was finally persuaded to enter Mayo's clinic under a pseudonym. After a series of shock treatments, he celebrated—in a telephone conversation with his friend, A.E. Hotchner—the fact that he was able, at last, to read again. The book he was reading was *Out of My League,* by the writer who, forty-three years later, will play Scott Fitzgerald opposite the man who is playing him. His wonderful blurb for it may well have been the last few sentences he'd write with ease. When he turned to his own work, attempting to finish *A Moveable Feast,* he was excruciatingly blocked. "There's no question," Mailer says, "that he devoted the best part of himself, not to love, not to his children, but his writing. I think one of the reasons he committed suicide was finally that he couldn't write well anymore. He was like a great lover who can't get an erection." Hemingway himself put it this way. "If I can't exist on my own terms, then existence is impossible. That is how I've lived, and that is how I *must* live—or not live."

When Plimpton—thirty-four years old—heard of his suicide, he walked around dazed for hours. Like many other writers, he felt as if he'd lost a "surrogate father" he'd also, literally, lost a friend with whom he'd fished, walked the beaches in Cuba, a man who always called when he came to New York. Though lacking such direct connection, Mailer, thirty-eight, was no less stunned. "It was as wounding to me as if one's own parent had taken his life. I can't call it life-changing, but it's something I've pondered ever since. I knew that, if a man with his strength, all the success he'd had, all the fame, could do this, then there is something seriously dangerous in being a writer. You better be aware of this danger. I think I have been, ever since."

* * *

Fitzgerald/Plimpton takes the stage and recites these well-known sentences:

> And as I sat there brooding on the old, unknown world, I thought of Gatsby's wonder when he first picked out the green light at the end of Daisy's dock. He had come a long way to this blue lawn, and his dream must have seemed so close that he could hardly fail to grasp it. He did not know that it was already behind him, somewhere back in that vast obscurity beyond the city, where the dark fields of the republic rolled on under the night.

* * *

Neither Mailer nor Plimpton were as affected by Fitzgerald's death as they'd been by Hemingway's, and neither knew much of Zelda, whose reputation would remain a kind of subtext of Scott's until Nancy Milford published her wonderful *Zelda* in 1970—*The Paris Review* gilded the lily with a feature on Zelda in 1983. For Norris, Zelda's influence is the dominant gift of the play. She will tell you that these evenings of inhabiting the always-surprising and often chaotic voice of Scott's wife—the woman who was a sort of demon for the man her husband plays—have changed her life. Focused as it is on the relationship between the three, the play's chronology ends with Scott's death. Zelda is forty at this time. It is ten years since she was diagnosed schizophrenic. She has spent most of the last decade in mental hospitals and is now confined to Highland Hospital in Asheville, North Carolina.

> It's ghastly losing your mind and not being able to see clearly—literally or figuratively—and knowing that you can't think and that nothing is right, not even your comprehension of concrete things, like how old you are and what you look like....

She and Scott have been separated for years. In the midst of her illness, she's finished *Save Me the Waltz,* had a one-woman show of her paintings at a New York Gallery, and experienced a soaring religious epiphany that Scott, like her doctors, takes to be one of her symptoms. "For God is the Actuality," Zelda writes to Scott. "God has evolved us from the beginning in Eden that we may ennoble our souls until they shall have attained a spiritual stature which can share His Beauty. That is the purpose of our lives, to increase our spiritual horizons." She will die eight years later in a fire that begins in the kitchen at Highland and spreads to her room through the dumb waiter shaft. Her last words tonight, delivered by Norris, are from the novel she was writing when she died:

> He was gone...they had been much in love. He had been gone all summer and all winter for about a hundred years...she wasn't going to have him anymore; not to promise her things nor to comfort her, nor just to be there as a general compensation...she was too old to make anymore plans—the rest would have to be the best compromise.

But the final words of this drama are Hemingway's—a summation of Scott and who knows how many other writers—from *A Moveable Feast,* the book he was trying in vain to finish a few months before his suicide. They are offered to the audience by Norman Mailer, who once said of him that "he was considerably more important, to those of us who wanted to be writers, than St. Paul was to Catholics."

> His talent was a natural as the pattern that was made by the dust on a butterfly's wings. At one time he understood it no more than the butterfly did and he did not know when it was brushed or marred. Later he became conscious of his damaged wings and of their construction and he learned to think and could not fly anymore because the love of flight was gone and he could only remember when it had been...effortless.

NOTE

The text of "Zelda, Scott, and Ernest: A Dramatic Dialogue" was shaped by George Plimpton and Terry Quinn in 2001, using a select group of letters and fictional writings from the three authors. Those who wish to look into the Rashoman that was this friendship and those who wish to think about the enduring fascination of these vexed relationships can find more information in the following books:

Bruccoli, Matthew J. *Fitzgerald and Hemingway: A Dangerous Friendship.* New York: Carroll and Graf, 1994.

———. *Some Sort of Epic Grandeur: The Life of F. Scott Fitzgerald,* 2nd rev. ed. Columbia: University of South Carolina, 2002.

Bruccoli, Matthew J. *The Sons of Maxwell Perkins: Letters of F. Scott Fitzgerald, Ernest Hemingway, Thomas Wolfe, and Their Editor.* Columbia: University of South Carolina, 2004.

Bruccoli, Matthew J. and Judith S. Baughman. eds. *F. Scott Fitzgerald on Authorship.* Columbia, SC: U of South Carolina, 1996.

Bruccoli, Matthew J. and Margaret M. Duggan, eds., with the assistance of Susan Walker. *Correspondence of F. Scott Fitzgerald.* New York: Random House, 1980.

Cline, Sally. *Zelda Fitzgerald: Her Voice in Paradise.* New York: Archive, 2003.

Donaldson, Scott. *Hemingway vs. Fitzgerald.* Woodstock, NY: Overlook, 1999.

Fitzgerald, F. Scott. *A Life in Letters,* ed. Matthew J. Bruccoli and Judith S. Baughman. New York: Scribner, 1994.

Hemingway, Ernest. *Selected Letters 1917–1961,* ed. Carlos Baker. New York: Scribner, 1981.

Milford, Nancy. *Zelda: A Biography.* New York: Harper & Row, 1970.

CHAPTER 11

Late Mailer: His Writing and Reputation since *Ancient Evenings*

John Whalen-Bridge

He had in fact learned to live in the sarcophagus of his image—at night, in his sleep, he might dart out, and paint improvements on the sarcophagus. During the day, while he was helpless, newspapermen and other assorted bravos of the media and the literary world would carve ugly pictures on the tomb of his legend.

Armies of the Night 5

A TALE OF TWO OBITUARIES

Norman Mailer died on 10 November 2007, and within a week hundreds of obituaries had been disseminated through the blogosphere. Just as Mailer set his personal vision against a representative official story at the beginning of his most influential work *Armies of the Night* (1968), it will be useful to begin with two remembrances. The first is from *The Independent*, and it is representative of many obituaries, though there were many that did not begin in the same backhanded way:

> Norman Mailer wanted to be the Hemingway of his generation, but it is not as a novelist that he will be remembered—even *The Naked and the Dead*, the Second World War story which made him famous at the age of 25, is rarely read today. Too often in the course of Mailer's career, celebrity triumphed over undeniable talent. (Rosenheim)

To say that Mailer "wanted to be the Hemingway of his generation" is to present a failed ambition—it should be remembered that Mailer, in presenting himself as a "poor man's papa," offered a parodic, postmodern rejuvenation and not a wannabe. To follow this sentiment with reference to the unread 1948 novel and the celebrity distractions are familiar aspects of a habitual narrative, one that has been circulating in the media for decades: Mailer had early success but then, like a Hollywood star who cannot handle sudden celebrity, burns out quickly in the most public way. The quotation is but the beginning of a mostly fair and representative 4,000 word review of Mailer's life and work, and it is not without admiration. In spite of the shocks in his life and failures in his career, "there was something moving about the unabashed way in which Mailer ignored these knocks and kept writing, though unquestionably his work had declined since its non-fiction heyday."

This letter appeared in *The Hartford Courant* on Tuesday, November 13, 2007:

> I have returned from the funeral in Provincetown of a beloved friend of forty years. It was a beautiful but emotionally exhausting experience. My friend was generous of his time, treasure and spirit. He was deeply loved by his nine children, most of whom spoke at the grave site. I never knew him to be less than great of heart and mind. He was known to the world in various degrees of exaggeration or oversimplification, and police were necessary to keep paparazzi from the dignified private ceremony. By the way, he wrote more than forty significant books, won almost every known literary prize (including the National Book Award and two Pulitzers), and left his indelible mark on American literature in his sixty year career. With the passing of this great man, an era ends. (Leeds 135)

Leeds wrote both one of the earliest (*The Structured Vision of Norman Mailer*) and the most recent (*The Enduring Vision of Norman Mailer*) book-length studies of Mailer. The latter is a much more personal collection of essays and, like the letter to *The Hartford Courant*, is a partisan review, if you will, of Mailer's life and achievement. Mailer readers such as Leeds know a different Mailer from the one created by media archives. The main purpose of this volume, however, is not to challenge the biographical representation. Mailer's executor J. Michael Lennon is at work on a full-length biography that will address such matters. Nor is there much question about Mailer's achievement in terms of American *writing*, that is, the creative nonfiction that came to be known as New Journalism. The essays in this volume mainly address Mailer-the-novelist and attempt to demonstrate that reports of his decline were widely exaggerated.

THE MAILER EVERYONE THOUGHT THEY KNEW

About two years before Mailer died, an article in the *New York Times* reviewed the New Journalism movement, and Mailer was mentioned. *Armies of the Night* (1968) won a Pulitzer Prize and National Book Award, and acknowledgment of these achievements are followed by mention of Mailer's "boozy antics" (Maslin). Everyone knows that Mailer started with a World War II novel, lost steam in the 1950s, gathered energy as a Beat/confessional/hip proponent of sex and violence as the 1960s counterculture coalesced, stabbed his wife and head-butted Gore Vidal. He wrote about the moon and Marilyn and Gary Gilmore, and he helped a man get out of prison who then stabbed a waiter and killed him; Mailer, everyone remembers, defended the risk of releasing a prisoner and offended the victim's family in saying so. He ran for mayor of New York, he was married a half-dozen times. Everyone knows what his lifestyle was, when all his stars were out, electric and dazzling. Everyone knows that he fell out of fashion and that it was perfectly acceptable to dismiss him as a stupid boor, as former comedians trying to be the next Bill O'Reilly did. And that he is not taught much any more.

Mailer was mentioned in the *New York Times* something like once a week for decade after decade. Everyone knows who he was, but people at the MLA looked at me funnily when I said I would be editing a special issue of *Journal of Modern Literature* on him. Outside of university English departments, Mailer was a major author. But, we all know, he was paid way too much to write books, and readers who lined up to get the first editions autographed were symptoms of America's fascination with mere celebrity. English departments have their own imaginary Siberia, and Mailer was in it, and it is not quite possible to deny Mailer's achievement. Toni Morrison's sometimes-charming, sometimes-backhanded National Book Award presentation to Mailer was a sign of this split. Here is how *The Book Standard* blog describes the 17 November 2005 event, "when Toni Morrison took the stage to present a lifetime achievement award to Norman Mailer":

> While heaping accolades upon the [then] 82-year-old author, Morrison also tossed in some barbs. She called out Mailer's "almost comic obtuseness regarding women and race"—a remark that was greeted by

barking laughter from Mailer—but declared him, in the end, to be a
"worthy opponent." (9 December 2005)

Mailer is at once the prizewinner and the opponent—what an odd
evening. At least he barked well.

One does not become part of a nation's vocabulary over decades
because of just one book and boozy antics. Mailer was widely considered a Herman Melville who never wrote *Moby-Dick*, though Joan
Didion famously claimed that he wrote his "big book" no less than
four times. Mailer intended for *Ancient Evenings* as an epic vision of
a man who manages to magically reincarnate himself through an ultimate act of sexual intercourse, so that his life stretches across four
lives. (He dies during the sex act and then is reincarnated in the womb
of his lover—imagine how flattering this must be for the woman.)
This book was a huge critical flop. In the summer of 2004, I spoke
with Mailer about *Ancient Evenings* and its relation to his subsequent
work. During the period from his Pulitzer Prize–winning "nonfiction novel" *Executioner's Song* (1979) through his last books, the
novel *Castle in the Forest* and his reworking of notions about God,
God: an Uncommon Conversation, Mailer wrote over a dozen books,
including five distinct novels, a book of political commentary about
Iraq, biographies of Picasso and Lee Harvey Oswald, and even a book
of cartoons. J. Michael Lennon notes in this connection that Mailer
is a "connoisseur of narrative forms" (Lennon 2). Boozy antics
indeed.

LATE MAILER

Harold Bloom responds in Emersonian fashion to the evaluation of
Mailer's accomplishment when he suggests that Mailer's greatest creation was "Norman Mailer," and Mailer's editor Jason Epstein has
suggested that he can be compared to Byron or even Stendhal.[1] It is
somewhat ironic that we must reach back to the nineteenth century
to understand a postwar postmodernist, one who has been regularly
dismissed by critics in the last two decades as "dated" or, to say it in a
Bloomian way, "belated." Mailer is belated in various senses, but most
importantly he is a late romantic, perhaps the last of the late roman-
tics. In his November 16, 2005 National Book Award speech he reiterated his true theology, which has much less to do with God versus
the Devil or karma versus practice and more to do with the novel as a
mode of understanding, a mode Charles Johnson calls "whole sight."[2]
Whole sight is a seeing that, at least, has the ambition of not leaving

anything out. A vision of totality risks wearing us out with tiny details, the significance of which we can only guess. And so all the details become pawns in a larger struggle, the struggle of The Good to come into being in a world in which it always seems to be in someone's interest to cheat The Good.

"God struggling with the Devil" can be taken in a literal way—and Mailer may mean it in this way—or, preferably, it can be seen as Mailer's Cold War metaphor for what happens in the world. However, for Mailer there is no clear line between "the world" and "the novel." He writes in *Of a Fire on the Moon* that each one of us unconsciously constructs a vast social novel. Our subjective experiences of the world—and thus the meaning of life as calculated by each individual person—is essentially novelistic: "It seemed to him that everybody, literate and illiterate alike, had in the privacy of their unconscious worked out a vast social novel by which they could make sense of society" (143). Mailer's worldview was thoroughly Bakhtinian, and so one can extrapolate and say that God and the Devil are locked in combat not just because that is how the world seemed to work during the Cold War but, more fundamentally, because this opposition of variegated sets of forces is for Mailer an excellent symbol of what happens *in a great novel*. In Mailer's Manichean, antiabsurdist view, the reader then matters most. Mailer is a literary consequentialist for whom the reader's aesthetic experience has political and even cosmological significance. And what if this simply is not the case? A literary atheist should at least be able to grant Mailer his *As If* logic: to read (and so to live) as if the world were at stake can only dignify one's choices and lead one toward economy and grace—a kind of morality that relies on no revealed truths whatsoever. Mailer grapples with the ghost of Hemingway or writes love letters to Henry Miller, all so that the spirit of novelistic comprehension—God's own calculus, as far as Mailer is concerned—may come into being. Mailer was one of the few writers (the best minds of his generation) who demonstrated an unfailing faith in literature, art, and imagination as vales of moral self-making. The idea of the heroic author is *ridiculous* in this "death of the author" age, but Mailer was our last quixotic/heroic writer. As the song used to go, "he's dead, but he won't lie down."

The anxiety of influence—or, rather, the anxiety that influence may end—may have driven Mailer to all sorts of great writing, but within contemporary criticism Mailer is as dead as a doornail, at least in terms of academic evaluation, and so Mailer is "late" in a second sense. He has, however, been *vigorously* dead; he continues to write into his eighties while undergoing heart-bypass operations and walking on two canes. In the year he turned eighty, he published three books—but he had, in terms of reputation, already been dead for some years. Some say he died in the mid-1950s, others at the end of the 1960s, and then there has been the long slow forgetting within academic criticism within the 1980s and 1990s when Mailer was dropped from syllabi and was left out of the *Norton Anthology of American Literature*. Melville said "Dollars damn me" and became unknown to the reading public, but Mailer made deals with the devil—the Marketplace itself, perhaps—and so he never knew what it was like to be out of print.

Third, "Late Mailer" can refer to the last third of his writing career, to those works he has written since his last publicly and academically well-received book, *The Executioner's Song* (1979). In Mailer's first phase, he was a novelist who created huge expectations with *The Naked and the Dead* before writing two less-well-received novels. In phase two Mailer was the postmodernist trickster who wrote novelistic nonfiction and novels (such as *An American Dream*) that clearly drew on his personal mythology. This period stretches from the late-1950s through the end of the 1970s. His third phase, dating from the completion of *The Executioner's Song*, includes works such as *Ancient Evenings, Harlot's Ghost, Tough Guys Don't Dance*, his book on Picasso, *Oswald's Tale*, and *The Gospel According to the Son*, and his imaginatively constructed omnibus *The Time of Our Time*. He has also published a book of cartoons and a book-length attack on Bush's war in Iraq in this period. Before I edited the special issue of *Journal of Modern Literature* on this part of his career, little or no criticism was published about the works from his third phase. This is a startling omission, and I can't say that the collection drew much attention to the final dozen witty and resonant works. Anyone working on postwar American Orientalism, the CIA and the Cold War, masculinity, novelistic nonfiction, the Judeo-Christian hyphen, and the cultural construction of the Author in postwar America will find rich possibilities in Mailer's third phase.

MAILER'S LITERARY KARMA

Ever since becoming suddenly famous at age twenty-five and until the day he died, Mailer meditated constantly on the ways in which celebrity and artistic power at once subvert and reinforce one another. In the twentieth-century, fame was a serious danger to Faulkner, Hemingway, and, of course, to Mailer himself. The "frenzy of renown" can doom the writer's art, and the writer who "fails to live up to his or her early promise" is a negative moral exemplar. Few will agree that Mailer had no choice or suffered bad luck, however. Since the mid-1970s, he became increasingly intrigued by the notion of "karma," an exotic concept that usually means, when translated into Western discourse, the comeuppance delivered upon anyone who fails to satisfy society's demands of self-effacing humility. The gods have been punishing Mailer (with bad reviews) for his egotism. In Mailer's own construction of karmic reincarnation and karmic consequence, systematized in *Ancient Evenings*, the scales of justice will balance *eventually*—meaning, after one dies. In Mailer's fictional reworking of Egyptian mythology, this tendency toward impersonal balance is personified by the Egyptian god Ma'at. Working from Mailer's own metaphors, a literary Ma'atist ventures the following propositions:

1. The scales of literary evaluation are currently out of balance.
2. Eventually, Mailer's work will receive more recognition than at present.
3. The current imbalance is, indeed, partly due to Mailerian karma.

"Mailerian karma," then, has two related meanings: the phrase can refer to Mailer's actions and the ways in which those actions have shaped his fame, his reputation among literary scholars, and the course of his own life. Mailerian karma can also refer to Mailer's orientalist revision of an Asian philosophical doctrine, his translation of that idea into specifically American terms—an action that may or may not have karmic repercussions in the former sense.[3]

Mailer salutes Dickens across "vales of karma" as a way of opening *Of a Fire on the Moon* (one of the many Mailer studies of the best and worst of times) and explores numerous permutations of the concept in *Executioner's Song*, but karma becomes the central structuring metaphor in more recent works, especially *Ancient Evenings*, a book about a man who has learned how to reincarnate himself through a magical sex act. The child is responsible for his own creation and cannot blame bad luck at all if circumstances prove harsh: karmic self-creation, then, is a fantasy of ultimate responsibility, of a world in which there really is no absurdity. Should the mother become distressed at the lover's denouement, and should the child suffer the mother's wrath, this particular child can never say, "Well, we do not choose our parents." In this way the karmic literary design bespeaks an ethos in which a person is able to take responsibility even for events otherwise understood as beyond an individual's power. In *part* Mailer's literary karma required him to engage with an American fascination with violence and with an aesthetic predicated on the ultimate social utility of the psychic outlaw (at least if we remember that "The White Negro" begins with a meditation on the death camps), and in *part* Mailer's action can be construed as having had disastrous results, which no amount of metaphysical speculation will negate. But in part it is also true that Mailer's work was an ultimately prophetic demand for a more responsible world. Which part is currently greater? Which part will matter more in decades to come?

Mailer claimed in interviews that novelist James Jones introduced him to the concept of karma, but Mailer certainly gave the idea, as it is deployed in his works, his personal stamp. The Buddhist/Hindic sense that consequences inevitably follow conduct is preserved in its colloquial American translation: what goes around, comes around. Mailerian karma is not the orthodox sense, however, since Buddhist and Hindu usage both warn that karma is an insidious echo of our actions that causes the repetition of personal being, whereas Mailer revises karmic recurrence and especially its biographical extrapolation "reincarnation" in a sentence that would surely puzzle any orthodox Buddhist trying to make sense of the matter: "I don't have this liberal, rational certainty, thank God, that once you die you die, and that's the end of it. On the contrary, I believe in a form of karma, I believe in reincarnation—not for everyone! I think reincarnation is a reward of a sort" (Mailer Newsweek).[4] From the standpoint of the central Buddhist traditions, coming back again and again is a painful chore and not a reward for virtue. That the West has borrowed aspects of philosophical systems (the nondualistic philosophies of Vedanta, Zen Buddhism, and Taoism, specifically) and has occasionally misunderstood these systems is not the particular worry here, but the divagations of "karma" and "reincarnation" in the Western context point to an underlying gravitational pull, a cultural desire that can account for the systematic shifts in the meaning of words that have crossed continents. The "mind of Europe," as hypostasized in Eliot's "Tradition and the Individual Talent"—an essay written in explicit defense of an impersonal aesthetic—craves reincarnation. Mailer points to this hunger too directly in his epic treatment of the ur-hunger that has become the West as we now understand it, and so his book has been ignored. Menenhetet I and Menenhetet II, reviewing the rise and fall of Egyptian, Greek, Roman, English, and later American empires, understand that these vast constructions of communal ego are each reincarnations of the last one—and Mailer, to his credit—was fully aware that the most anti-imperial voices of the current world partly draw sustenance from such communal modes, or they would not be heard. Mailer creates a vast imperial fantasy like *Ancient Evenings* while also publishing no-holds-barred attacks on Bush administration imperialism (*Why Are We at War?* 2003). That the two books were by the same author only seems a contradiction because readers do not understand that Mailer was not identical with Menenhetet, that his books (especially in the third phase of his writing career) were elaborate, ironical, and thoroughly dialogic constructions. When reviewers dismissed such achievements by saying that Mailer wrote too much about himself or that his works expressed too much hunger for regard—then the culture doth protest too much.

To say that Mailer was neglected because of "Mailerian karma," then, is a blade with two edges: Mailer's eccentric and syncretic mixture of ideas and approaches makes him something like that "three-pronged phallus of Osiris" in *Ancient Evenings*—a magical force that, unlike the other limbs that are scattered in all directions in Mailer's mythical method, can be found precisely because it is indigestible. Mailer, like Melville a hundred years before, was so rich that he gave us a kind of cultural indigestion. And he also stuck in our craw because of his lifelong penchant for flouting rules and for finding out the limits by crossing them. In both senses, Mailerian karma helps us understand why Mailer was such an uncelebrated literary phenomenon. We must acknowledge Mailer's own actions. Some of his extra-literary activities directly contributed to the neglect of his writings and to the sometimes vindictive hostility with which his books were reviewed; but our speculations about Mailer's next few afterlives spring forth from an idea drawn from the notion of karma, an idea that may be true or merely useful, namely that the mechanisms behind literary reputation are *ultimately* impersonal.[5]

If we allow Mailer to set up the scales of judgment according to his own metaphors, what will be Mailer's fate when he swims across the river (called the Duad by ancient Egyptians, as readers of *Ancient Evenings* will recall) separating this world from his literary afterlife? Mailer, who has had an effect on postwar American culture that is arguably as profound as that of his biographical subjects Marilyn Monroe, Henry Miller, or Muhammad Ali, has excluded from the *Norton Anthology of American Literature* for several editions, supposedly because no one is teaching him. However infrequently his work is taught in the first decade of the twenty-first century, Mailer has been a cultural landmark among *adults* for five decades. Much has been written about him, but the work after *Executioner's Song* has been severely neglected—and it awaits readers who are ready to doubt the official story of his life and work.

"There was that law of life," Mailer wrote in his 1955 novel *The Deer Park*, "so cruel and so just, that one must grow or else pay more for remaining the same." The work from the two decades of Mailer's writing life demonstrates that he not only maintained his powers as a writer—he continued, against all expectations, to grow. If Mailer was right about Ma'at and karma and growth, then his life-gamble certainly paid off, and he ought to do fairly well in the afterlife. If he was wrong, he remains interesting as an author who bet the rent on his own best ideas and produced a dazzling array of work as a result.

NOTES

1. Bloom finds that Mailer has written no "indisputable book" along the lines of *The Sun Also Rises* or *As I Lay Dying* and that, perhaps, "he is his own supreme fiction. His is the author of 'Norman Mailer,' a lengthy, discontinuous, and perhaps canonical fiction." See his "Introduction" to *Norman Mailer: Bloom's Critical Views*, 2; also see Epstein's foreword to this volume for the comparison to Byron.
2. According to MSNBC's coverage of the ceremony, "Mailer has long lamented the decline of the novel and continued to do so Wednesday night, likening himself to a carriage maker helpless before the arrival of the automobile." See "Joan Didion Wins National Book Award." On "whole sight," see Charles Johnson, 1–6.
3. It is important to keep in mind that "Mailerian karma" is part of Mailer's creative syncretism, with strands of his creative web reaching outward to existentialism, Manicheanism, Gnosticism, aspects of Hassidism, and even (in *Harlot's Ghost*) suppositions of a possible "sophisticated Fundamentalism." Mailer's uses of concepts like karma and Manichean are eclectic and creative; readers have to resist understanding such terms too quickly. We should also keep in mind that Mailer didn't merely make social mistakes—he gambled with socially risky situations. See Shainberg's essay for a discussion of the ways Mailer's gambling crossed between typical betting situations, social situations, and creative engagements.
4. Clearly the *Egyptian Book of the Dead* and its myths have been more important to Mailer than any specific Buddhist or Hindu text— see Hume.
5. For examples of hostile reviews, see anything about Mailer's work by Michiko Kakutani of the *New York Times* excepting perhaps the obituary, which was half-way nice. For a discussion of the verb "to be kakutanied," listen to "Writers Respond to Book Critic Kakutani."

Works Cited

Bloom, Harold. "Introduction," in *Norman Mailer: Bloom's Critical Views*, ed. Harold Bloom, 2nd edition. Broomall, PA: Chelsea House, 2003. 2.

The Book Standard Web page (now closed). 9 December 2005. http://www. thebookstandard.com/bookstandard/news/author/article_display. jsp?vnu_content_id=1001524145.

Hume, Kathryn. "Books of the Dead: Postmortem Politics in Novels by Mailer, Burroughs, Acker, and Pynchon." *Modern Philology: A Journal Devoted to Research in Medieval and Modern Literature* 97:3 (2000): 417–444.

Johnson, Charles. "Whole Sight: Notes on New Black Fiction." *Callaloo* 7:3 (1984): 1–6.

"Joan Didion Wins National Book Award." http://www.msnbc.msn.com/ id/10077214/, 9 December 2005. Accessed 9 August 2009.

Leeds, Barry H. "My Friend Norman Mailer." *The Hartford Courant*, 13 November 2007. Republished as "The Death of Norman Mailer; the Birth of the Norman Mailer Society." *The Mailer Review* 2:1 (Fall 2008): 135.

Lennon, J. Michael. *Critical Essays on Norman Mailer*. Boston: G.K. Hall, 1986, 2.

Loy, David. *Nonduality*. New York: Humanity Books, 1998.

Mailer, Norman. *Armies of the Night*. New York: Signet (New American Library), 1968.

———. "Miller and Hemingway," in *Pieces and Pontifications*. Boston: Little, Brown, 1982. 86–93.

———. "Norman Mailer Approaches Eighty." *Newsweek* 121:5 http://www. kingfisherpress.com/Mailer_at_80.htm. Accessed 8 August 2009.

———. *Of a Fire on the Moon*. New York: Signet (New American Library), 1970.

———. "We Went to War Just to Boost the White Male Ego." *The Times* (London), 29 April 2003, 20. http://www.timesonline.co.uk/tol/comment/columnists/guest_contributors/article871969.ece. Accessed 8 August 2009.

Maslin, Janet. "When Interesting Times Made for Idiosyncratic Journalism." *The Gang That Wouldn't Write Straight* 5 December 5, 2005. http:// www.nytimes.com/2005/12/05/books/05masl.html. Accessed 8 August 2009.

McDonald, Brian. "Post-Holocaust Theodicy, American Imperialism, and the 'Very Jewish Jesus' of Norman Mailer's *The Gospel According to the Son.*" *Journal of Modern Literature* 30:1 (2006): 78–90.

Rosenheim, Andrew. "Norman Mailer." 12 November 2007. *The Independent*. http://www.independent.co.uk/news/obituaries/norman-mailer-400006.html. Accessed 8 August 2009.

Vaihinger, Hans. *The Philosophy of "As If": A System of the Theoretical, Practical and Religious Fictions of Mankind*; translated [from the 6th

German ed.] by C.K. Ogden, 2nd ed., reprinted. London: Routledge & K. Paul, 1965.

"Writers Respond to Book Critic Kakutani," originally broadcast 7 December 2003 on National Public Radio, http://www.npr.org/templates/story/story.php?storyId=1536561. Accessed 8 August 2009.

AFTERWORD: NORMAN AS EDITOR

Norris Mailer

Norman Mailer was one of the best editors I knew. I got an education in editing from Mailer U by living with him for nearly 33 years and reading his manuscripts, which sometimes would change so drastically from the first draft until the final as to be almost unrecognizable; there might be 6 or 7 drafts in between. Sometimes more. Norman always said that the real writing was in the editing and the first draft was just the raw clay, which is a comfort to writers who struggle to get those first words onto the blank page. As I often say to new writers or wannabe writers, "No one has to see what you write except you. You are free to show it or change it or take it out later, so just let it all go onto the page, then decide what to keep."

Norman had a group of trusted friends who read his books at every stage and offered their suggestions. I was lucky to be among them, so I have read every draft of every book he wrote after *The Fight*. Sometimes I would offer a suggestion he actually accepted, which was thrilling, but more often he would ignore my red pencil marks. If all of us trusted readers were of the same mind on a particular point or edit, he took it more seriously, but that didn't mean he was going to change anything if it went against his gut feeling.

One basic disagreement we always had was about digression. He loved it, and it drove me crazy. A prime example is the Russian section in *The Castle in the Forest*. At a certain point in his research, he began to read about other events that were transpiring during the period of his boy's, Hitler's, life, and became engrossed in Rasputin and Nicholas and Alexandra. It was irresistible for him to leave the Hitlers and write about the Romanovs, which I thought was a mistake. I, the reader, was immersed in the grittiness of Germany and the molding of the young monster, and to be yanked from that to the sappy love letters between Nicky and Alex was jarring, to say the least. My suggestion was to write a separate book about the Romanovs and Rasputin, which he had always wanted to do, and leave the Hitlers to the Maestro who was bringing them along nicely. But he resisted, as he had in *Harlot's Ghost* when he went off on such a long digression from the story that he never came back. That was another one I fought for and lost. Others shared the same opinion of the Russian section in *The Castle in the Forest*, but the most he would do was cut it down. It's not that the digressions were unworthy or uninteresting, they were just meant, in my humble opinion, to be another book.

Unfairly, I didn't give him the same privilege with my own writing. I was too vulnerable to his criticisms, and I wanted to be able to say I had done the whole thing without any help from him, which was certainly true. After patiently waiting, he finally asked to read my first novel, *Windchill Summer*, when it was in galleys, which I thought would be safe, but after an hour or so he called me upstairs to the office and handed me a stack of pages—covered with his pencil marks.

"Here," he said, "start putting in these changes and I'll work behind you."

I was aghast.

"No," I said. "You can't edit this book, sweetie. It's done."

He was quite perturbed by that and answered,

"If I can't work on it, I can't read it."

"Fine," I answered. "You can read it when it comes out in hardcover with everyone else." Which he did.

He always said the book would have been 5 percent better if he had edited it, which I think was the highest praise he could have given me.

CONTRIBUTORS

Mashey Bernstein holds a PhD in American Literature from the University of California, Santa Barbara, where he currently teaches in the Writing Program and in the Film and Media Studies Department. He has written extensively on Mailer in *The Mailer Review, Studies in American-Jewish Literature,* the *San Francisco Review of Books,* and the *London Jewish Chronicle.* He also writes on film, especially Jewish aspects of the media.

Scott Duguid is in the process of completing his Doctoral Thesis on Norman Mailer and the aesthetics/politics of the avant-garde at the University of Edinburgh. His interests include twentieth-century fiction, with a particular focus on America; intersections between literature and art history; theories of modernism and postmodernism. He has published articles on Norman Mailer, and on Warhol's films.

Jason Epstein was Editorial Director at Random House for forty years, where he developed the Vintage paperbacks series and published Norman Mailer, Vladimir Nabokov, E.L. Doctorow, Gore Vidal, Philip Roth, Elaine Pagels, and Richard Holbrook. In 1952 he created the Anchor Books imprint; in 1963 he cofounded the *New York Review of Books,* and in 1979 he became one of the cofounders of the Library of America, which was intended to market archival quality editions of American classic literature. The first volumes were published in 1982, and the company now prints about 250,000 volumes per year. Epstein is the first winner of the National Book Award for Distinguished Service to American Letters (1988) and, in 2007, he has won the Philolexian Award for Distinguished Literary Achievement. Currently he is running On Demand Books, which he cofounded in 2004. This company markets the Espresso Book Machine.

Ashton Howley teaches literature and writing at the University of the Fraser Valley in British Columbia. He has taught at the University of Ottawa and at Yonsei University and Jeonju University in Korea. His publications include "Mailer Again: Heterophobia in *Tough Guys*

Don't Dance" (*JML* 30.1, 2006) and "Squaring the Self: Versions of Transcendentalism in E.E. Cummings's *The Enormous Room"*(Spring 12, 2002).

Brian J. McDonald holds the PhD in English Literature from the University of Edinburgh. His research interests include post–World War II American and British fiction and the relationship between imaginative literature and liberal political thought. His essays have appeared in *Studies in American Jewish Fiction, Journal of Modern Literature,* and *Gothic Studies.*

Norris Mailer has worked as a high school teacher, a model, a film and theater actress, a painter, and as the artistic director of the Provincetown Repertory Theatre. She is the author of the novels *Windchill Summer* and *Cheap Diamonds,* and she has just completed a memoir of her life with Norman Mailer entitled *A Ticket to the Circus.* It will be published in April 2010.

Jeffrey F.L. Partridge is Associate Professor of Humanities and Chair of Humanities at Capital Community College in Connecticut. He is the author of *Beyond Literary Chinatown,* a 2007 American Book Award winner from the Before Columbus Foundation. His articles have appeared in the *Journal of Modern Literature, MELUS,* and *Studies in the Literary Imagination.*

James Emmett Ryan is an Associate Professor of English at Auburn University; he has been researching the ways American writers and literary cultures have been shaped by transformative historical forces such as religion, politics, technology, and commercial media. He also has studied topics in American Studies such as disability and authorship, Herman Melville's fiction, nineteenth-century American Catholic literary culture, modern architecture, and New Journalism and has recently published essays and reviews in *American Quarterly, American Literary History, Religion and American Culture, Leviathan: A Journal of Melville Studies, the Journal of Modern Literature, American Literature, Early American Literature,* and the *Encyclopedia of Alabama.* His new book *Quakers and American Culture, 1650–1950* is was published in 2009 from the University of Wisconsin Press.

Lawrence Shainberg was born in Memphis, Tennessee. His works include the novels *One on One, Memories of Amnesia* and *Crust,* as well as nonfiction writings *Brain Surgeon* and *Ambivalent Zen.* His stories and articles have appeared in *Paris Review, Esquire, Harpers,* the *New York Times Magazine*, and other publications. He lives now in Truro, Massachusetts, and New York City.

John Whalen-Bridge is Associate Professor of English at the National University of Singapore; he has written *Political Fiction and the American Self* (1998). He has also published articles on American literature in relation to Buddhism, Orientalism, the Cold War, and pragmatism. With Tan Sor-hoon, he coedited *Democracy as Culture: Deweyan Pragmatism in a Globalizing World* (2007). He coedits the SUNY series Buddhism and American Culture with Gary Storhoff, which includes *The Emergence of Buddhist American Literature* (2009) and *American Buddhism as a Way of Life* (2010). He is currently working on "engaged aesthetics" in the work of Gary Snyder, Charles Johnson, and Maxine Hong Kingston.

Heather Wolffram is a Postdoctoral Research Fellow at the Centre for the History of European Discourses at the University of Queensland. She is the author of several articles on psychical research and parapsychology in the German context as well as a book titled *The Stepchildren of Science: Psychical Research and Parapsychology in Germany, c. 1870–1939* (Rodopi, 2009). She is currently working on a project that considers the use of hypnosis by European psychiatrists during the late nineteenth century as a "cure" for homosexuality.

INDEX